cosa nostra

cosa nostra

NICCI HARRIS

also by nicci harris

The Kids of The District

Facing Us

Our Thing

Cosa Nostra

Her Way

His Pretty Little Burden

His Pretty Little Queen

Their Broken Legend

ISBN ebook: 978-1-922492-04-3

ISBN print: 978-1-922492-03-6

Edited by Writing Evolution. @writingevolution. www. writingevolution.co.uk

Internal graphics by Nicci Harris

Cover design by Books & Moods

Nicci illustration holding kindle by @katiereadingcorner

for guitars.

—*For playing them.*
Making them.
Buying too many of them.
Without you, my husband would have noticed my absence.
And Cosa Nostra may have never been written.

cosa nostra

song list

Kids of the District
Our Thing & Cosa Nostra
Book one & two

1. Dance of the Sugar Plum Fairy – Royal Philharmonic Orchestra
2. Riptide – Vance Joy
3. The Way You Look Tonight – Frank Sinatra
4. Rosaries – Nbhd Nick
5. Numb – Linkin Park
6. Nothing Else Matters – Metallica
7. Wild Horses – The Sundays
8. Somewhere Over The Rainbow – Leanne & Naara
9. Tears in Heaven – Eric Clapton
10. The Unforgiven – Metallica
11. M.I.A. – Avenged Sevenfold
12. Over The Rainbow – Judy Garland
13. The Bones – Maren Morris
14. Tangled Up In You – Staind

15. Nothing's Gonna Hurt You Baby – Cigarettes After Sex
16. Angel – Theory of a Deadman
17. All I Know So Far – P!nk
18. Remember Everything – Five Finger Death Punch

Go to Spotify to listen.
Our Thing & Cosa Nostra

"everyone is made up

—*of little contradictory pieces and you should never judge another person's decisions because you don't know the pieces they have to choose from."*

CHAPTER ONE

MOST OF OUR dirtier jobs go down outside of the city, at Capel Grove—Jimmy's abattoir. But Mickie happened to be at the wrong place at the wrong time, and we needed to get the deed done before he left the District. Or worse.

This is why I'm in downtown Connolly, freezing my balls off in the walk-in freezer at Sergio's Meat Market. I cross my arms over my chest. My breath marks the air around me with grey clouds of vapour. The freezer fan above me creates a drone—a kind of white noise.

Our cleaner, Armad, moves to the metal table in the corner, a bounce to his every step. He is a slender man who walks with a peculiar gracefulness. Outside, in the real world, he could easily be mistaken as an easy target—gullible. A fool's mistake.

I watch him as he hums a soft tune and rolls his tool sheath open, displaying its sharp, shiny contents. Carefully, he selects the implements needed to complete tonight's job and then places them gently on display. He takes a moment to caress the polished blades one by one. A ritual I've seen many times. He told me once that it's like greeting a colleague.

He's fucked in the head.

Glancing to my side, I notice Bronson is watching Armad, his blue eyes sparkling, his fingers stroking his palms. But it's not our job to cut. As much as he may enjoy getting his hands bloodied, I frown at him, reminding him he's not a soldier.

Armad and his two boys sling Michael's bound feet to the hook hanging from the ceiling. There is a big, viscera-encrusted grate directly below him on the cold cement floor, so when he finally wakes, it'll be a chilling sight to behold. A hint at what's to come.

Bronson moves in beside me, chomping at the bit to get his hands dirty. He'll watch every moment of this, reaping satisfaction from Michael's pain. I look down at his feet as they shuffle with a kind of anxiety. A kind of anticipation. All I feel is bored.

Michael now hangs from his feet like a carcass ready to be divided into muscle groups. Armad steps back as one of his boys throw a cold bucket of water onto Michael's head. The water drips from his face and hair and then slides down the drain.

As Michael comes to, the rhythmic hum of the freezer fan is interrupted by his panicked whimpers. Fast gasps follow snivels follow stutters of words that make no sense. Then his body gyrates as his adrenaline spikes. As his body tells him something is wrong. He grunts with exertion while he attempts to dislodge himself from the hook. His own weight and small muscles prevent much success. And with his shirt hanging partially over his chin, he can't see our faces. Not that it matters. He knows who we are.

As he continues to flip around on the hook like an overfed goldfish, I sneer. What a sack of shit. What a weak, useless waste of space. I've known a lot of dirty bastards in my twenty-four years of life—that's part of being a Butcher—but a man can be nasty and crooked and still have honourable qualities. Their integrity. Their pride. Often, they even have traits to admire. Strength. Loyalty.

This piece of shit is as empty as his pockets.

He lets out a guttural, incoherent groan. "Oh God, please. Please don't do this."

When he's met with further silence, he shudders. My heart beats steady and rhythmic, but when he starts to cry, I cringe. There is no place for tears in my world. Fight us, for fuck's sake. Threaten us. But don't whimper like a little bitch.

"What is this?" he cries. "Where am I?"

"We ran out of pigs," Bronson states simply. "I promised my family a spit roast. You like spit roasts, don't you?"

Michael whines. I roll my eyes at my brother's wide, soft smile. Taking a step closer to our hanging friend, I only stop when his eyes lock on my shoes. "Where's Jimmy's truck"—I tap my foot—"and where are our diamonds?"

He tries to jolt his body around, attempting to catch our eyes or a glimpse of our expressions. "I don't know. I told you. I was—"

"See, we know you're lying," I drawl, rubbing my forehead and temple with my index finger and thumb. Dropping my hand to my side, I sigh roughly. "Would you like to know how?"

"I swear it. Max. Bronson. I swear—"

Bronson's boot nails Michael in the face. His head snaps backwards. Eyes closed. Mouth agape. And now he's unconscious and swaying on the hook as if he's already dead.

"Fuck's sake, Bronson," I mutter.

"I don't like it when they say our names," he states

plainly, grabbing another bucket of icy water and splashing its contents over Michael.

I completely agree. Hearing anyone say my brother's names or Butch's or—*especially* —Cassidy's, pisses me right off.

As Michael stirs again, I signal Armad. He moves in, slicing him with quick, trained precision, parting his flesh from bicep to wrist. It's a relatively shallow incision. Blood trickles down, painting the grate, but it's not enough to bleed him dry. Michael's eyes snap open. As blood and pressure build within his cranium, he spits and drools and reddens.

He lets out a long, half-incoherent moan. "*Fuck.*"

"Do you know how the butcherbird got its name?" Bronson asks with a smooth and steady voice.

Fuck's sake, not this butcherbird crap again.

"Once they spear their prey with their massive knife-like beaks, they then impale them on thorns, fences, any place they will hang, leaving them with their guts exposed to rot in the sun."

A rumbled sigh draws everyone's attention to me. Bored of this shit already, I jump straight to the point. "Yesterday, while I was balls deep inside your wife's arse, I saw the prettiest pink diamonds hanging from her ears. And I'd know our product anywhere."

"Stay away from Jess!" He chokes out the words.

She may be a loyal lady, I wouldn't know. I've never spoken to her. One of my men followed her and noticed the earrings. It just makes me chuckle to think he may believe that I was rearranging her guts while he was stealing from us.

"Where are our diamonds?" I snap.

Bronson kneels in Michael's blood and knots his hair

between his fingers. Michael can finally see a face, but by the growing whites of his eyes, perhaps he wishes he couldn't. Bron strokes his slick hair and it makes me sick. "We're not threatening you today, mate. I want to make that crystal clear. You will be leaving this freezer in bags," Bron states. "But my brother has a massive cock, and your wife won't like the way he uses it on her tonight if you don't tell us where our diamonds are."

Even though it's bullshit—I'd never hurt an innocent woman—Michael seems to believe I would. He begins to vibrate with panic. For his life. For hers.

Clearing my throat, I say, "We want the location and the names of the people involved." I look over at a metal rack coated in icicles in a corner of the freezer. Ice used to remind me of my childhood. Of soaking in a half-frozen bathtub with Bronson to lessen the bruises our mother had kindly left. But now it reminds me of my little ballerina—Cassidy. And that's a name I can't let infiltrate my conscious at this moment. Forcing her aside and growing quickly impatient, I scowl at Michael. "Ready to share?"

As Michael begins to talk—really share—I stare at the ice forming around me.

"But people like you have people like me that love them."

For a second those words slip into my consciousness— Cassidy's sweet naive words. And there is truth in what she said that night, but she doesn't understand the depravities in this world. And he is not a good person. And fuck, I'm letting her in again. Well, too bad, it's done. This is nothing personal. This is business. Still, for reasons I can't explain, I turn towards the door and push the latch open, moving out into the process area.

Loosening my tie and collar, I exhale loudly. Plastic curtains sway in front of me, leading into the shop front. I frown at them as I roll up my sleeves. This room smells like formaldehyde and I fucking hate that smell. It lingers.

Rubbing the coarse stubble on my jaw with my palm, I think about how I left Cassidy alone in my bed *again*. I growl at my wandering thoughts.

Carter is just outside our room—*my* room. Even though I trust that man—I do fucking trust that man—I still want to get back there. Back to her world. Whenever I'm with her, I end up in her world.

I'm in foreign territory with her. All I know is that I'd kill for her. That I want her sweet little body sprawled out above my sheets when I come home. And—of course—that being with her is enough to make me hate myself. For all the parts of me she hasn't seen. Doesn't want to. If she had, she wouldn't be in my bed right now, and she wouldn't have that bruise under her eye because she would have high-tailed it at the first sign of danger.

Xander is suddenly in the processing room with me, having come in from the storefront, a look of worry on his young face. And I realise now just how dangerous my affections for her are. How easily the thought of her in the wrong moment could get me killed—or worse—get one of my brothers killed.

"What is it?" I ask, meeting him halfway.

"We have company, Max," he says, a slight shake to his voice.

Quickly moving past him, I pull back the plastic curtains and stare across the shop, through the glass windows, at an unmarked car with two men inside.

Fucking Jacks.

"What do we do?" Xan asks.

Fucking Xander.

Clearing my throat, I wander past him and into the shop

front. I press my back to the counter and cross my ankles in front of me, staring directly at the Jacks as they pretend to mind their own business. I watch them for several seconds. Recognising the driver, I know what to do to subtly remind them who they are dealing with.

Wandering behind the counter, I grab a roll of butcher paper. Xander follows me into the room but doesn't ask what I'm doing. Normally, he's a cocky little shit, but he knows I'm still pissed at him. Knows better than to fuel the fire.

I grab a handful of pork chops and throw them into a bowl before pouring barbeque marinade on them. I toss the meat as Bronson appears in the shop front with an unnecessary amount of blood on his white collared shirt.

He's an emotional man, my big brother. Far more emotional than me. There are two sides to him —one that charms the world and one that most people never see twice. He can sever his morals to protect the people he loves. To seek revenge. To claim what's his.

I can't quite compartmentalise like that. I would kill Michael. Quick like. But Bronson enjoys the act in a way I do not.

"Couldn't you have just cut him clean?" I say with a frown.

"It's the dirt that makes the man appreciate the sparkle." Hearing Jimmy's words spouted from my big brother's mouth only tightens my brows further.

"And what sparkle do you have to show for all your dirt, Bron?" I bite out angrily.

Amused and unaffected by my tone, he smiles at me and then at Xander, who is now sitting at one of the small circular tables. "My beautiful brothers."

"Does he know where they are?" Xander asks, and I snap

him a look of disapproval. Fuck's sake. Why is he asking questions when he should be seen and not heard?

"Jimmy's not gonna like this, but he said Marco and his mob orchestrated the whole thing. Our stock is already on its way to India," Bronson says, looking at me despite the question having come from Xander. He glances at the bowl in my hand. He doesn't appear the slightest bit concerned with why I'm all of a sudden interested in the culinary arts. He leans on the display fridge between us and watches me. "I'll tell Jimmy tomorrow... He's gonna want us to hunt them down. You know that, right?" Bronson states; a grin that is anything but nice works his lips.

"Yeah." At that, I'm pissed. Michael has cost us more than money and time. Jimmy is going to expect me to go with Bronson, find our stock, and leave a trail of messages in the form of bodies. And I can't do that. I won't leave Cassidy.

Grumbling to myself, I crack some salt and pepper over the chops, then further coat the flesh with a flip of the bowl.

"Armad is finishing off." Bronson stares at the meat that I am now wrapping up in butcher paper. "I'm hungry. I'm glad you salted those fuckers. You always under season my meat."

Shaking my head at him, I tape the paper shut. It takes Xander until I'm on the shop porch to realise what I'm doing.

"Max, no," I hear him say as I stroll outside and onto the sidewalk. The shop door swings shut behind me. I make my way over to the Jacks. The streetlamps light my path while the sound of my footsteps interrupt the quiet of the night. Their eyes shift to me. They slouch down in their seats.

Stopping beside the driver's door, I tap the glass with my knuckles. They look at each other sideways. After a few seconds, the driver finally winds the window down.

I squat to meet their line of sight. "Evening, officers. Would you like to come in? We are just gutting a pig."

They share glances full of meaning. "No, Max. We are fine here."

"Alright then. Well, take this home to your pretty wife and son." With a smirk, I offer Constable Hall the pork chops. "These are the best fucking chops you'll ever eat."

They don't just take the paper package; they also thank me for it.

Tucking my hands into my pockets, I step back and watch as they pull away from the sidewalk, and then cruise off down the street.

Wandering back into the shop, I notice Armad and his men have joined my brothers out front. Bronson is now seated opposite Xander while the others stand by or lean on the counter. Armad quite rightly minds his own business as I approach, keeping his head downcast. I don't dislike this man—they are all our men. Nevertheless, I find most people struggle to hold my gaze.

Bron chuckles. "Should have given them some sausages as well, mate."

Xander groans a little. "Why provoke them?"

I sneer at him. "But you're going to be a big-shot lawyer soon, so I shouldn't have a problem, right?"

"You are your own worst enemy sometimes, Max," he mutters as Armad and the others sneak slowly outside.

"You need to toughen up!" I snap at him, and he winces. "We need a fucking man. Someone we can count on." My voice gets louder as I feel heat hitting my temples. "Trust with what's important to us!"

Trust—I don't think I trust anyone anymore. Jimmy. Butch. My own brother who walks and talks like a man but disappoints me at every turn.

With sad eyes, he shakes his head and says, "I'm so sorry for what happened, Max. I said I was sorr—"

Before he can finish his sentence, I lunge at him, dragging him to his feet and pinning him against the wall. "You're fucking sorry!" I bark as his chest vibrates with fast heavy breaths beneath my forearm.

He swallows nervously but holds my stare. "I tried to go after her, Max. She told me she'd be okay. Dustin had guards watching my every move. I tried to stop it."

Fucking Dustin.

I haven't forgotten about his apparent involvement in the attack on Cassidy. He thinks he can toy with what's mine; he's got another thing coming.

The presence of Bronson standing just behind me is palpable, but he's allowing this to play out.

Inching in a little closer to Xander, I hiss, "And yet, there's not a scratch on you. So tell me, my tough little brother, how hard did you really *try*?" His eyes drop, finally cowering beneath my livid mien. "If you weren't my brother, I'd *kill* you," I whisper before letting him go with an angry shove. For a second, he looks at me as though I've just ripped his heart right out of his chest, and that fucking wrecks me. I growl at the ground. Taking off towards the exit, I glance at Bronson, who appears stoic. As I shove my way outside, the murmur of their voices follow me through the open door.

"No, let him go," Bron states calmly.

"I'm sorry, Bron."

"I know you are, buddy."

CHAPTER TWO

AS I MAKE my way to the Rover, I clench my fists at my sides. All I feel is rage again. Rage, yes, and fucking regret. And I hate regret; it's a useless emotion and I know better than to suffer it. Know better but feel it, nonetheless.

I try to ignore the dark voice in my head that stokes my volatility. A voice that tells me to trust no one with her. To suspect everyone. I jump into the Rover and start the engine, turning the music up in an attempt to drown that voice out.

Now that business is done, every muscle in my body twitches with the need to get back to her, an irrational response to her absence these days that I'm still not accustomed to. *Fuck*, how I used to like my independence. My solo existence. Now, though, I breathe deeper when she's around.

During the drive home, I relive that night. The night I truly realised what was at stake. Finding her half-broken on the floor. Finding him metres from her with a blade of glass shoved through his carotid artery. She'd fought him, alone, in the dark—without me.

I let her down.

By the time I get home, I'm ready to go several rounds on the bag. But when I walk into my room and see her asleep above the covers on my bed, my anger stills. I freeze in my tracks. Sighing roughly, I map her little figure with my eyes. She's the tiniest thing. She's on her side, facing the window that occupies the full length and height of my bedroom wall. The glow from the city below us shines onto her naked arms and legs. Her hair is in a low ponytail, and I have an urge to pull the elastic away, to let her long, thick, almost-pink blonde hair spread across the pillow.

When I'm beside her, she sleeps naked, but right now, she's in white panties and a singlet. Wandering around the bed and towards the window, I sit on the two-seater lounge in a corner of the room and look at her. Part of her face is in the shadows, but the part lit up by the moon and city is relaxed, soft, and lightly frosted in freckles. They might be my favourite part of her. Those freckles. And I've licked every one of them.

My gaze traces the curve of her shoulder, down to her tiny waist, and over the small swell of her hips.

Leaning back into the cushions, I crack my knuckles. My attention is suddenly snagged on the tattoo on my finger. The one that reads 'ardent one'—fiery one.

My fiery one.

Realising now that I'm not angry anymore, I fold my arms across my chest and continue to watch her sleep.

"MAX."

Although I don't move, my eyes open instantly to the sound of her voice. She sits up slowly in bed—lazily. Moaning sleepily, she rubs her eyes. "What are you doing?"

Taking a few moments to adjust to being awake, I realise I'm still on the lounge.

"Go back to sleep, Little One," I instruct, but she's already climbing from the bed and crossing the room towards me, her little face questioning and concerned.

She stops just short of me, and all I can concentrate on is the slip of white skin between her panties and her single. I lick my lower lip and then look up at her face. She smiles softly at me and fuck—just, *fuck*.

Batting her long soft brown lashes, her bow-shaped lips curl into a sweet smile—as if she has me all figured out.

As she sits on my lap with her legs to the side, I lean back to get a better view of her face and body.

"Why are you on the couch?" she asks, her voice huskier than normal in a half-wake daze. I like it. My cock pulses.

"Didn't want to wake you," I lie. Didn't want to crawl into bed with you while I smell like formaldehyde. Didn't want to lose my mind over your scent and take my frustrations out on your sweet body. Some fucking bullshit truth like that.

I fix my eyes on her lethargic hazel ones, the flecks of gold and amber in them shining despite her sleepy state. My gaze drops to those velvety full lips and they part immediately. She follows my line of sight as I look down at her perfect thighs pressed together. I don't like the way she's sitting. I grab her waist and lift, manoeuvring her until she's stretched open over my lap. *Better.*

Gripping her delicious soft backside, I draw her towards me. She gasps when her soft axis meets my hard one. When her forearms rest on my shoulders, her nails move up along my neck and she strokes my skin. A shiver runs the length of my spine. *Fuck me.* What do I do with her? I'd never been touched like this before meeting her. Not sure any previous girl would have dared to.

Her eyes—adoringly—study my face, and it's welcome and needed and uncomfortable at the exact same time. I'm just thankful she can't see what I am.

Leaning forward, I rest my forehead on her shoulder and take a deep breath.

"Max, tell me," she pleads softly. Straightening back up, I look down at the thin piece of fabric between her legs. Stare at it, actually. Her fingers still in my hair. My hands stroke from her knees to that fabric and stop just shy of it, but I can feel her heat. I push her panties aside, exhaling roughly when I see her smooth bald pussy lips spread open a little due to the position she's in. She is breathing heavily now. Her whole body rocks slightly with each big breath. My cock starts to fill, pressure building inside it as I touch that soft opening with the tip of my finger.

She whimpers slightly—not in a good way. I stop my finger from going any further but don't move it away. I stare up at her beautiful face just as a single tear slides down her cheek. My jaw tics. I want to fuck that sorrow out of her. Her sorrow makes me want to set the earth on fire. She must see that rage building through me because she's kissing my tight lips now. I can taste the salt from her tear.

"I'm sorry," she says against my mouth. I've heard that far too much today. And from her, it's the last set of words I need to hear. Her breath, so sweet, floats into my mouth as she says, "I still hear his words."

My teeth grind. *Fucking Erik.* If he wasn't in pieces already, I'd consider digging him up just to cut his flesh off myself.

"What words? Tell me what he said."

She shakes her head once, timidly shifting her gaze to the ground. "I don't want to repeat it."

"*Cassidy*." I lift her chin and press my lips to hers quickly. Lingering close, I brush our mouths together as I speak. "Think about me. My fingers touching you. Pleasing you. Now tell me what he said that's keeping you from me."

Swallowing nervously, she takes a few moments to answer. "He said I'm weak and that men enter women. Like the devil does."

Fuck. I breathe raggedly. "You don't think you enter me?" I snap, but my aggression isn't meant for her.

She sucks another breath in. A strained breath. "He said you control me with my body. With this part of me."

I want to both howl in anger and burst into laughter at the pure inaccuracy of that statement. Leaning into her almost-pink hair, I speak into her ear. Her cheek moves into mine affectionately as I do. "Every time I come, I think about you. You're in my head." I breathe her in. *Cassidy*. She doesn't wear perfume; her scent is simply feminine. Clean. Natural. My breath on her neck causes her to gasp and then pant. "This soft wet skin." Gradually, I tunnel my fingers between her pussy lips, and her startled moans resonate in my cock. My other hand nearly spans the width of her slim back, pushing her trim abdomen forward and arching her the way I like. "These strong responsive muscles that grip me like a fist. The freckles on your inner thighs. Your smell. Taste. I don't control you, Cassidy. Nothing is further from the truth. You control me. My fingers. My lips. My cock." I shake my head against hers. "You own me, Little One." She's crying now, so I pepper kisses all over her face, tasting the saltiness of her tears as if I were licking her wounds. "Control me, Little One," I tell her.

She blinks at me for a moment, lips open and eyes hesitant. Understanding my gentle command, she swallows nervously and then begins to roll her little pelvis on my lap, stirring my fingers inside her tight, pulsing pussy. She stabilises herself with my shoulders, delicate fingers holding my tight muscles—tight with restraint.

She's tense, but with every forward wave of her hips, her expression becomes more captivated by the moment. I admire her body as her hips start to sway with a rhythm and grace like nothing I've ever seen before. My little ballerina dances on my fingers like it's an enchanting, beautiful act. And with her, it is. My cock strains with yearning in my trousers. Needing to fuck her. Feeling possessive and in need of reassurance she's still mine, I press my teeth together to stop from growling the following words. Instead, I demand gently, "Whose fingers are inside you?"

The tops of her pert milky-white tits flush as heat spreads across her skin. "Max's." She pants my name. Leaning in, I take her taut, aroused nipple into my mouth, my teeth gripping it through the little singlet she's wearing. Groaning at the feel of her rolling body and circling hips, I suck on that tiny bud. Her sweet breast is so perky, so pointed—perfection. When I twist my fingers against her rhythm, I feel her buck slightly with pleasure.

"*Max*." She whimpers my name.

"Max who?" I press.

"*Max Butcher*."

"Tell me you love me," I order, not understanding or analysing why I want to hear it, but goddamn it, I do.

"I love you, Max." Little whimper-mixed moans leave her parted pink lips, so I swallow those sounds, but although muffled, they only get louder as I steal her breath.

While I finger her slowly, she responds to my penetration, sucking my fingers in and kneading me out with those strong internal muscles of hers. "What do you want?"

She starts to shake. "*More.*"

Using my thumb, I press down on her sweet little clit, massaging it back and forth while the two fingers inside her work at a steady pace. "You feel so good wrapped around my fingers, Little One."

Her lips are soft and confused as they strain to kiss me and moan and pant simultaneously. Her body starts to tremble, and I break our kiss to watch her little tits jiggle beneath the white fabric and her face come apart with pleasure.

"You're so fucking beautiful."

Her pussy locks onto my fingers. My cock pulses. Anticipating her recoil from the orgasm thrashing through her, I grab the side of her throat and squeeze lightly, holding her down so she remains deeply impaled on my fingers. As I curl them onto that spot twitching inside her, she cries out loudly. Fuck me if she isn't the sexiest thing I've ever seen. How she can look so incredibly sweet—innocent—while purring out her orgasm on my lap like a little kitten, I do not know.

My fingers continue to fuck her, drawing her orgasm out. Not giving up my repetitive motion, I wring every last sensation from her. And goddamn it, if I'm not in physical pain with the need to bury my cock deep inside her. Feeling her orgasm on my fingers, her body vibrating, overwhelmed, I groan through gritted teeth in unison with her peaking cries.

When she finally stops shaking and the pleasure she just riding flattens, she stares blankly at me.

My brows draw in tight at the sight of her blinking, confused expression.

That's not good.

Then her eyes widen with uncertainty. She's breathing

like she's just run a marathon, and it's now apparent to me that this is a fucking bad thing. A *very* fucking bad thing.

Clenching my jaw, I pull my fingers from inside her. "Cassidy, what's that look?"

While my breaths mingle with anger at the crumbling state of the girl on my lap, hers are all of a sudden short. Quick. Shallow.

Panicked.

I sit up and cup her cheeks while her eyes bounce around in a kind of stupor. "Little One?"

"I'm fine. I'm fine. I'm fine," she chants, but tears burst from the corners of her eyes. Fucking tears. And fuck me, does the sight of them slice me up.

"What happened?" I growl, wanting to shake her back to coherence.

"I don't know," she says, her voice faint and unsteady. I pull her against my chest, shielding her little frame with my arms. Tightening with the need to protect her. Too tight. Not tight enough.

I can fix this—I'm going to fix this.

Moving forward, if anyone so much as upsets her, makes her shuffle on the fucking sidewalk for them, I won't be leaving the freezer with a clean shirt.

CHAPTER THREE

cassidy

I BLINK at the blonde girl staring back at me in the vanity mirror—her reflection strange and foreign in a way I can't explain. With her big hazel eyes and matching coloured freckles lightly dusting her nose and cheeks, she doesn't resemble the kind of girl who would shoot someone in the face. Less the type to feel no remorse in the wake of that person's death. I'm not sure what that kind of girl looks like, but it isn't this.

Max's bathroom is my favourite place in his house. Although I haven't even seen half of his home, this room is full of fun memories and love. Today, though, it looks different. I can't explain how. That's all I know—different.

Running my fingers through my hair and scooping it to one side, I note how long it is. How wavy. I don't think I like it anymore. Flicking it back over my shoulders, I decide I'm going to cut it off. Maybe dye it.

If Max won't mind...

I glance down at the Carrara stone vanity top, touching the dusty brown veins that run through it like marble. Next, I stare at our toiletries all laid out together—his aftershave and deodorant alongside my many cans and creams. My toothbrush is next to his in a little navy-grey ceramic cylinder, and for some weird reason, I find that oddly painful. Which, of course, is a completely ridiculous emotion to feel in regards to the placement of a toothbrush. Ignoring my silly feelings, I pick it up and begin to brush my teeth.

As my mouth gets a good cleaning, I can't help but let my mind wander to the events of last night. What it should have been and wasn't. How I ruined it. My emotions shifted uncomfortably fast from wary to needy. I remember his voice being raspy with sentiment as he whispered words to me. And yet, he might as well have yelled them because they held that much power. 'I own him.' We own each other. And I enjoyed that thought enough to allow the lust to take over. But then, as I came off the precipice of the man-god that is Max Butcher, a boulder of complete self-loathing dropped into every fibre of my being.

Clearly, my mind is in a state of anarchy.

Freezing my thoughts, Max strolls leisurely into the bathroom, wearing only white cotton boxers. His penis is hard to ignore in pants; in underwear, it's damn right impossible. Shaking my head to try to focus, I ignore the growing need inside me. My body wants his, but my mind isn't so sure, and the two are giving me whiplash.

Last night was the first time we've been intimate since Erik attacked me, and it didn't exactly go well. What must he think of me? Riding his fingers that desperately and then bursting into tears? *Oh my God*, poor Max.

Like a little voyeur, I watch his reflection as he pulls his boxers down and moves into the shower. He's the most beautiful thing I've ever seen. As he begins to wash, I find myself fixated on the ink that encompasses his strong arms, back, and shoulders. Each tattoo shares a little piece of his soul with the world, and yet, no one has any idea how to interpret them. Myself included. Besides the cross on his chest, there is no real straightforward image. It's like beautiful black, white, and red abstract art.

On a normal day, he's not the talkative type. He's the master of the single-word response. And yet, the silence right now is ear-piercing. I stop brushing my teeth and spit into the sink. Deciding I can't go to ballet class, leaving him all day without something *good* to remember me by, I pull off my shirt and pull down my knickers.

When I step into the shower, he turns to face me with a brooding expression. Anyone else might call it a scowl, but I know it's merely a warning. Warning me not to push him too far. I peer up, craning my neck to see his narrowed, turbulent grey-blue eyes, which cloak so much emotion. I know it's there. Hidden deep where no one can touch it.

Hot water splashes off his shoulders and down onto my breasts. Unable to hold that powerful gaze, I drop to my knees on the tiles and he exhales roughly.

His sigh is almost pained as I trail my hands up the tight muscles of his thighs to the thickly defined V-shaped cords between his hips. They pulse in response to my caress. So perfect. Beautiful.

I reach for his large, growing penis, but he catches my wrist.

"No," he growls.

My eyes seek out his, finding them angry and darker than before. "Please."

"Don't you fucking dare do that just for me!"

My breathing picks up at the sight of him—tormented between lust and guilt.

Swallowing down my heart as it tries to beat up my throat, I say, "I want to, Max."

As the muscles in his cheeks pulse, he releases his grip on me. He nods once stiffly, giving me permission to touch him again. And then I see something I never thought I'd see in his expression *bullshit*. He's a lot of things, my Max. A towering, broody man with a physique built for destruction and dominance. He's a powerful heir to a corrupt empire. A boxer. Rugby player. Brother. Menace. To name a few... But he's not fake. Max doesn't do bullshit and yet, there it is, allowing me to armour my broken pieces. Hide them. He's allowing me to pretend that last night didn't happen, to be powerful and free and in the moment.

I hide that realisation by dropping my gaze to his erection, which is now nearly as long as my forearm and almost as thick too. I still have no idea how he puts that inside me. His foreskin has bunched below its smooth head, and as I lick up the full length of it, Max shuffles his feet apart. Placing both palms on the tiles in front of him, he leans some of his weight forward. My tongue meets the smoothest pinkest skin I've ever seen and when a bead of precum slides out, I lap at it eagerly.

Working the underside with my tongue, stimulating his tight ridge, I enjoy the taste of his skin.

I feel good doing this—in control.

Wrapping my hand around the base of his erection, I try to take him into my mouth as far as I can. I close my eyes as the feel of his girth strains my jaw. He feeds one of his hands through my hair. Gently at first. Then fisting lightly to urge me deeper, to open my jaw wider. As I relax my throat and let him slide down further, he groans low and long.

Max's thrusts meet my inward strokes, but he's still being careful not to go too deep. For a second, I wonder if he was gentle like this with other girls, and somehow, I know he wasn't. From what I've seen, his soft side is a temperament only reserved for me. He pants roughly, guiding me with his fist, down and out.

He takes control.

He begins to pump into my mouth faster, still seemingly concerned with not going too far, but he's slowly starting to get a little carried away.

I press my palms to his taut thighs, bracing myself. Focusing on breathing through my nose, I swallow around his erection, and he uses that moment to slide in further still.

"*Fuck*," he hisses. His pleasured groans spur me on, so I try to use my tongue to massage the underside of his penis in time with his rhythm. Then something shifts. His movements become more chaotic and relentless as pleasure takes hold. He's nearly there. I feel for his balls as they draw up. The muscles of his thighs twitch. His abdomen crunches. And now he's cradling my cheeks and really thrusting into my mouth. I blink up at him and he trains his dark eyes on me before closing them and dropping his head back. He shudders. Groaning and holding my mouth around his erection, he releases inside me in three powerful pulses. I keenly swallow what he gives me, feeling desire thrumming between my legs even though my mind won't allow for any kind of pleasure. I feel ripped apart between my body and my psyche.

He doesn't release me for several seconds. The throbbing of his erection slows in unison with his heavy breathing. When he finally pulls my head back, his penis slides out and hangs half-erect by his thigh. Slowly, I stand up. He reaches for my neck, envelops it with his hand, and pulls me to his lips for a soft, quick kiss.

A little light-headed, I try for a smile. "That was really deep."

His brows draw in. "Did I hurt you?"

He always asks me that. Shaking my head slowly, I say, "You never do."

Warmth moves through me when he pulls me into his chest and holds me there as if he loves me. As if he's fighting some kind of battle. As if he's afraid of something. But Max Butcher isn't afraid of anything.

And I don't *think* he loves me—I know he does.

As he strokes my hair, I rub my cheek against the shadowed wall of his hard chest. *Ugh*, I wish last night would disappear. Wish I wanted him to touch me the way he used to. Take me without asking. Worship my body.

I think I'm a little broken. A little lost.

More than anything, I want Max and Cassidy's world back.

Wrapping my arms around him, I squeeze tight. As if my tiny, little grip can possibly hold us together.

CHAPTER FOUR

I TAP the top of the Chrysler with my palm and then step back as Carter slowly cruises away with Cassidy in the back seat. She twists around, her golden eyes wide and fixed on me.

As I watch them exit the driveway and disappear out of sight, it takes every piece of restraint to stop myself from chasing after her.

Things are not right.

I jump into Romeo—*fuck*, the Rover, and drive off before I start to think too much. Think about her soft mouth stretched around my cock in the shower, taking me deeper than most girls can. Think about her teary eyed and swallowing around my thrusts.

I shouldn't have allowed it.

But I was a selfish bastard.

It's a ten-minute drive to Jimmy's, but it feels like a split second. His security waves me through the boom gate. Large hedges border the driveway like looming barricades, and atop every light pole there are many sets of eyes watching my approach through cameras. We have good security at home, but nothing like what Jimmy has. It's a good thing he has it too. He's got enemies—more than he thinks, perhaps.

I park in my spot, beside Butch's car, and jump out. I take note that Bronson's bike is missing, but I don't need to speculate as to why. He doesn't have the levelheadedness for this side of the business.

As always, the front door opens for me before I can ring the bell. The young maid, who I'm sure gets down on her hands and knees and wears a collar for Jimmy, ushers me inside. His love of submission is well known.

I stride past her and head straight towards the boardroom, growing further agitated with every step.

We'd set this meeting a few days ago, but due to Cassidy's delicate condition, I cancelled. At that mere thought of her, heat rushes into my head.

As I approach the boardroom, Jimmy's thick Sicilian accent sounds through the door. "This is distasteful business."

My teeth mash together. Him speaking in English means he has Australian soldiers in there ready to intervene if things turn south.

"He threatened my family, Jimmy," Butch states, his tone harder than normal but not hard enough given the crux of the conversation.

I push the door open, causing it to hit the brick wall with a thud. The sound renders the room silent. I didn't mean to do that. Happy accident.

Clay and Butch turn to acknowledge me with tight smiles while Jimmy stares deadpan at me from across the room. Two overweight soldiers sit casually on stools at the small bar. Hostility gathers around us. My eyes stay fixed on Jimmy as I round the table, sit beside Clay, lean back, and fold my arms across my chest. I should have been here earlier, but I was with Cassidy—I don't rush those moments.

Jimmy ignores my rude interruption and looks back at Butch. "You don't know, se? The boy had ulterior motives. He could have organised this alone."

Bullshit.

Butch drains his whiskey before pressing, "He sent her down there. Xander confirmed it. I trust my son's instincts; you should too."

Her. I bite my tongue to stop from growling.

Jimmy tsks. "And you're so sure he knew what would happen?"

And now I want to lunge across the table and rip out his *tsking* tongue.

Jimmy leans back into his seat. "I don't want my family at odds. I will talk with Dustin—"

"That's not enough," Butch interrupts, glancing at me sideways, knowing I'm losing what little restraint I have. I'm glad he can see it. My aggression feels tightly coiled, and the grip I have on that coil is slipping.

"Luca." Jimmy appears almost exasperated. "You know he's got the Australian blue-collar fucks wrapped around his finger. *Iddi sù devòti.* Just like us. You know they won't work with Sicilians. We lose Dustin, or worse, he takes up alliances elsewhere; we lose the truckers, our mines, our diamonds."

Clay nurses his whiskey instead of drinking it, keeping his mind sharp and his temper in check. He's a tall, business-type man now, but I remember the egotistical cut-snake he was at my age. Although, it'd be hard to believe that looking at him now. He's annoyingly polished these days. Logical. This is the first time I've seen him since he got back from his honeymoon, but I imagine Butch has filled him in. He is his heir, after all. His heir, yes, but my brother and our code of loyalty is impenetrable.

"I could do it," Clay says smoothly. "I could make the deals up in the Kimberley."

"No, my boy." Jimmy dismisses him with a wave of his hand. "You're going to need to keep squeaky clean if you're to run for a councillor position next year. And not just you, all of you. We can't afford any attention." He looks dead at me. "Keep your business clean."

He best be referring to his business and not my relationship with Cassidy. "*Your* business," I mutter angrily.

"*Our* business, Max," Clay corrects me.

Butch notices my expression, the heat now spreading to my neck.

"Jimmy," Butch snaps, drawing Jimmy's attention back to him. "I want to deal with Dustin myself—"

"We are not having this conversation," Jimmy says, feigning composure as he cracks his knuckles in front of him. "No one is to discuss this with Dustin."

"I have spent the better part of my life making uncomfortable truths disappear for you, but this one will not just disappear," Butch states, his brows weaved in tight.

"No, I believe it won't," Jimmy replies.

"Let me take care of it then," Butch says, his voice low.

"No." Jimmy opens his arms to us, pretending to welcome our concerns but squashing them all the same. "It pains me. I'm not happy with how things went down. I am very fond of our Cassidy—"

"Don't fucking say her name," I hiss.

Jimmy stiffens. "I think that's just about enough out of your mouth today, boy. Not another word."

My fist hits the table, rattling whiskey tumblers.

When I stand up, all eyes lock on me, as do two Glocks

which are pointed directly at my tight forehead. I couldn't care less. As I scowl across the Marri boardroom table and into Jimmy's brown eyes, I feel no fear. I used to fear this man—not anymore. And for a moment, just a split fucking second, Jimmy's throat contracts, and through that fleeting gesture, the truth is exposed—he's a little intimidated by me.

I hiss low through my teeth. "No one is to go near Cassidy."

He attempts to interrupt me, but I don't allow it. "She is out of this! She stays out! No one is to talk to Cassidy. No one is to so much as look at her with goddamn indifference, or I swear to your God, Jimmy, I swear it, I'll bring your whole fucking empire down."

Jimmy's gaze sears holes through mine. He lifts his hand to signal the soldiers. "Do not point guns at my family," he orders, his voice calm, annoyingly so. His soldiers lower their weapons. "You disrespect me, Max. Do you think so little of me that you treat me with suspicion and hostility? I think of you as a son, se? Your father—a brother. I have given you everything you have ever asked of me. Given you opportunities, and this is how you treat me?"

My body vibrates with adrenaline. Blood thrashes, feverishly and volatile, through my arteries and veins. "I. Want. Dustin. Dead!"

"Dustin has left the District," he states plainly. "He is taking care of an issue I have up north."

"Even better. Let me meet him up there," I bite out.

"Max, think about this," Clay says, still seated casually. He swirls his whiskey around the glass; not a drop is missing from its initial fill. "Go home. Be with Cassidy. Let the matter settle."

I look at Butch, who is now completely unreadable, and

then back at Clay. Jimmy has big plans for him. Perhaps that has infiltrated my big brother's honour as a Butcher. Am I wrong to think his loyalties lie with us? No. He's sly. And he's cut throats for me before.

"The fish rots from the head," Jimmy says, drawing my scowl back to him. "We are the head—Storm and Butcher. Don't be the *rot*. Do as Clay says. I give you my word that whoever disrespects my family will never do it twice."

I bite back my growl, turn my back on him—knowing just how much he fucking hates that—and stride from the room. The door slams behind me.

I may be punished for that. But he needs to know that if anyone disturbs her peace, gets in her way, derails her progress out of the fucking nightmare I've put her in—*Fuck.* If she so much as feels unsafe. Even a hint. A murmur of unease. I'll rip his world apart. Dismantle it. Dirty deed by dirty deed.

Passing the maid, who I'm sure will look delicious on all fours—I suppress the urge to fuck my anger away. Not too long ago, a different version of myself would have dragged that girl into a room, buried myself deep inside her, and made her scream my name. But now I ignore my cock, jump into the Rover, and speed off towards the gym.

***

WHEN I ARRIVE, the gym is near empty. My guards usually call ahead, anticipating my destination while I drive. We are all followed: Xan, Clay, Stacey, Bron sometimes, but he slips them on his Ducati when he wants to be alone. Butch likes to have eyes on each of us around the clock. Given we can't even trust our own at the moment, it's a good thing too.

And I have eyes on Cassidy now...

I grab my pager and send a quick message to Carter.

> Max: Get someone on Dustin Nerrock.
> Watch him.

Glaring across the gym, I note both training rings are free and there is only a handful of men in the weights area. I clench my fists. *Dustin fucking Nerrock.* Craving the ache and fatigue, I head straight for the bags.

After a three-hour weight and boxing session, my mind has relaxed somewhat. My muscles are on fire, but my mind is cool—settled. I'm about to finish up when Butch storms in, his voice booming across the room. "Everyone out!"

Fuck.

He enters like a goddamn nuke exploding; people fly off like shrapnel in the opposite direction and out the nearest exit. Although he's in his fifties now, his frame thicker and movements heavier, that doesn't weaken him. He is ever-more fuelled by determination and pride. And while a lesser man might tire of such an exhausting level of expectation, he is only ignited by it.

Gripping the bag on either side, I slow its movements before pressing my forehead to it. I sigh harshly, stealing a second before the mayhem starts. Sweat pours from my brows and down my nose. Time's up. Turning to face him, I brace myself for what is to come.

A lesson in respect, I am sure.

"Gloves off! Get in the ring!" he orders.

Fuck.

Caught between wanting to show him no weakness and wanting to keep all my teeth, I stand strong. He doesn't even bother to remove his shirt and tie, ready to mess me up dressed like a fucking accountant. With determination in his eyes, he strides past me and into the ring. I follow him, working on removing my gloves. As soon as I enter, he swings at me.

"Fuck's sake," I growl as I duck under his fist.

"You fucking amateur!" Butch growls. Lunging towards me, his head bobbing, he lands a right hook into the side of my jaw. Pain shoots through my face and into my eye socket. "I thought you were the smart one!"

Dodging another punch, I fumble around with my sweat-soaked gloves, trying to get them off. They finally drop to the mat.

He jolts towards me. His fist flexes. Keeping my arms high, I block his quick swing to my face. That pisses him off.

"I told you I would take care of this!" Butch growls.

I take a few light steps around while he darts from foot to foot. There is nothing but 'The Butcher' in his deep-set scowl right now, and defence is my best bet. Still, I throw a few punches his way, connecting on the third, but then he charges at me, shoulders lowered and arms on guard. I hesitate. He slams me into the mat with a loud thud.

Dropping on top of me, straddling my hips, his weight pins me down. I'm a fucking big guy, but he's heavy with rage and disappointment. I hold my forearms up, shielding my face as he beats the living shit out of me. His fists feel like a wooden bat to the side of my head. A few vision-blackening blows rain in, and my eyes are forced shut due to sweat, drool, and sticky blood.

My every sensation is now felt in the dull smacks of his knuckles. Even though my forearms are shaking with exertion, I keep them high, blocking the strength and destruction of each one of his swings. Our collective grunts and growls are animalistic and raw.

Pain shoots through my cheekbone, but I wait. Wait for

an opening. For the moment he tires. Straight after his first sloppy blow, I drop my guard for a moment. Lowering one fist, I take another knock to the face. I ignore the pain and jab his right rib hard.

His thighs release their hold on me.

He rolls onto his back.

Lesson settled, we pant side by side, flayed open on the mats. Blood trickles down my face and into my mouth. When I taste the warm metallic substance, I spit it out.

Clenching my teeth, I bury my groans deep in my chest. "Not bad for an old man," I rumble.

"You're getting good," he states emphatically, his voice steady and unaffected. "You should consider boxing. Get you away from freezers."

Wiping the blood and sweat from my forehead, I point out, "I don't want to box."

He jumps to his feet without a single show of discomfort. But when his blood-stained white shirt catches his eye, he scowls with disapproval.

With furrowed brows, he states, "We don't always get what we want, Max."

As he turns to leave, I sit up on the mat, lifting my knees up and leaning forward on them. "I'm going to kill him."

"I know you are, son," he says over his shoulder as he approaches the door. He stops with his hand on the door handle. "Can you wait?"

"Do I have a choice?"

"We always have a choice, Max." He turns and levels me out with stern eyes. "I told you I would take care of it. I told you to keep your cool head. You made the choice not to listen."

CHAPTER FIVE

"WOW, Max has really lost his mind over this," Flick says, staring through the window and across the moonlit street to Carter's parked car. Max wasn't kidding when he said Carter doesn't sleep. It's ten p.m. and he's out there. Of course, I can't see him through the tinted windows, but his car is there either way.

Closing the lounge room curtain, Flick sighs and wanders over to me. "So he's always going to be around? You'll never be alone?"

I don't want to be alone. It's a truth I can't say aloud because it's completely embarrassing and completely not me. I used to love being alone. But now I take great comfort in Carter's lingering presence. "He gives me privacy. He barely looks at me, and for such a big guy, he seems to be able to make himself invisible."

"And what if Dad calls the cops? Have you spoken to him about your new shadow?"

"No," I admit. "Not yet." It's a fair question. But even though my dad is a protective man, I know he won't call the cops. He knows more about Max's family than he's letting on. The secrets around us are like an intricate web. At times, I'm eager to put a torch to it just to see if I can burn it all down. But I don't know who will burn along with it.

My big brother, Konnor, maybe?

Max, definitely...

Flick sits down opposite me, her hazel-green eyes pinned to me, holding back so much emotion. She drops her line of sight to my bruised cheekbone and then to the jagged gash running the length of my forearm. "The guy that did that—" She winces and takes a big breath in. "He's dead... isn't he?"

Swallowing hard, I nod. It's all I can manage.

Her eyes widen even though she's clearly not that surprised. "Max killed him?"

I nod again, hating that I do, even though it's what he would have wanted. The fact that I pulled the trigger is a secret between Max, Bronson, Xander, and I. Carter probably assumes as much, but he never saw the deed done. Butch might suspect it, but the words were never uttered aloud.

She breathes out fast. "That's so fucking heavy."

My heart picks up pace when the idea of Flick sharing this information hits me. "You can never tell anyone. No one." She's quickly beside me as my body beings to tremble a little.

Her arms go around me. She rests her cheek on my head while her molten-red hair cushions my face on her shoulder. "I won't tell anyone. I promise. Does Stacey know?"

"I don't know." I sigh. "I haven't seen her since the auction. I presume so. I presume Xander would have told her everything."

A stream of light moves across the curtain as another car parks across from our house. My arms release their hold on Flick and drop to my sides. I stand and wander over to the window. Sweeping the fabric aside, I see Max's Range Rover idling beside Carter's car. He switches the headlights off.

My heart pirouettes. I already miss his smell. His touch.

Flick moves in behind me, peering over my shoulder. "I don't like this, Cassidy. You are being almost *owned*."

Peering up at my sister, who is at least six inches taller than me, I say, "It's not like that. He's protecting me, that's all."

"And Carter is reporting to him... like you're his property. If I'd known, I'd never have..." I feel her sigh against my back. "I'd give up Stacey in a second to get you out of this mess."

"I'm not in any mess, Flick. Max—" My attention is snatched by Max's car pulling into the driveway. Moving away from Flick and towards the door, I suddenly stop at the handle. "I love Max. He didn't choose his lifestyle."

But before I can step out onto the veranda, Flick says, "Yeah, but you still can."

I don't like how those words ring in my ears.

Stepping outside into the warm dark night, I wait for him to park and switch the ignition off. I literally have to jump when exiting Romeo; he's like a few feet off the ground. Max, on the other hand, steps out with ease.

He strides with purpose towards me, cloaked in the occasional shadow.

"Max—" I begin, but when his face comes into view, I'm shell-shocked. Covering my mouth with my palm, I gasp into it. "Oh my God, what happened to your face?"

I rush to him, feeling the need to touch his beautiful face and kiss it back to health. Wrapping my arms around his waist, I nuzzle his chest. "What happened?" I can tell something is wrong. His body is taut. Feverish. When his arms go around my head, holding me to him, I rub into his body further. "Max. Did you get into a fight?"

Dropping his arms to his sides, he says, "Boxing. Let's go."

His fingers entwine with mine, but when he turns to pull me towards his car, I resist.

He has bruises all over his face. Blood on his lip. Yet, he wants me to just accept that he's been boxing recreationally when I know it's more than that. That someone has hurt him. Intentionally. That knots my stomach.

So secretive.

My fingers slip from his.

When he freezes with his back to me, I try to stand strong. Wanting to know what happened. Wanting the truth. Slowly, he faces me again, the light from the veranda highlighting his bruises and the cut on his lip and—

My breath catches.

And even though he's my Max. *My Max.* For the briefest of moments, I see Erik.

His scarred face lit up between the tree limbs at the wedding. His defensive, distrusting expression. His eyes full of revenge as he stroked between my legs.

Women were created to be so weak. Small. Fragile.

Max's brows draw together slowly. "What's going on?"

Slowing my breaths, I try not to heave.

"I miss my family," I blurt out before I can analyse why. Max's gaze darts to my feet, narrowing on them as I take a tiny step away from him. His fingers twitch as if he's resisting the urge to grab my hand again. "I just want to stay here tonight," I say, but the words are not strong and true; they are brittle and confused. As his expression darkens with suspicion, my heart twists. For him. For the confusion in my own actions.

I glance at the ground, my throat filling with heat. I've never denied him my company before. But I can't... not tonight. Not when he looks like—"Don't overthink this, Max."

He straightens. "Get in the car, Cassidy."

I meet his gaze again and try not to see the bruises. The lies. "Max." I say his name, hoping it'll ground me. It doesn't. "Stop it." Fierce stormy-blue eyes narrow on me just before he grabs my arm. "Max!" As he drags me towards his car, I dig my heels into the grass. A futile attempt to slow him. How easy it would be for him to throw me around. Control me.

Max controls you too.

My pulse ignites.

Manoeuvring me until my back is pressed to the passenger side door, he cages me in with his body, his palms meeting the car either side of my face, his muscular arms flexing as he leans forward, leaving me very little room to move.

My breaths come in hard and fast.

Dipping his head, his heavy exhales hit my neck as he whispers, "Don't make me beg, Little One."

Trying to control my racing pulse, I squeeze my eyes shut and focus on Max's smell. He smells like sweat and our sheets and home, not like herbs and tobacco. Not like dense, pungent dark clouds of tobacco. This is Max. *My Max!*

I take a big breath in.

Out.

And I realise, something is wrong with him tonight. Something has happened. He needs me, and it's that need that drags me back to him. I bat my eyes open. He's staring down at me in a world of pain, turbulent and chaotic. Volatile and yet, deeply vulnerable. But Max is never vulnerable.

He needs me.

"What happened?" I whisper, ignoring the chaos in my head. The fear that makes no sense. He presses his forehead to mine, and I feel as though our hearts ache together but for different reasons. Neither of which we can explain to the other. His body vibrates with anger and restlessness around me.

"Just get in the car," he whispers, his voice deep with emotion. "*Please*."

Oh God, he is literally begging me. "*Shh*." I cup the back of his neck, feeling the ridge of his shoulder muscles react. Pulse. They are on fire.

I stroke him soothingly, summoning all my will to remember that this is the man I love. That the fear I'm feeling isn't associated with him. Not at all. Even though that is all true, I can't stop the tremble in my voice. Or the sob that wants to burst out. I can't be there for him tonight. I just can't. Not when it is taking every piece of will I have to not flinch from his touch. To hold his gaze. "I want to spend the night here."

"Why?" he barks, and I immediately recoil.

Growling low at himself, he takes a step backwards as though he's wrestling with something internally. He breathes angrily as he eyes me up and down. Max is often unreadable. For the most part, he doesn't reveal. He's closed off. But not tonight. Tonight he's radiating emotion. Pain. Desperation. Anger... *Need*. He needs me right now for whatever reason and I should—

When Max fists his hands, wincing ever so slightly, my attention shifts to his clenched fingers, the bruising on them visible even in the gathering night. The bruising from punching someone. I lift my hand and touch the remnants of the bruise under my eye.

He looks at me, brows weaving with confusion. With

anguish. "I'm sorry, Little One. I just need to know why you're still here? Why didn't you get Carter to take you home?" he asks roughly.

I breathe slowly, craning my neck to catch the intensity in his eyes. I want to say, 'But I am home.' The words seem to burn my throat because maybe... I'm not. "You know things aren't right with me. Something huge happened to me—"

He bares his teeth, leaning down to press his cheek to mine. "What happened to you is making me murderous, Little One. I assure you, I haven't forgotten."

I shake my head. "I just need to process it, Max."

He grabs the top of my arms and squeezes lightly—a warning. *Controlling.* "You made me want this, Cassidy." His voice deepens. "Now you think you can just take it away?"

My shoulders move as I take shallow breaths in and out.

Erik's body cages me. "I want to take something from him."

I squeeze my eyes shut, holding them like that as I fight the onslaught of Erik's memory. "I'm not taking anything away from you, Max," I say, my voice choked. "I promise. I love you—"

My eyes fly open while his narrow at the sound of my sister's voice. "Get your hands off her, Max!"

And Max's resolve shatters.

Detonates.

I don't think Flick understands that our thing is our thing, and people can't get in the middle of it without being torn apart. Max tightens his grip on me as if she were physically prying me from his hold.

Bending his head to the side, his eyes burn, piles of embers being stoked by her presence. His body unmoving, he hisses, "Walk back inside, Felicity, or they'll never find your body."

Oh my God!

Something inside me snaps.

I shove at his wall-like body, barely making an impression on his chest, completely ineffective in shifting him. He turns his head to frown down at me.

My heart beats frantically. "Go inside, Flick," I say, swallowing hard, feigning anger but feeling weak...*weak*. Like I want to shrink into him where I am safe and hide from him all at once. It hurts. It stirs my insides. Wanting to clutch at my stomach as nausea rolls through me, I curl a little in on myself. "Don't"—I shake my head slowly—"ever threaten my sister, Max."

He fastens his eyes shut, muttering under his breath. "*Fuck*."

He's not Erik.

I force myself to press my shaky palm to his cheek. Force myself to remember who he is to me. "*Menace*," I whisper, the word breaking. Trying to steady my voice in the face of his anger, I call over to my sister again. "Flick, go inside. I'm fine."

Peering past him, I watch as she moves inside the house unhappily.

He opens his eyes, seeking out mine. "Don't take this away from me," he says, his voice tightly coiled.

God, my emotions run riot inside me—a little fear, a little discomfort, and a bucket-load of confusion. "It's just one night," I say, but I know things won't just go back to normal tomorrow. I also know he needs to hear that they may.

He's not Erik.

My trembling fingers move up to caress the swelling on his cheek and under his eye. "What happened to your beautiful face?"

"Boxing."

I lift onto my tippy toes and press my lips to his bruised cheek. "With the hulk?"

He lets out a sound that toes the line between a scoff and a chuckle. "Say, this is what I want." His feverish lips meet mine in a chaste and yet, helplessly needy kiss. Need takes control. His lips become punishing against mine. Demanding something I can't give him tonight.

I recoil.

Stilling, his mouth freezes on mine.

He leans back to gaze at my face, eyes moving around each aspect of my expression. His mien turns dark, distorting into one of pure fury. "You're hearing *him*, aren't you?" He growls.

He pushes off the car and moves around to the driver's side, every piece of him radiating with rage.

My world tilts a little at his sudden absence. "Don't leave things like this." I rush after him, but when he turns around to meet me, I stumble backwards, my feet taking me away from him. Away from his dark, bruised face. Narrowed eyes.

"*Fuck!*" he roars. He tears himself away again, ready to just leave, to take away the thing that has my pulse shuddering through my veins. *Him.* He's scaring me. And it's *killing* him.

It's breaking me.

How could I let this happen to us?

"Max!" I beg, the heat of tears tightening my throat. "Not like this." My heart leaps out to be with him, but my feet stay rooted to the ground.

Opening the door, he puts one foot up on the step. "Little One, if I don't walk away from you right now, you'll end up over my shoulder. And after that, I don't know what I'll do."

I cover my face, tears bursting from my eyes. I cry for Max. For me. I move away from the car while he climbs inside, knowing I can't push him away and pull him back and mess with his head anymore. The lights flick on, illuminating me in the dark. Through the windscreen, he stares at me for a few seconds as if he's worried it might be the last time. But it won't! That's not what's happening here, is it?

I can't breathe through that thought.

But then he pulls away.

CHAPTER SIX

I TOOK two Phenergan last night to help me fall asleep.

I still woke up before my alarm.

And the antihistamines make me foggy. I welcome the feeling.

After a quick run followed by an even quicker breakfast, I am now on my way to my ballet academy. To keep from analysing what happened last night with Max, I stare at my phone, idly flipping through photos and messages.

Carter doesn't peer back at me. Cautious to keep his eyes on the road, he navigates the residential streets before turning onto the highway.

So apparently, my mind can take in pictures and scenery and also thoroughly dissect my anxieties. The fact that Carter is still here. That he picked me up to take me to my classes means I haven't lost Max. Or is this protection now due to his guilt and not his love? I swallow the thought.

Last night was restless. A night filled with yearning.

My insides are all tied up at the mere thought of spending another night alone in my bed. Without him.

Wondering whether he's still so angry. So hurt... His pain had manifested the only way it knew how. Max Butcher doesn't cry. Or act weak. He doesn't have a flight mode...

I have already foreseen the scenario where he charges into my bedroom and drags me out by the arm. What's more uncomfortable to imagine... is if he doesn't. I mean, I'm not exactly my charming, playful self lately. He might enjoy our time apart.

My stomach rolls.

God, that thought makes me feel sick.

Focusing on some selfies of Toni and me, I force my brain to analyse them instead. When my phone rings, I jump. I lift the handset to my ear and answer, "Hello."

"Is this Cassidy Slater?" a young female voice asks.

"Yes."

"We have been trying to get hold of you since you were discharged," she says with a little exasperation or maybe it's nervousness, I can't tell. "I'm a nurse from the District Central Hospital. We wanted to know how you're feeling?"

Shame hits me. I've been ignoring numbers I don't recognise. Every flashing nameless number fills me with fear, reminding me of Erik. Of his anonymous texts. Of how ignorant I was to ignore them.

Through a sigh, I answer, "I'm feeling a lot better."

"Is there any discolouration or pain around your sutures?"

Glancing down at the jagged slice on my forearm, I shake my head even though she can't see me. Erik threw me through a glass table—he made his mark physically and emotionally that night. "No."

"That's great. There is another thing, Cassidy," she says, sounding a little strange. "We were unsure whether you knew at the time... you left quite abruptly."

Sitting up straight, I frown at the rear-view mirror. Wary of Carter while he focuses on the road, I lower my voice, but I'm not sure why. "Knew what?"

"Well... your blood test revealed that you're about six weeks pregnant, well, seven now." She keeps talking, but the words are suddenly foreign, her voice muffled and distant.

Between my ears, my heartbeat hammers like a drum.

Oh God.

Saliva builds up in my mouth, forcing me to swallow hard. This can't be happening. Not now.

I'm eighteen.

I want to dance around the world.

I'm eighteen...

The phone starts to vibrate beside my ear from my hand trembling so fiercely. I blink at Carter, who is now glancing at me in the mirror. Hearing the tick tick tick of the indicator, I barely register that the car is slowing down and rolling into the strip lane.

"Did you know?" the lady on the other side of the phone asks. Apparently, we both speak English again. Well, this explains the whole crying over the position of a toothbrush thing. The sick feeling. The confusion.

I decide to lie in order to cut the conversation short. "*Yes.*"

The phone call ends or I hang up or she does, I don't know which.

Pregnant.

Through the front windscreen, I see cars flying past us.

Oh God.

We can't bring a baby into *his* world.

The blare of horns snaps me back to reality. Staring at the mirror, I acknowledge Carter and say, "Why have we stopped?"

For a man who wouldn't need a mask to dress up like Freddy Kruger, it is amazing how comfortable I am in his presence. Unable to see his mouth, I watch his eyes as he says, "That's big news, Miss Slater. Congratulations."

"Could you hear her?"

Nodding, he confirms, "Yes." When he glances at my ear, I realise I'm still clutching my phone to the side of my head. I lower it to my lap. Looking at it, I'm reminded that Max doesn't have a phone. He doesn't like to be contacted. Bothered. That's the mentality of a man who doesn't want to be tied to the world. Restricted. Not that long ago, he thought having a girlfriend was worse than polio. And now...

I glance up at Carter. "I can't dance Sugar Plum." The words come out at the same time as my realisation. Uttered without context, they must be such peculiar words to him. In two months, I'll be expected to perform a very physically demanding role—one that I'll never be able to do four to five months pregnant. I mean, I could. But not to the standard I would want. That truth sinks like a boulder to the pit of my belly, my body slumping in the seat as if its presence is a tangible thing.

How big will my belly be at five months pregnant?

I'm so small.

Max is so big...

I don't know enough about genetics to know whether the size of the parents play any role in the size of the foetus...

Should I call it a foetus?

Can I?

Is it wrong?

It's a baby—

"Max said you like carnival rides?"

Carter cuts into my complete freak-out. Peering into the rear-view mirror again, I can see his eyes are smiling. And even though it's a bizarre question or statement, I'm not sure which, I still nod.

He explains, "They have a festival down at Stormy River. How about you skip ballet and I pick up your friend, Toni, and take you both there?"

CHAPTER SEVEN

EATING my fairy floss on a stick, I walk alongside Toni as we meander along the boardwalk through a noisy sea of people. To my right, there are local nick-nack stalls one after the other; to my left is Stormy River. Flanking me on both sides... are two fricking prams. They are, like, the tenth babies I've seen since we arrived half an hour ago.

What's that all about?

They are coming for you, Cassidy.

The mothers silently chant 'one of us' with their eyes and the babies mock me with their cuteness. I'm like the pregnant woman's version of the crazy cat lady phenomenon. Babies start appearing randomly in my path. On the benches I pass. In the windows of the coffee shops. On a nearby fence... Okay, maybe not on a fence...

I drag Toni off the main deck and onto the grass, hoping the terrain will mean fewer prams. We move up a bank towards the glowing lights and the hustle and bustle of the showgrounds. As we head towards the screams and laughter of people enjoying the main rides, Carter follows several metres behind us.

My best friend gets scanned from head to toe by almost every oncoming female. While Toni is undeniably gay to me, to strangers, he is equally as beautiful as he is masculine. He is clearly ethnic, but most people have a hard time placing his ancestry. Being both Chinese and Italian, he's just a lovely blend. He is built solid from spending most of his time at the gym, and he's confident and funny without restraint or care.

He looks over his shoulder at Carter. "Is it weird that I kinda want to pull him into The House of Mirrors and blow him?"

How am I still surprised by the words that come out of Toni's mouth? "Oh my God, Toni, you have a boyfriend."

His beautiful dark, almond-shaped eyes thin further as he grins. "And? There is something kind of kinky about that man I just can't ignore."

Not wanting to think about Carter like that, I avoid the thought altogether. "He's Carter. He doesn't have any sexuality as far as I'm concerned."

"Oh, Golden Girl." Toni sighs. "He has sexuality. He is dripping in sexuality."

I cringe, now staring at my fairy floss with revulsion. "Don't say dripping."

He lathers his lips and purrs, "*Dripping*."

"*Ugh*." Walking to the nearest bin, I dispose of my sugar-wrapped stick. "He's very professional. And kind. It was his idea to pick you up."

Toni rolls his eyes. "Nice to know someone thinks about me."

Ignoring his pity party, I say, "I need to talk to you. Serious-like."

He stops. Facing me, he folds his arms across his chest. "As serious as a heart attack?"

Breathing the warm spring air into my lungs—it's a floral aroma blending with butter and salt from the popcorn stand beside me—I nod. "As serious as pregnancy."

"No way..." His voice trails off and his arms drop to his sides. "You're pregnant!"

Glancing nervously around the crowd, I mutter, "Please tell all of Stormy River."

"You're pregnant!" Toni's eyes leave mine and dart around desperately. "I really need to find The House of Mirrors, like, right now."

I study his tight expression. "Are you mad?"

"Fuck." He grumbles, still searching the area with strange intent. "Yes, I think I am. That careless prick."

"No." I reach for his arm, trying to draw his attention back to me. "It isn't like that. This is on both of us."

He scoffs. "What about ballet?"

My breathing gets a little shallow. "I don't know. I'm still processing."

"Well, I'm your processing partner. Oh look"—he gestures over my shoulder—"The House of Horrors. That's fitting. Let's go."

The house has cracked glass windows set into steep black walls. A tiny door acts as the entrance, opening for each rail cart. Theatrical—eye-rolling—groans and howls echo from within its depths. Before we can approach the ticket clerk, someone touches my shoulder. I spin to see Carter, up close and personal. I crane my neck to meet his shaded eyes.

A light grin adorns his rough features. "Sorry, Miss Slater, I can't let you go on *that* ride. Another ride, maybe?"

Toni's eyes widen. "The House of Mirrors okay with you, Carter?"

I stifle a giggle. "Why not this ride?"

Carter takes a few steps away from me. "Any other ride? One less dark, perhaps."

I contemplate arguing with him, but it probably won't get me anywhere. "Okay." I wrap my hand around Toni's arm. "Let's go find the teapots. Will you come on them with us?" I beam at Carter. Seeing him in his black suit and men-in-black sunglasses, spinning in a pink teacup would literally make my day—maybe my month.

He nods. "If you want me to, then I will."

Toni and I grin at Carter's expression, a stoic mask covering an amused and maybe light-hearted glimmer.

Toni laughs. "Ha. He almost said that with a straight face. Don't worry, big guy, we wouldn't do that to you."

Pulling me alongside him, Toni leads us away from The House of Horrors and towards the main oval. We sit down on the grass mound circling it just in time to see the start of some sheep dogs herding their flock through an array of obstacles.

Toni stretches his long, denim-covered legs out in front of him. He begins to rip at the grass beside him, a sure sign he's a little anxious. The topic of my pregnancy sits heavily between us. "How the hell are you so calm? 'Cause you're gonna get *so* fat."

"I don't know," I admit, ignoring his last sentence. It's as if I've just heard life-altering news about a stranger. Not about me. Me: pregnant. With a Butcher baby. Maybe, with a Butcher boy—

"Oh my giddy aunt, are you smiling?"

Lifting my fingers to my lips, I stroke the curve they now form. Yep, I'm smiling. "I have no idea why. Usually, it's *your* mouth and brain that aren't connected." I laugh.

"*Meeeow*. Up-the-duff-Cassidy is a mean girl."

I shake my head, smiling for no reason at all. "Sorry."

"So, do you want to have Max Butcher's baby?"

Pulling my knees up, I cuddle them tight. "It's happening anyway."

"You could abort," he states with ease. Those words lodge themselves in my throat. Immediately, I look around for Carter, finding him a few metres away. Swallowing hard, I turn back to Toni. "I couldn't."

"What if Max doesn't want it?"

"I—" Realisation hits me. "I can't abort. No matter what. I'm kind of afraid he'll secretly hate me for this, but I still can't. He's still getting used to me and now this? *Gawd*. Have I ruined his life?"

Toni twists to face me, lifting one knee to the side. "Firstly, you couldn't ruin anyone's life, darlin'. Secondly... I presume by what you have just said that you haven't told him yet?"

Cringing a little, I shake my head.

His mouth drops open. "Fuckidy fuck. Why not?"

I glance away, staring off into the distance. "I only just found out and last night... I didn't stay at his."

He hums with contemplation. "And... why not? You've been getting humped by that man-god every night since—"

"Since the attack," I blurt out, "we don't. I mean, we try, but it never ends well."

"Is that why you went home? Is he pressuring you?"

"No. God no." I smile at that truth. "He'd never."

"So..." He tilts his head knowingly. "You started to talk and then stopped. Last night what?"

"Last night, Max came to me." Feeling uneasy about sharing this intimate information, I squirm a little with discomfort. I keep Max's secrets. His vulnerable side is just for me; sharing this... it feels like I'm betraying his trust. And yet, I need to tell Toni something. I hate lying to him. "He was really tense. Really... I can't think of another word. Like, intimidating... And he has all these bruises and cuts on his face, and he wouldn't tell me the truth about how he got them. I... saw—" My eyes flicker with unease. Angry eyes. Scarred skin. Dark mien. "Well, the guy who attacked me had all these scars. And I saw him. I couldn't unsee it. And I just... couldn't be with Max last night."

He wraps one long arm around my shoulders, and I lean into him. "Don't feel guilty. You're allowed to feel however you want to."

"Max said the same thing." I sigh, thinking about how patient he's been. How understanding.

Frick, what is wrong with me?

Trying to rationalise an irrational thing, I say, "He's a lot, you know? And he's gone a lot. He disappears some nights." I laugh contemptuously. "I'm not allowed to know what he's doing. I always feel a little lost in his world. Like I'm in a maze."

"A maze?" he confirms, lifting a perfectly manicured eyebrow that usually only proceeds mockery. "With like a minotaur and a fairy?"

I groan with exasperation. "Yes."

He nods as if he's on my wavelength, but the whole concept is a big joke to him. "Is Max the minotaur?"

Rolling my eyes, I just agree. "Yes."

He grins. "Am I the fairy?"

"Yes," I groan, releasing my knees and rubbing my temples with my forefingers. "Thank you. I'm so glad you could stay on track with this analogy."

"Sorry. Okay, so you're in a maze. I get it. You're lost in the big, sculptured hedges of his being. Isn't the maze exciting though? That's why you went in in the first place."

I smile at that. "It *is* exciting."

"Good." He squeezes my shoulder. "Don't let them win. Control those fucking memories. They are yours. Push them aside. Don't let them win, darlin'."

Control.

It's always about control.

I watch as the cattle dogs steer the flock with little effort around the field, controlling them..."Do you think sex can be used as a form of control?"

And there it is.

"Of course. But I don't see how that will help you control your memories unless you are thinking about something way above my kink spectrum."

I shake my head at that, feeling a little better already. Feeling like my best friend is now sharing part of the weight of this memory with me. Just having him know about it makes the memory feel lighter. Staring at a black and white border collie that is bending the sheep to its will, I expose more fears in the hopes he'll lighten their hold on me too. "Is Max controlling me?"

Toni cracks up laughing and I kind of want to slap him. That's probably the Butcher baby in me, spiking my hormones. "Oh, Golden Girl. Hell no. Your lady parts have *him* hog-tied; don't you worry about that."

"Stop it, Toni. I'm serious." I turn from the oval and face my beautiful chow-mien-biscotti bestie. "Does being a woman instantly make me weak? Because men literally enter women. Max entered me. My body. Heart." I shuffle on the grass. "And now, a part of him grows inside me. I've never thought about it before, you know, but it's true."

He frowns at me. "That's a really perverted way of viewing your relationship. Where is this coming from?"

I scratch a piece of pink nail polish off my index finger.

"It's just something I read," I lie. I lie because I know that listening to the words of a psychotic dead man is absolutely ridiculous...

Yeah, Cassidy, it really is.

His eyes suddenly brighten. "Put your finger up his arse. Even the score."

"Oh my gawd, Toni! Seriously?"

"Sorry," he mutters as if ashamed, but I can see he has more to say. It's so blatant on his too-excited face. Unable to hold it back, he blurts out, "If you do though, please film it for me."

I slap my forehead. "I need a new best friend."

He lets out a soft, serious sort of exhale. The kind that means he understands me. Understands what I need to hear. "Alright, Golden Girl. No, Max isn't controlling you with your vag. You are not weak. Women control men, Cassidy. With class and heels."

I sigh. It's not control we offer... It's comfort.

Frick, my Max.

That's what he needed yesterday. He gave me what I needed—space—and in doing so I denied him what he needed. Comfort. I'm a place he can be himself—honest, raw, guard-less. I'm his gentleness in this dangerous world and that doesn't make me his weakness—it doesn't make me weak.

Maybe... I'm his strength.

Toni continues, "And as for the baby topic, Jacinda Ardern had a baby while the prime minister of New Zealand. If she can do that, then you can work it around ballet. My queen is way ahead of the competition. It's only fair to give them a chance to catch up. You were getting a bit too fabulous anyway."

I smile softly. "I can't dance Sugar Plum." Remembering

the sponsorship I was offered, I groan. "And Jimmy's sponsorship is out of the question. He was going to pay my way through Europe, but now... I can't go."

He nods slowly. "Maybe not this year. But you will. One day."

Breathing smoothly for the first time in what feels like days, I begin to silence the irrational thoughts. I won't let trauma consume me. Let it blanket darkness over the good things in my life. The good people in my life. People I trust. Love.

I take a big breath in and steadily breathe out Erik.

CHAPTER EIGHT

SHE WAS SCARED of me last night. For the first time, perhaps ever, there was a glimpse of true fear in her golden-hazel eyes. That rips at my guts. I fucking force that down, the way I begged her, the way she rejected me, the way I left, the way it made me feel... fucking helpless. Fuck. Yep, I ram it all fucking down.

I glance out the window of my Chrysler 300 and take a sip of my whiskey neat. All my attention should be on the mob at Stormy River. The fucking Italian trash that won't last the night. Won't be going home to their families.

Cassidy.

I can't stop seeing her wide, confused eyes. Can't stop recalling how she lied to me about why she wanted to stay at home. Home. That place isn't her fucking home anymore.

I take another sip of my whiskey. My fingers tighten around the glass. Tighten with the urge to shatter it in my fist. To feel the shards pierce my skin. Open me up. Like she does. Fucking Cassidy Slater and her gentle, sweet nature. Hopeful. She pressed her little palm to my cheek and bared me down with that simple, mundane action. She opened me up. It's a dangerous thing she is doing to me. She is making me want her too much. With that, my skin crawls with the need to get back to her. To order my driver to turn around so I can fix whatever is wrong between us. I don't.

I can't.

I am being escorted to this perceived casual meeting, my car following the convoy of black, bullet-proof, high-end vehicles—Cadillacs and Chrysler 300s. I know that a few cars ahead, Jimmy is drinking red wine and being sucked into a good mood.

As is his style before an execution.

Butch will be stoic—I still don't understand that man.

Clay will be all business; to him, this is nothing personal.

Bronson is probably bouncing with anticipation.

Xander will most certainly be nervous.

I couldn't care less how Salvatore feels.

As we roll through the fencing towards the abattoir, I see Marco and his mob jump out from within a black van. All nine men were crammed in, shoulder to shoulder, and I can't think of anything worse, except... maybe polio.

I exhale through a growl.

My car pulls up behind Clay's, but before we step out, we sit for a while. The sight of nine tinted boss cars looming in front of the heads of them is like a warning. The Stormy River mob straighten. Puff up.

Once again, our differences are bleedingly obvious. While I watch my family step out wearing suits and ties, the Stormy River Italians shuffle around dressed like they are hitting the clubs—shirts open, gold chains, fucking sneakers. It's an embarrassment.

Before leaving the car, I pull my jacket off and lay it over the leather seat beside me. It's a fucking hot night for October. Usually in the back of my mind, I am calmed by the peaceful thought of Cassidy in my bed. My little piece of purity in this world. Of goodness.

Tonight though, as I walk into the abattoir, flanking Clay, Bronson, Butch, and Jimmy, I'm reminded that she isn't in my bed, and my angry mood is stoked by that thought.

When I stop within a few metres of our 'associates', Xander appears beside me, his demeanour measured. Salvatore quickly moves to stand beside Clay—the little fucker's way of trying to claim a spot on the hierarchy. Even though not a single soul in the Family would promote that piece of shit.

This is a soldier-free interaction.

And we've kept our end of the deal.

Jimmy and Butch take the few steps needed to embrace and kiss our guests like well-mannered Sicilians. Although I find it distasteful, I move forward to do it too, and I do it with confidence. It's an insecure man who doesn't plant those kisses firm and hard. There is often aggression in that greeting. A silent show of power; we can just as easily kiss their ugly faces as we can slice them the length of their smiles.

It's all the same to us.

"Marco," Jimmy coos, his tone welcoming and warm and anything but.

"Jimmy, it's been too long." He greets Butch and then us, the gold in his teeth flashing as he smiles widely.

I size our company up, noting their skills, and calculating our plan. Beside Marco is his twin brother, Paul. Both men are overweight, but they're strong. On the other side of Marco, with gold rings on his fingers and dense, curly, black chest hair visible between the V of his white shirt, is his right-hand man, Gabriele 'The Fist' Russo. He's been known to one-punch men to death on several occasions, and I've often wondered how he would stack up against Butch.

As they all exchange pleasantries, catching up on the latest deals, business, and women, or in The Fist's case, boys, I slowly meander around the abattoir, leaving my brothers feigning engagement beside Butch. If Bronson had been the one to step away, the pricks might have suspected something. But I'm the uninterested Butcher. The one who appears bored at most meetings, and I know this because the bastard Italians have said as much to my face.

"I suppose you heard what happened? *Se?*" Jimmy finally gets to the fucking point.

"—stolen on the road," Marco mutters with a tsk, and I move a little closer, still pretending to be preoccupied with my own thoughts.

"Se, I'm here to offer you some work. I need five good men to accompany my nephew Salvatore to India." Salvatore steps forward, pride on his smug face as he gets the first important job in his weasel existence. "That is where the product has landed."

Jimmy wants to keep us on the front line while important things are taking place in the District. While Clay works his way up into the spotlight, we need to keep things peaceful on the streets. It's what Butch wants too. To keep us all together in this city he has built alongside Jimmy. And it's what I want. I want to be close to her.

Peering over my shoulder, I see The Fist's lips twitch with a smirk and then it's gone. At that, I move behind them, making a fair amount of noise so they feel comfortable with my presence. Obvious. Unthreatening.

"Your boy still bored of shop talk, Luca? Or is he thinking about that cute, barely legal pussy he's been seen with lately?" Macro sneers, and I'm so very glad he does. Coming up behind him, I sling my garrotte wire over his head and pull him with me as I step backwards. I hear gunshots from Clay and Salvatore. See Bronson pull his Glock out and release bullet after bullet into The Fist's chest and cock. Am aware of Xander now holding Paul with a machete to his throat, forcing him to watch as we destroy his firm.

Jimmy and Butch stand coolly and still, observing the chaos like fucking mafia kings.

The fat fuck flailing around in front of me howls, his hands clawing at the wire shredding his flesh. Blood drips over his glistening gold chains and slithers down his shirt like little snakes before splattering onto the floor.

Jimmy steps forward like the reaper himself, and I make certain not to kill Marco before he can hear what he has to say. "Have you ever had blood drained from your body before? I often give blood, I'm that type of man. But I've never been drained of it. I hear it's quite a spectacular sensation. Your heart rate becomes frantic. Head beats like a drum. You lose all senses. My pretty face will be the last one you see." He moves in closer. "If you tell me where they landed, I will give you one life."

I loosen the wire so he can speak. "Trichy," he manages to choke out between bile and blood.

Jimmy leans in and kisses Marco's forehead. "You'll only steal from the Family once." Then he straightens and nods at me. "Remove his head."

Marco lets out a loud howl, his back vibrating on my chest as I saw at his flesh, through his carotid artery, blood blanketing the both of us. He is silenced completely when I sever his vocal cords. I keep rocking the wire from side to side, slicing through muscles and tendons and vessels. I grit my teeth as what he said about Cassidy repeats in my mind. As I think about how he's probably beat one out fantasising about her small tits and petite physique, which, yes, to some, may appear barely legal—he likes them young.

My eyes see red.

I keep sawing.

Once I feel the wire snag on his spine, I drop his body like a sack of potatoes. I taste the fuck's blood in my mouth. Feel it sliding down my forehead and chin. This isn't usually my way. But after spending last night alone with only Cassidy's scent, I don't feel much like myself. So maybe I *can* compartmentalise like my brother can.

Maybe.

I look up from the bloodied mess as Paul wails with grief. In my peripherals, I can make out that most of his men are now merely bodies spread out around him. I pull out my gun and shoot between the flaps of Marco's neck, aiming for his exposed, crimson-coated spine.

I finish the job and walk the dripping head over to Paul. When I place it at his feet, the sliced and hacked neck flesh, gummy and wet, slaps the concrete, smearing a wing of blood in front of him.

Falling to his knees, Paul cradles the severed head of his twin as if it were a baby. We all stand by and allow him to grieve.

After a few minutes, his time is up.

"I gave him one life. You. And now, I'd like to offer you the same job," Jimmy says smoothly. "Five men. India. Get my product back."

Tears fall quickly from him. They don't make me roll my eyes; instead, for a moment, they make me glance away. Marco got off easy. Paul, on the other hand, will have to work alongside the very people who killed his men and with me, the one who decapitated his brother in front of his very eyes.

It's a reality I would never live. I wouldn't drop to my knees while my brother's murderer breathed the same air as me.

AS THE CAR pulls away from the curb, I study every flourish of the cursive writing on my finger, which is now tainted with track lines painted in another man's blood.

Ardent One.

In Latin it means 'to burn.' And she does burn me down to my core. I inhale deeply and exhale even louder. The shrill wailing of screams now gone only seems to make the silence more vivid. More unnatural.

As the car cruises slowly through the streets, its tyres spinning, rolling, its movement becomes rhythmic. The engine hums. Soothes. And I think about hazel freckles. Slouching into the seat, my head drops back against the rest. I close my eyes.

And I see hers full of fear.

CHAPTER NINE

THE FIRST TIME I saw this house, I was in awe of it. Even though its grandeur hasn't dwindled, another feeling holds more prominence—a homey feeling. When I step out from the passenger side, Carter is already there, holding the door open for me as though I am some kind of princess.

I stare up at Casa Butcher. It is hard to believe that the single-liner, brute and boxer, sex god, gym junky, rugby playing Max Butcher also has enough space in his talent toolbox to be... creative. I mean, that is what this is. He's an artist. My Max.

Ugh. What can't that man do?

Staring up at it as if for the first time, I take in the steep white walls lit up by external lights and the modernist shape and feel. It's impressive. Not one feature is overlooked; that man likes perfection. That man is *perfection*.

Grinning to myself, I wander up the steps and through the front door. A man, suited in all black and holding it open, smiles as I move past him.

I wave at him. "Hi."

The Butcher guards are very polite and conservative, almost as though they have very little personality, but I doubt that is the case. They are just professionals.

As I round the sleek black and white kitchen, I see the reflection of the television lights on the hallway walls. Knowing that means one of the boys is awake, I wander down the corridor.

If I thought for a second that Victoria or Butch might be sitting in front of that television, I wouldn't have dared to join them, but they are mostly out of town, at hotels or one of the other houses on their vast real estate portfolio. Despite that being unusual, I never thought too much about it. But right now, I do. I mean, it makes sense that she —*Victoria*—that vapid woman, would purposely keep Butch from his sons. She must get swallowed up by their presence.

When I see the relaxed, large, and gorgeous form of Bronson Butcher lying on the couch, watching *The Bachelor*, I laugh to myself. "I can't believe what I'm seeing."

"I know, it's so romantic." He feigns a coo, not moving a muscle.

Rounding the couch and sitting on the single recliner, I'm all of a sudden desperate to tell him he's going to be an uncle. Of course, I can't. Not until I tell Max that he's going to be a dad. Although Bronson is an enigma—both charming and easy-going, dark and unpredictable—he's also the one person I'm positive will be nothing but excited about this baby. It's the reaction I want.

Need.

He looks so much like Max and strangely, so very different. While Max is closed off, Bronson seems welcoming and daring. Max has black, white, and red tattoos. Bronson has vibrant designs covering almost every inch of his skin. I stare at his tattooed forearm, where a purple clock and owl are etched into the surface.

Still unmoving, his hands tucked under his thick, strong biceps and his boots crossed up on the cushion, he says, "Did you know that Max named Xander?"

I pull my legs up, crossing them in front of me. "No."

He doesn't divert his eyes from the television. "Yeah. Mum couldn't be bothered. Personally, I wanted to name him Ned, after Ned Kelly. But Max wanted it to be Xander. His name has a loose translation—'defender of men.' Max liked that idea at the age of five. We practically raised that kid together. Like emperor penguins, ya know? The guys all get together and look after their young."

Are we talking about babies? Can he read minds? My palms get moist, so I rub them on my legs. Bronson Butcher never ceases to amaze me to the point of near speechlessness. "Emperor penguins?" is all I manage to say.

"Yep." His bright, opal-blue eyes shift to me and he grins, his lips a tick of mischief. "They're really good fathers."

Oh my gawd. How does he know? I need an aluminium foil hat to stop him from infiltrating my thoughts. Or does that only work with aliens? Maybe some garlic? Or silver?

Focus, Cassidy.

My lungs begin to strain. "Does Max know?" I breathe hard.

When his eyes drop to my belly, his whole face smiles. "Know what? About emperor penguins? No. But I make it my business to know everything about them."

A laugh of relief bursts from me, but I have no idea why. Shaking my head, feeling tongue-tied, I take in his beautiful, comforting presence. I don't know how he knows... *Ugh.* Yes, I do. *Carter.* I frown at Bronson. "Carter told you?"

Grinning, he states, "He had to report it to one of us." I

want to be mad, but I'm not. Because Bronson's smile fills my heart with the courage it needs to tell Max.

"Is Max in his room?"

"He's exhausted. Go easy on him."

Beaming from cheek to cheek, I stand to leave but stop abruptly. Peering back at Bronson, still casually slung over the couch, I say, "One day, you're going to tell me why you're single."

He chuckles. "Emperor pigeons."

I laugh again. I have no idea what that means.

Taking the staircase, which I now know is made of Jarrah wood, I navigate my way up to the third floor and through the carpeted hallway to Max's room.

The best part about sneaking into his room at near midnight is being able to watch him sleep for a few moments. It's been a fascination of mine since the first time we slept in the same bed. When he's awake, there is no mistaking who is in charge.

But when he's asleep, he's almost—exposed.

The window is open, but there is no moon tonight, so it's just a black square dotted with what looks like fireflies spread across the horizon. The only light floods in around his bathroom door, but it's enough for me to see him.

I make my way over to his big bed, noticing that he's sleeping on my side with his head resting on my pillow. I smile harder. I breathe in Max Butcher, dark-brown hair, tanned skin, and the tattoos I like to trace with my fingertip. *My Max.*

I slide my shoes off quietly, pull my dress over my head, and crawl onto the mattress in my underwear. My nails lightly graze his thigh as I move in close to him.

Suddenly, he jolts up, seizes my throat, and throws me under him. Pressing his heavy body to mine, he pushes the air from my chest, leaving me gasping for it. As fear and arousal swirl through me, my pulse beats hard against his hot, tight grip.

It's me!

But I can't speak with his fist squeezing the air from me. I was stupid to sneak in here. Because taking a sleeping Max Butcher by surprise might not have been the best idea. I didn't even think about it. Didn't consider his defensive stance on an unknown person in his bed.

He measures me up. His eyes are thin black cuts set into his hard expression. As the big arm pinning me down shakes with restraint, Max slowly comes to. Blinking at me, realisation gathering in his mind, he loosens his hold on my neck but doesn't move his hand away. When his lips press against mine, I catch some breath from within his mouth.

Oh my God.

"Am I dreaming?" He hums—raspy and deep—into our kiss.

"No, Max. I'm here," I whisper, feeling a tidal wave of love. As a tear slides down my cheek, I just feel too much. In deep. And while the heat from his body is so intense it's like I'm being smothered by the sun, his mouth, as it moves on mine is gentle with adoration.

Closing my eyes, I hum and focus on his soft lips as they massage mine. I think about Max Butcher. Only him.

Cupping his rough jaw, I deepen our kiss.

As his fingers twitch around my throat, he exhales a rough, lust-filled growl. "Don't fuck with me."

"I'm not." I breathe against his lips. "Take him away, Max. Please. Take it all away with your touch. Your smell." Thrumming on my leg now is his steel-like erection, and I start to pant into his kiss, wanting it, needing it. Without hesitation. "*Max*, I want you."

Flipping us over so that I'm on top of him, he pulls me to straddle his hips. He releases my throat, and I inhale sharply, not realising that he had still been squeezing ever so slightly.

God, he smells good. We don't break our kiss.

As if he doesn't believe my conviction, he states, "Stay on top of me, Cassidy. I don't trust myself with you tonight. Not while you're saying shit like that."

My fingers slide up his strong chest and into his messy hair while one of his hands cradles the back of my head and the other strokes down my spine to cup my backside.

I slowly slide my tongue the length of his lips, invoking a groan of pent-up yearning from within his chest. "I trust you with me. I'm sorry I forgot for a while—"

He cuts me off. "I'm not doing this, Cassidy. Not again."

"*Please*," I whimper. "Take me. I'm yours. If I'm yours, then no one else can touch me. Make me yours again."

He growls at that. "You have always been mine!"

"Show me," I say, my voice barely a whisper, a flutter against his mouth, but no doubt a siren in his soul. I am desperate for him. Desperate to have him consume me until all the mess in my mind is swallowed up by his being. Incinerated in the fire he lights in my heart with his loving embrace and possessive touch.

He rolls me under him, a smooth movement that leaves me pressed between his hard body and the mattress. His mouth works on mine. Lips gentle. Loving. When his tongue trails down my chin to my throat, tracing the beat of my rapid pulse, I tilt my head back. Combing my fingers through his hair, I press his lips to my skin harder and breathe heavily.

So heavy.

All of it. The moment. The anticipation.

His movements are leisurely, his tongue savouring. As he

licks down my chest to one of my breasts, he cups the other in the gentle, warm vice of his palm. He removes my bra and laps his tongue over my nipple, long and slow, and so gentle it's almost painful.

I want more.

My fists tighten in his dark-brown hair. My nipple is flicked over and over, bringing shockwaves of sensation to the delta between my thighs. I moan. The muscles between the lips of my sex squeeze at the emptiness in a silent plea.

But he's taking his time.

The casual exploration of his mouth on my breast is so excruciating in its tenderness, I want to cry. He slides down my body, his tongue tracing the ripples of my abdominal muscles. He dips lower. The anticipation of his mouth between my legs is so unbearable, I moan long and low and thrust my hips up. He growls with restraint. His biceps pulse.

But he denies my wordless plea, sliding his tongue down my thigh.

I melt into the soft sheets, my body jelly for him to consume and mould.

His tongue and breath are hot on my skin as he strokes down the full length of my leg. I buck when he gets to my foot. I squirm at the sensation of his tongue sliding down to my toes. "Mine," he murmurs, "Every inch of you, Little One."

He moves on to my other leg, painting a hot, wet trail with his mouth and tongue.

My belly warms.

As he nears my sex with his hot mouth, I press my thighs together.

After being worshipped by him so thoroughly, I gasp when he rolls us over. He flips me around to face the other way and then places a hand on my back, pushing me down.

Oh God.

My cheek meets his taut, ribbed abdominal muscles. As he moves me until the silky skin of my thighs cup his rough jaw and my core is on his lips, my heart thrashes around inside my ribcage. I still have my knickers on, but that somehow makes the feel of his hot breath fanning the material between my legs even more intense.

His hands span my bum cheeks, fingers squeezing and spreading the smooth, plump flesh. At the feel of his tongue lapping at the fabric between my thighs, soft sounds of pleasure escape me.

While all of my body is on the hard wall of his, while he licks at my wet knickers, his groans are that of someone indulging—low, deep, and primal. His feather-light caresses send me out of my mind with need.

The sound of my knickers ripping sets the warmth in my belly to boiling. He slides them aside and, oh my God, his tongue. Both palms knead my bum, forcing my wet lips into his mouth as he eats me in a frenzy.

And he's no longer slow.

My head is suddenly dizzy.

And I've never loved being short and petite more than I do right now. Even though I can't reciprocate, I'm literally laying on a Max Butcher mattress while he devours the flesh between my thighs.

I try to keep up with all the sensations now overwhelming me, but whereas Max is usually methodical, precise—like licking me to a climax is an art form—right now he's wild. Completely animalistic. I roll my hips into his tongue's shallow thrusts and firm licks. His mouth doesn't insist on, but instead demands my orgasm. The coarse texture of his jawline creates the perfect friction on my sensitive, smooth skin.

It comes without warning. The wave of my desire hits my thighs with a jerk. My legs squeeze against his face. Erupting inside me, pleasure fills me. I let out a longing cry as the muscles between my legs pulse around his tongue.

My body tingles from my toes to my scalp. Max keeps licking me even as I become more sensitive. *"Max,"* I plea, pushing up so that I can suck his hard ridge, which is only inches from my face.

He squeezes me harder, holding my pelvis to his face. "More."

His finger teases my bumhole, drawing circles around it. I can't help but pucker against him. Sliding his hand down the crease of my backside, he replaces his tongue with his fingers. He strokes me, collecting up the slickness of my desire.

"You're always so wet." He cups me firmly, and I pulse against his palm. "*Fuck*. This is mine. Don't ever take it away from me again. You're going to sit on my face all night. And I'm going to fuck both your holes with my tongue and finger until you pass out." His fingers move back to that private part of me while his mouth moves back to my clit.

I press my cheek into his hot, firm abdominals as, inch by inch, he slowly fills me with his finger. The sounds coming from me now are more like yelps. I should be embarrassed, but I'm not. For the first time in a week, we are alone in our world again.

A trusting world.

His teeth latch onto my clit, his tongue flicking the pinched bud. His finger stills inside me as the muscles surrounding it beat and squeeze. He releases my clit. "I'm going to fuck this with my cock one day, Little One." He curls his finger inside me. "Then you'll really feel me everywhere." He starts to massage his finger in and out of me.

My orgasm thrashes through me. I scream, clenching my fists, feeling the pleasure set fire to my insides. It hits my ears and stars my vision. It's a beautiful, overwhelming feeling that is so rocking I'm mewling around on top of him.

Gradually, Max guides me off the precipice. He slowly pulls his finger from inside me but continues to lick up the result of my arousal. I nuzzle his abdomen—high on him—while he strokes my backside and kisses my clit softly.

As the night continues, he brings me to two more orgasms. All the while, I lay on his body in a daze of pleasure.

After the third, I feel myself drifting into a coma of exhaustion.

Easing my sluggish body from him, Max moves me around the mattress until my cheek sinks into his pillow. As my senses flutter away, chasing the sweet closure slumber brings, I hear him whisper, "You're all I want."

CHAPTER TEN

AS I SHIFT from asleep to awake, the words Max whispered to me last night float through my mind. Did he literally mean 'I'm all he wants'? Like, he doesn't want anything else?

Or *anyone* else?

Does he know? Does he know that a whole new identity will soon be demanding my time and his?

Knowing I have to tell him this morning, flutters begin to build in my chest. My heart beats so hard I'm scared I'll wake the gorgeous, broody man sleeping beside me.

I want him to be okay with this. When I tell him, I want him to say that it's okay. That we'll work it out. Together.

I just need to hear that because people are going to speculate. I know how they will view our situation, gossiping to no end about how I've snagged Max Butcher by getting knocked up. But what worries me most of all is... will he think that too? I pushed him into wanting this—me. *Frick.* That truth hurts even though it shouldn't. I should accept my truths, and yet, they are often overlooked—purposely overlooked. Had I not pursued him, he might have lost interest in me. He said as much himself a few nights ago. I made him want this. I don't want to *make* him do anything...

As the light glows through the thin sheath of skin over my irises, my eyes flutter open. The dawn peeks above the rooftops of Connolly. I'm on my side, his warm body curled around me. I wriggle against him, feeling his legs shuffle to accommodate my movements.

"Don't move," he groans sleepily.

I still and watch the horizon as it explodes in colours so vivid they almost seem unnatural. I think about my new future. Think about the baby in my belly.

The light moves into our room, creeping across the floor and onto the tattooed arm slung over my waist. He breathes rhythmically behind me, asleep once more, leaving me to watch the sun fully rise.

Taking a big breath in for courage, I shake his tight hold enough to spin towards him. I burrow my face in his chest, my nose twitching against soft hairs, my cheek vibrating in time with his beating heart. And that smell, frick. It's enough to make any girl drop to their knees. Pressing my chin to his rising chest, I peer up at him. His eyes are closed, but his brows are furrowed as if the light has invaded his slumber too.

"Good morning," I whisper.

Warm hands move up the length of my spine and into my hair. With his eyes still closed, he strokes me from my crown to my neck, and I watch his face as he does. His sigh rumbles against me. A knot rolls down his throat as he grips my hair, squeezing his fingers into his palm to lock the strands in tight.

When a soft whimper leaves me, he relaxes his hands. "*Cassidy*."

I stroke my fingertips softly down his cheeks and wriggle up the mattress until my lips meet his. The edge of his pillow supports my head as I kiss him. Lazy kisses that slowly draw him from his sleepy state. His tongue moves across my lips and he releases a longing groan. The hand hooked over me slides down to cup my backside, lifting me up against his erection, before pulling me on top of him.

"Wait," I breathe into his mouth. But while he stops the direction of his hand, his hips still roll as if he can't control them.

"I'm going to fuck you, Little One," he growls, opening his eyes, and oh my gawd, *his eyes.* They're so blue right now. Usually, they are clouded with shades of grey, but in the direct sunlight of dawn, they are piercing.

At the feel of his erection tapping against me, my eyes nearly roll into the back of my head with lust. "I need... to talk to you."

His nose meets mine. "Talk."

Frick. So, Max, I'm pregnant. I'm pregnant. Stop doing that with your hips. We are having a baby. Ugh, stop touching me like that. There is something you need to know; I'm pregnant. I somehow got pregnant...

"I'm"—the words expand as I force them through my larynx—"*pregnant.*"

Oh.

My.

God.

He stills.

The fingers spanning my hips freeze. Nose to nose, the increase in his breathing is palpable on my cheek and against my chest. But at least he's breathing; he's not paralysed by the idea.

My throat tightens, an involuntary response that often

precedes tears. Heat hits the back of my eyes, but I ignore it, not wanting my tears to fall down on his face. He continues to breathe deeply.

Finally, after what feels like the longest few moments of my life, he clears his throat and speaks against my lips. "What about ballet?"

What?

Slowly sliding me off him, he sets me down on the mattress. Within seconds, he's on his feet and moving across his room, pulling his clothes on.

I breathe in fast and hold it.

As he walks from the room, I watch the door shut behind him. Hot tears squeeze from the corners of my eyes. He's just processing, right? Like I had. Just taking a few moments to organise his thoughts.

Did I do this wrong?

I knew I had to tell him before he went downstairs because Bronson would have expected as much. But now that I have, I'm alone. And his absence makes my heart sting.

I stare at the closed door as if my answers lie there.

I finally breathe out hard.

After several minutes, I lie down and curl in on myself, clutching my knees to my chest. Blinking tears from between my lashes, I wait for him to come back. Not overanalysing this is the key to remaining calm, to not completely break down into a sob—the threat of which stokes my ragged breaths. I just need to take his sudden absence for what it is —processing time.

Remain calm, Cassidy.

I will my heart to stop burning.

The door swings open and Max strides in with a phone clutched to his ear. As I sit up, the sheets drop to expose my naked torso. The cold air tweaks my nipples. Max's demeanour, hot and powerful like a live wire, causes my heart to beat in an erratic cadence.

But he is far too preoccupied with the gruff voice on the other side of the phone to notice me. He stops by the bed and, with one hand, begins to remove his clothes again.

"That wasn't a question. I will need more men." His tone is all business. The person on the other side of the phone speaks, but their words are muffled by Max's cheek. "Right." He hangs up and finishes removing his clothes.

As the last item of his drops to the floor, all I can do is tilt my head in confusion. The sequence of events that have just unfolded isn't exactly what I had imagined. They are rather weird to say the least.

"Max?" I say because what else do I say?

A physique made for destruction crawls onto the bed and up my body until I drop back to allow him to hover over me. Intense, searching grey-blue eyes bore into mine as he settles himself up on his elbows. With his hands in my hair, warm fingers stroke my face and trace my freckles.

"Yes?" he whispers, watching his fingers map my every feature.

I giggle at the absurdity of this moment. "Did you hear what I said?"

"Yes."

I swallow hard. "I'm sorry, Max."

His brows form a tight line above his penetrative stare. "For what?"

"Cause... um..." I falter. "I don't know."

He studies me as if he's unsure of what to say. Max Butcher is a man of few words. He doesn't shower ideas or confessions or inspirations around for all to enjoy. But he usually has a stance. Right now, though, he's contemplative.

He gazes at me. "I should leave. I should leave you and this baby, and you'll be safe."

My whole world shifts, and I whimper. "You won't do that though," I say, my voice panicked, my throat burning.

"No. I won't," he states definitively. "Because I'm a selfish prick and I want you."

I try not to weep with the feeling of relief. "I want you too."

"You shouldn't."

"I'm not afraid of your world anymore, Max. The only thing that scares me now is not being there for you. With you."

He exhales, following his finger as it moves across my cheek, gazing at my hair winged out around his pillow. "This will be your decision then."

Air seems to thicken, so I open my mouth.

He continues, "I'm not going to let anyone make decisions for you anymore."

I shake my head. "I don't understand."

"Say, Max, let's make a baby."

And the air is now like tar—so dense I can't draw it in. "What?"

He dips his head down, his lips meeting my ear. "Say it, and then I'll fuck you."

I'm actually panting now. "I—I don't—" I stammer. "I still don't understand?"

Oh my God, what is he saying? What is he talking about? Is he okay with this?

He pushes himself up, leaning on one forearm. Grey irises nail me to the mattress, demanding, dead fricking serious.

And yet, I struggle to form words.

"I told you, Cassidy," he says, a hint of some kind of emotion knotting his voice up—anger, maybe, guilt, perhaps. "I fucking swore it. I'd never let anything happen to you again. I fucking said it and now something has. I need you to say it. Or I've failed you again."

Tears squeeze from the edges of my eyes, painting salty streams down my temples and on his pillow. "No, Max," I say, pressing my hand to his perfectly coarse cheeks. "I know you are still getting used to me being a constant in your life. This can't just be my decision—"

His face tightens. "Who said that?"

My breath catches at his suddenly fierce expression. "What?"

"Who fucking said I'm still getting used to you?"

Blinking the tears out, I shake my head once. "No one, but—"

"Have my actions not been clear?"

"Um, yes," I say because they have. I think. "I just feel like this is all a lot for you. Up until a few months ago, a girlfriend was worse than polio and now—"

The fingers in my hair twist, tethering me to his fists. "I'll spell it out then, Cassidy. I want you here. Every day. In my fucking bed. I'm not getting used to you. You are what I want. I thought I made that clear already."

He leans down and kisses a tear as it falls. This is all too much. I think he's saying he's okay with this? That this is happening? That he supports my decision? Is that what's fricking happening right now? "And the baby?"

"Just say the words."

Knowing this is his way of gaining a sense of control, claiming the situation we have found ourselves in, I slowly say, "Max, make a baby with me."

He grips my jaw, his fingers pressing into my cheeks. His lips meet mine softly, completely contradictory to the firm hold he has on my face. As his tongue touches my lip, I open my mouth and massage his with mine. Kneading. Dancing together in a collective rhythm of need and love and acceptance.

When one of his hands moves down to hook my leg over the back of his thighs, he begins to stroke his body against mine. His lips journey around my face as he releases my jaw. Careful not to lay too much of his weight on my body, he moulds me, manhandling me into position. His erection is pressed, hot and hard, between the lips of my sex. My core clenches in anticipation of being filled so fully at any moment.

He rolls his hips up and down, stroking himself between my wet lips. Groaning at the sensation, his mouth becomes more frenzied. Nipping. Licking.

I drag my fingers lightly up his back while he moves to grip his erection. Holding me stationary with one hand, his fist picks up pace, the brunt of it meeting my sex. I hold my breath, helpless against the pressure of him on top of me, caging me. And when he moves his hand away, nothing separates us.

His hips pump shallowly into me, forcing his huge pulsing erection in, spreading me wide. Letting out long, whimpering moans, I grip his biceps. Brace myself. He pushes in. Pushes further. I thought I would get used to the feel of his girth, the breadth of his hips, the heat of his body, but I haven't.

It's as all-encompassing as it was the first time.

He sinks into me until I'm full of him; a dull ache inside me warns me of his depth. "Don't underestimate my feelings for you, Little One." He grunts, thrusting in a possessive way, wanting to claim, to mark. "Nothing could be more dangerous."

He draws back a few inches and pushes in again. I cry out, my core locking around him, clamping down tight.

"*Yes,*" he growls, starting to really move. "So tight, Little One. I wouldn't fit if you weren't so fucking wet for me all the time." He buries himself in deep, my lips hugging the root of his erection. He abruptly pulls out only to thrust in again. And again.

"*Max.*" I mewl beneath him, holding on to him as he rocks us. Fills me. Empties me. The power in his legs can be felt against my thighs. His balls slap at the puckering hole of my bum—the sensation so subtle and yet so arousing. Long, strong arms caress every inch of my body.

"You're perfect." His lips meet mine and we kiss, our bodies moving in time now, sliding together. Synchronised.

Every thrust seems to connect us deeper, push him further into me until the onslaught of my orgasm begins to gather in a hot ball in my belly.

It explodes.

The pressure of which moves through my legs, forcing them to squeeze his hips. As it crashes down to my toes, they curl in tightly. Shaking uncontrollably, I pulsate around his thrusts, crying out and actually crying because I've missed this so much. Too much. I don't want to separate us again. I do trust him with me.

His mouth stills against mine as he concentrates. As his movements become more urgent, I know he's close too. The beat of his hips gets faster. He thickens. One of his hands fists the skin at my backside while the other seizes my neck, and he begins to pump cum inside me. Filling the room with his groaning, he doesn't slow down until the pulsing of his orgasm mellows.

He rains kisses down on my face, over my lips, jawline, and neck. Slowly, we ride the wave out together, settling down into a sensual pool of chaste caresses and gentle touches.

Still inside me, he thrusts slowly.

"I love you, Max Butcher," I whisper.

"I don't deserve you,"—he presses his lips to mine—"Cassidy Slater. I'm keeping you anyway."

CHAPTER ELEVEN

MY FINGERS SKATE over her beating heart and down to her trim abdomen, where I know something profound is taking place. Something she's not ready for. Something I did to her and can't undo. As she sleeps soundly on her back, I softly trace the smooth white skin on her stomach. My chest contracts, tightens, burns, and it's a feeling I'm not interested in analysing. She is in my bed again and after what I did last night, fuck.

She shouldn't be.

And yet, this is her fate now.

In *our* bed.

Cassidy.

She crawls into my brain and makes me contemplate a different life. I focus on her lovely little tits, slopped to small peaks and moving with a gentle sway as they rise and fall. She is out cold. She must be exhausted. For a few moments, I simply watch her breathing. Moving my gaze to her face, I notice her eyes flicker slightly. Lips pout and, *fuck me.*

She's beautiful.

Soft. And inside, in her mind, so fucking silly I want to wrap her in cotton wool and never let the world taint her. Not like I have—

With that thought, I slide out of bed and pull a pair of jeans on, making sure to tuck my cock in properly before I pull the zipper up. It's not easy having a big cock sometimes... I chuckle coldly at that. Such a fucking burden.

I leave the room shirtless and with my jeans hanging at my hips.

As soon as I notice Carter standing at the bottom of the staircase, I'm instantly reminded that he let her sneak into bed with me last night without any warning.

Halting at the bottom step, I fold my arms across my chest and scowl at him. He's a tall, fucking ugly piece of work, but I like him. For all the right reasons and a few wrong ones. "Didn't think to warn me she was coming up? I could have shot her."

He isn't scared of me. That's always been refreshing, but he is professional. A face like a smashed crab—workplace injuries—and biceps like my head, he's a fucking monster. Under that, though, is a finely tuned moral compass. I believe he ignores the arrow on occasion, but it's there anyway, guiding him.

"Bronson knew, boss. I told him," he states adamantly.

And that pisses me off. "And why did you do that?"

"Sorry, boss." He hesitates. "You wouldn't have shot her."

"Maybe not." When I note the slightest grin on his face, I pause. This fucker knows. "You know." It isn't a question and yet, it still demands an answer.

He nods once. "Yes. I overheard—"

"I don't care. Shit changes now." I step to his level.

"Understand? I want you to get your guys, go to Cassidy's house, and pack up her shit. She's moving in here. I need Life360 installed on her phone. Also, I need a phone. So sort that out for me. And a bigger room, I think. And a fucking list of obstetricians and—" Faltering, I rub my face before cracking my jaw with my palm to relieve the pressure. I shake my head, feeling unprepared, and I fucking hate that.

Carter studies me. "Shouldn't Miss Slater come with us, advise us what she wants to take?"

I walk into the kitchen, expecting Carter to follow. "Take it all."

"Does she know what we are doing?"

Stilling at the fridge, I slowly step to face him again. He's on the other side of the island bench, all professional in stance and appearance, but his tongue is a bit too inquisitive for my liking. "You're asking a lot of fucking questions, Carter. What's that all about?"

He straightens further. "Nothing. Just..."

"Oh fuck, please don't hold back now, you ugly bastard. Spill."

"You should ask her to move in, Max," he says, sounding more like my father than my employee and I both dislike and like that familiarity. "Not tell her."

Carter has been working for us for over fifteen years. He is a few years younger than Butch and has proven himself to be loyal beyond his contract. Beyond what we could have imagined. I turn my back to him and open the fridge door, pulling out an orange juice. "I don't need to ask."

I hear him shuffle his feet with apprehension. "In this case, you should anyway."

When I spin back, I'm met with a glint of nervousness. "I should, should I? Are you in love, Carter?"

His teeth flash as he laughs. "Good thing I'm ugly."

"Yeah." I grin at him because... who can't she charm? "Good thi—"

Suddenly, I hear the sound of voices—Butch's and someone else's. Usually, I don't care to involve myself in Butch's business, but in this case, the other voice has piqued my interest. Putting my glass down on the island bench, I stride past Carter and head down the hallway towards Butch's office.

"I thought you would protect my daughter. After everything I have done for you—"

With that, I push open the doors to the office, making my presence known. Ben Slater and Butch both look over at me, neither overly taken back by my attendance. Which in itself seems far too forced. Butch shifts his weight slightly—a gesture that on any other man would seem like unease. He taught us boys from a young age to be the impartial man in the room. To keep others guessing as to our intentions. As to our interests. Never show anyone what affects us. At times, I am good at this. When it comes to Cassidy though, less so.

Whereas I'm half-dressed, both men are in tailored dark suits. That doesn't faze me at all. I didn't even know Butch was here. And Ben isn't powerful in a suit. He isn't powerful at all.

"You discuss Cassidy with me. Not Butch," I state, growing further irritated that Cassidy's father came over here but clearly didn't respect me enough to address his issues with me. I cross my arms over my chest and wait for him to do just that—discuss Cassidy.

Butch leans on his desk casually. "Ben is sharing his concern for Cassidy's wellbeing."

I stiffen, but despite my annoyance, I try to keep my voice level. "Cassidy's wellbeing is my business."

Ben Slater is a lean man with an aura of wholesomeness that I couldn't feign even if I wanted to. I highly doubt Ben Slater finger fucks his wife at dinner, surrounded by some of the richest, most autocratic pricks in the District. He'd be an in-the-bedroom-missionary-style man, for sure. Everything about Ben is hopeful and gentle and boring. From his unguarded generous hazel eyes to his open stance and neat appearance. He is anything but the impartial man in this room.

He smiles sadly at me. "How did she hurt her arm?"

Her arm. That fucking slice. My hands twitch, but I try to keep my face straight. "She was attacked. Nothing like that will ever happen again. I have taken care of it."

I narrow my eyes at them as they share a glance, the non-verbal exchange rather odd. Filled with meaning. Secrets. I don't like it. Why Butch is even entertaining this conversation is beyond me. Not that I know all of his dealings. Or want to. But still—

"She's my daughter, Max. I love her very much. I just want her to be safe," he states, openly expressing his affections like the sentimental man he is known to be. Of course he loves his daughter. She's his daughter.

His *daughter*.

That dull ache moves through my chest again at the thought of having a daughter. At having a son. At either of them getting hurt. He has every right to be worried. This *is* his business, goddamn it. *Fuck.* I'd be hunting down the bastard who cut my little girl. I'd be burning houses to the ground indiscriminately.

I unfold my arms. "Nothing is more important to me than keeping her safe."

"Can you?" When Ben takes a step toward me, I grit my

teeth, then have the urge to put my hand on his shoulder and reassure him. But I don't. "Keep her safe for me."

I nod once. "I can."

For you.

For me.

CHAPTER TWELVE

WALKING DOWN THE THIRD-STOREY HALLWAY, I tip toe towards the sound of banging and laughter and music—some kind of gangster rap. I stop mid-step when I hear the easy-going chuckle of Bronson filling the gaps between the profanity-filled lyrics. Glancing down at my pink silk pyjamas, I consider going back and covering myself in a robe.

Another bang pulls my gaze back to the room ahead.

Max's voice, more relaxed than I've heard it in a long time, greets my ears like a warm hug. His tone makes my heart pirouette. With that lovely feeling, I'm too intrigued to turn back.

The door at the end is open. Its walls are painted a bright white, reflecting the natural light. When I reach the entry, I peer around, trying to catch a glimpse of who is inside before they notice me. Bronson's dressed casually in a pair of jeans and a blue shirt the colour of his eyes. I notice Butch at the exact same time as he notices me.

Frick.

My cheeks warm at his welcoming smile. He's in a dark fitted suit, looking oddly out of place, standing on the blue tarpaulin that covers the floor. "Girl of the hour."

Butterflies break loose in my stomach.

Bronson uses his watch to turn the music down. He grins at me, that mischievous dimple indenting his cheek. "Good morning, sister Cassidy."

"Hi," I say, waving a little, like a complete weirdo.

Max steps out from around the corner, his strong tattooed torso bare, abdominal muscles moving as he lowers the big mallet-type object in his hand. "Little One, too loud?"

My mouth drops open, partly because he's a sight worthy of a statue and also because he appears to be putting holes in a wall. I stare at the holes in the plasterboard, timber beams exposed, dusty residue lingering around.

I shake my head, glancing back at Max but find all three eyes fixed on me. "No."

Butch moves towards me, stopping an arm's length away. "Congratulations. I can't tell you how pleased I am for you both."

Stunned, a response literally refuses to form in my mind. I didn't expect Butch to be *pleased*. Although, he is Sicilian. They like big families, right? Maybe. I don't know. That's a stereotype, perhaps a falsity. But he *is* Catholic, so it can't sit well with him that we are having unprotected sex out of wedlock. Wedlock... Who uses the word wedlock anymore? I start blinking really fast, unable to stop.

Bronson chuckles and is quickly upon me, banding his arms around my middle and lifting me off the ground. He squeals like a little girl getting a new toy. "We're having a baby."

Unable to ignore the clear approval of the Butcher family, my cheeks burn hot with equal parts happiness and embarrassment. When Bronson places me on the ground, I stare at Max. A veil of feigned exasperation at his big brother covers the hint of a grin.

"Pick her up like that again and I'll remove your arms," he says, revealing that smirk.

Bronson's silly cavalier smile only grows. "Ah, Maxipad. I'm so proud I'm rubbing off on you."

I shift in place, still confused by the moment. Still coming to terms with everything myself. Still...isn't it a bit early to tell people? Shouldn't we have informed people together? I should have told my mum first. Or Flick. I find myself staring at the cracked plasterboard in a kind of daze. "Why are you putting holes in the wall?"

Butch moves towards the hallway, stopping to catch my line of sight. His eyes are blue and full of fierce confidence, still managing to make me swallow even though he's not intimidating right now. "I will leave you to it. You need anything..." Nodding, he stares over at Max. "Nothing takes precedence over this."

Butch strides down the hallway, flanked by a swaggering Bronson. Max tilts his head at me, making a show of lapping up the sight of my scantily covered body, toe to crown, his eyes somehow managing to stroke me until the sensation is palpable. My knees buckle. "Don't wear that outside of our bedroom, Little One."

I glance at the wall. "What are you doing?"

His eyes fix onto mine and beneath their stormy-blue depths is something I haven't seen since before the auction. Hope. "Making the room bigger."

Feeling as though I already know the answer, because Max Butcher is all about telling me how he feels, what he wants, and what to expect with gestures and actions, I ask anyway, "Why?"

"For us." He swings the mallet into the plaster to reveal more of the space on the other side. "And him," he states, glancing at my belly. Immediately, I press my palm between my hips, over the spot that has his attention. It's the first time I've done this. Touched my belly, knowing someone else is forming on the other side. I don't know why women do this when they're pregnant, but here I am doing it.

It's like a little hello—an acknowledgment. I know you're there.

Hello, little baby.

Pinpricks hit the backs of my eyes, and tears quickly flood my face, but I think I'm smiling too—crying and smiling. That would be appropriate given my emotional state.

Max drops the mallet. The weight of it hitting the floor causes vibrations beneath my feet. "Don't do that." He quickly envelops me in his arms, cloaking me in his manly scent that is all Max Butcher. All hot. Sweaty. Consuming.

As big hands move up into my hair, pressing me to him, I cuddle his waist.

"This is a lot," I whisper.

He holds me still for a few moments in this room, which smells like paint, dust, and wood. After a few moments, he pushes me out in front of him, searching my confused—overly—ridiculously emotional face. "You're moving in—" He stops for a second, grumbling roughly at himself. "You should move in."

I divert my gaze to the view from the window. It is just like the one in our old room, but with a better view of the canals to the south.

In our old room.

Glancing away from him, I look at the hole in the wall, then back to him again. I gather my thoughts. Channel my emotions. Is this really happening? A few months ago, the mere thought of this would have excited me to the point of frenzy. Now though, after Erik, after all the secrets, the excitement at the prospect of sharing my daily life with Max Butcher is also coiled with concern. Tainted with it.

"I LOVE MAX. *He didn't choose his lifestyle.*"
    "*Yeah, but you still can.*"

WORRY WINDS itself around my heart and lungs, making it hard to breathe. I want peace for him—burden free and open. The man I see smiling after a game of rugby. The one content in my arms after an intimate moment. The one with *me.*

My Max.

I seek out his gaze. "I want a normal life for us. For you."

Those tempestuous deep-set eyes fix me with their intensity. "Tell me, what does that look like to you?"

I sigh, a little sad that he doesn't already know what that means. I don't really know what Max Butcher, son of Luca, heir to a corrupt empire, looks like after he leaves me alone in his bed. I'm not sure I want to. I do know, as clear and true as my love for him is, what *my Max* looks like. "A nine-to-five job. Home for dinner every night. Holding each other all night long. Rugby on the weekends... Bruises that can be explained." I touch the red-purple discolouration on his jaw. Wincing as if his pain were my own, I say, "I don't want violence to be so trivial to you, Max."

He threads his fingers through mine, lowering my hand. The tunnelling grey eyes of the man who consumes me soften further as they search my face. "The bruises are from boxing. I told you that."

"And the rest of what I said?"

"That's a fairy-tale."

"It doesn't have to be," I state adamantly, thinking about how my parents have dinner together every night with fresh-cut flowers, settings and placemats on the table. Even when their children are too preoccupied or busy, they still spend dinner together. I think about how they still shower together every night. Still steal touches and kisses when they think no one is looking.

"I'll give you everything I have to give," he murmurs, stroking his palms down my cheeks.

I press into his firm, possessive touch, closing my eyes to feel the warmth of those hands. Suddenly, I'm fraught with the vision of Max and his brothers soaking in ice baths, beaten and bruised. My eyes bat open. He's lived in a kind of emotional poverty. I'll show him it's possible. A real and sweet, however normal, existence. I'll give Max Butcher the fairy-tale.

I'll give him peace and placemats. "It *is* possible."

Searching his eyes as they scan my face affectionately, I want to ask if he's in danger, want reassurance he will come home at night in one piece because God, I won't survive losing him. And this is it now. A big leap towards a forever with Max Butcher, and oh my gawd, that sinks in. This isn't life-changing news about someone else; this is *our* life-changing news. Life-sealing news. Life-fricking-cementing news. Instead of all that rambling, I simply agree, "I'll move in."

His lips curve, setting into that magnetic yet menacing Max Butcher grin.

I smile back, unable to refuse him when he's like this. When he's calm. Relaxed. "You're so happy right now... why?"

"Wallabies won against the All Blacks," he states with a shrug, picking up the mallet and throwing it through the wall. When white clouds of dust fly around the room, Max's eyes snap to me. "Leave until it's clean in here, Little One." When I giggle at that, he lets out a long, satisfied sigh. "I've missed that sound."

"Why are you so happy?" I repeat.

He slowly runs his tongue along his lower lip. "I can still taste you."

I bite back a nervous smile. "*Max*."

"*You* make me happy, Cassidy. Remember?"

CHAPTER THIRTEEN

WITH A PAIR of angel wings strapped to my back, I rush around, trying to find candles and a lighter as the party carries on around me. This is the very first party I've ever hosted. *Ever.* My mum and Flick usually do the honours. They are the queens of hosting parties with their extensive lists of friends and their expert tastes in food and wine.

Luckily for me, though, Bronson's birthday falls on Halloween, so I got away with making fun spooky-inspired food and silly multicoloured beverages. I'm all over that.

As for the guests, it wasn't exactly hard to get most of the District here given The Butcher Boys' social status—especially Bronson's. He's, well... he's a paradox. There isn't a girl here who wouldn't climb him like the tall, muscular, colourfully carved tree that he is.

Well, besides me, Flick, and Stacey.

Of course, it was me and my big mouth that insisted on throwing him a twenty-fifth birthday party. I love my Bronson bear, but I also wanted to showcase my being a part of the Butcher household without actually coming out and saying it. Loudly. Proudly. So every fricking person in the District can hear and see.

Turning to look in another drawer, I take a step forward. I'm immediately jerked back, my wings snagged on a black chrome pantry handle. Laughing at myself, I pull my wings free, then riffle through drawer after drawer.

"If those white jeans were any tighter, I'd be concerned about your fanny dropping off from the lack of blood," Toni says to me from the other side of the breakfast bar.

A few days ago, I found the most beautiful sparkly white jeans at an op-shop. They are like Lycra on me, clinging to every curve. I'm wearing a white crop-top, fricking big white wings with sparkles and lace, and six-inch white stilettos. I have glitter smeared all around my exposed shoulders and over my exposed belly.

"Max likes my bum in jeans," I say whimsically.

"You seem to have settled in." When I hear Victoria's posh British voice coming from around the corner, my back stiffens.

Toni spins to face her, and I plaster a wide smile on my face when she appears. "Um, I've been here full time for a few weeks now." Not that she would know; she's *never* around. Her head tilts as she bats her false lashes and smiles insincerely at me. Subtly and quickly, her eyes then scrutinise my body, stopping briefly at my exposed midriff before bouncing back up again to meet my gaze. I suppress a shudder.

She usually looks at me with disdain, but now that disdain has a tight red bow wrapped around it and is glued on with honey, probably from wasps *she* stung with the venom of her speech. And then ate. *Ugh.* I hate this woman. She hasn't even bothered to dress up for the event. She is in her usual body-fitted power dress. Nails long, red, and manicured as if she's never worked a day in her life. I wonder where this feigned nicety has come from.

Butch.

Yep, it must all be an act for him.

"You're not showing," she states softly. "That must be nice."

I glance at Toni and we communicate with our eyes —*awkward.*

"Actually, I can't wait to show," I admit proudly. The past few weeks have been close to perfect. I've been given a choreographer position for the *Nutcracker* production this year, allowing me to oversee my second while she trains for Sugar Plum. Max has only left at night once, returning soon after and in a great mood. He finished his research paper and submitted it this morning, which is one less weight on his shoulders.

Right now, though, Victoria's presence in front of me is like a looming toxic fog. I relax slightly when I see Xander approaching the kitchen, his joker makeup slightly warped from the heat. He's still handsome though. Even with the green hair and gash of red paint cutting his face in half. As Toni stares at him, his eyes go sleepy with complete, unabashed lust.

"Mum." Xander clears his throat as if the word was uncomfortable to say. "Dad is looking for you." I've never heard Max refer to her as Mum before. It saddens me to hear it from Xander, knowing he manages to find the term appropriate enough to use when Max would probably rather cut out his own voice box.

Victoria tips her shoulders. "It's been so nice to catch up."

Balancing on the points of her stilettos with ease, she

strides away from us, through the rear sliding doors, and out into the alfresco.

"She is terrifying and fabulous in equal measure," Toni mutters to himself.

I smile at Xander. He winks in return.

He's been the star of my pregnancy so far. He has somehow anticipated my needs over the last few weeks, knowing what steps Max should take, and the things he needs to know and learn. He's given us books on parenting and always has something to say on the subject. But there is a rift between the two Butcher brothers. And although it's never been blatant in the form of an argument or discussion, it's apparent in Xander's obsessive need to please Max and in Max's curt response to anything he does.

"You are *too* fine," Toni says to Xander without a care in the world.

Xander just grins. "Ah, cheers? I think."

Giggling at Xander's chilled response, I turn and start opening cupboards. "I need to find candles."

I hear Xander's laughter as he moves in next to me. "Can you scoot away? You're going to poke my eye out with one of those things."

"Wouldn't want to do that. They are so fucking pretty," Toni coos.

"Oh my God, Toni. Leave him alone."

"You're getting dangerous to be around, ya know that, Toni?" Xander says with a chuckle. Toni has been a frequent visitor since I moved into casa Butcher. Although they would never admit it, I think the Butcher boys kind of like the added dynamic. This house was all alpha male and testosterone. Now, though, there is little ol' me and my bestie sprinkling in the weird like wildfire.

Toni smirks. "You like danger, don't you, Xander?"

My cheeks pinch with a big smile as I watch Xander ignore Toni's blatant objectification. "One, you have a boyfriend. Two, he's straight. So leave Xander alone."

Toni plucks up a single perfectly tweezed brow. "I'm just enjoying the view, Golden Girl. I'm appreciating the effort that must go into creating that tight—"

"I am so cutting you off there!" I state, covering my face with my palms. "Please, please stop talking."

Toni laughs. Having successfully embarrassed me, he casually sips his bright green Martini. I step out of the kitchen and around the island bench. Leaning into Toni a little, I watch the youngest and sweetest Butcher chuckle to himself as he searches for some candles. "I suppose I can't really complain. Get a few drinks in me and I've been known to have a pretty filthy... *Ah*—" He turns and places a box of candles on the breakfast bar. "There ya go. You know you can get the maids to do this stuff, don't you? I don't think any woman besides them has been in this kitchen in years."

"A filthy what? A filthy what?" Toni bounces on the black and chrome bar stool.

Xander leans over the counter, his blue eyes narrowing, his lips curling up on one side. "*Mouth*."

Toni nearly falls off his stool as he flings the back of his hand to his forehead. "Get this man a few drinks, asap!"

Laughing so hard, I am quickly brought to tears.

As we all chuckle together, Stacey and my sister strut in, dressed in a couple's costume: O Ren and Gogo from *Kill Bill*. Stacey has her dark-brown hair pulled into a tight Japanese bun, her fringe swept to the side and pinned back with a white flower to match her kimono. Flick is dressed in her old preppy high school uniform, complete with blue blazer and all. She was ecstatic to discover she still fits into it. With white stockings folded neatly below her knees, a pleated skirt, and a white dress shirt, she looks the part and fricking gorgeous. With the long black wig and bangs, her face looks even paler than usual, emphasising Gogo's emotional void.

"You two look so hot!" I grin at my sister, who is still a little uncomfortable with everything that's happening. She still needs more time to accept that I really am happy. That Max isn't a bad person, he just sometimes misdirects his anger. And when it comes to me, he has no filter.

She smiles back at me. "You, my little love, are glowing... I wonder why?"

I giggle. "It's the glitter."

"Yeah, that's all it is," Toni quips.

"Has anyone seen Bronson?" I ask, peering out and through the crowd. They shake their heads. "What about Max?" They glance at each other sideways before shaking their heads again. I frown at my friends and sister. "They are party poopers; I'm going to find them."

Moving through the ocean of guests, my wings offering me a wide breadth, I search the house.

At the end of the hall, I swing the entertainment room doors open, and oh my God, Betty Boop is being nailed from behind by the Mad Hatter.

She is slung over the billiard table, her head arched back, her breasts stroking the green cloth as Bronson, dressed as the Mad Hatter, thrusts into her hard and fast and ruthless. He's got one white-knuckled grip on her hip; his other is in her hair, the strands tightly coiled in his fist. Her mouth is wide open, alternating between panting and yelping after every slap of his hips to her curvaceous backside. My mouth drops open just as Bronson turns his head and notices me.

"Sister Cassidy!" He grins, moving faster. "This is Laura. Say hello, Laura."

She growls. "Fuck, Bronson." A sound that is both exasperated and on the brink of climax falls from her agape lips.

"I am fucking you, sweetheart," he says, just pummelling her harder. He looks at me. "You okay? Need anything?"

"Oh my *gawd*." I rush from the room, unable to stop the blush engulfing my cheeks. He *is* mad. No costume is needed to show that. Mad and amazing and lovable. I laugh to myself; I'm not sure why. I think I'm happy to see him with someone.

As I move back down the hallway, I feel the surrealism of this moment seep into me. I can't believe that I am here. That these boys are my family. That Max chose me. I touch my belly, smiling as I head back into the kitchen.

When I enter, I feel my skin start to simmer. The heat from a pair of eyes on me strokes my flesh to the point of scolding. Of fever. And only one set of eyes can do that. I search the room, glancing over small groups of people before landing on Max.

He's in a black V-neck and jeans, the kind of casual attire he would wear if the house was empty of visitors. The sleeves of his shirt bunch above his elbows, banding tightly around his strong biceps and showcasing defined, inked forearms.

I breathe faster as he tracks my movements. He leans his head to the side, lapping up the stilettos, the fitted jeans, the wings, and all the shimmer.

When I stop in front of him, his slow, menacing grin all but sweeps my legs out from under me. My belly flutters. I know what that man is thinking. His eyes have a promise. A dare. One I will be eagerly accepting. That gaze makes me blush so hard even the butterflies in my belly have bright crimson cheeks.

"You don't have a costume on," I manage to say.

His eyes narrow on mine. "Yeah, I do." He points to a

white sticker on his jeans. Written on it in black Sharpie is 'God.' He's *my* God, there is no doubt about that. "I plan on fucking one of my angels tonight."

My whole world shines. "We have a couples costume on!"

Shaking his head, he lets out a soft chuckle; it's the best sound in the whole world. A breath-taking sound that is as rare as it is meaningful. "Only you."

Slowly, I take another step towards him until I can feel the heat from his body. "Only me what?"

He drinks me in, and when I lower my eyes to his hands, I see his fingers massaging his palms, wanting to grip me, anxious to do so. Craning my neck, I kiss his chin softly. But he lowers his head, taking my mouth hard and hungrily. We kiss and pet each other, fondle and ignore the other guests as they move around us.

I break our kiss, and Max grumbles. "Don't smite me, my lord, okay? But I have to get the cake ready," I say, beaming at his tight face.

Skipping around him, I finish the final touches on the cake while he stands a few metres away, beside some men I don't know. He sips his whiskey, but his eyes never leave me. I can feel them.

As a group of girls slide past him, they make eyes, say hello, and try to engage him. With a slight frown in their direction, he nods his head once in response to their eager approach. They look offended. He's basically waving them off, and I hate how much that makes me smile. Because I don't want him to be rude to people. Don't want him to be an unapproachable, unfriendly person, and yet, that's Max. I've come to realise that. He chooses the people who deserve his attention, and he's ruthless in his selection. And this group, which includes a tall, leggy brunette dressed as Cat Woman, doesn't seem to have the prerequisites.

The cat girl follows Max's stare, locking on to me as I try to focus on fixing the frosting on the cake. Focus on the frosting and not her. Or how interested she is in my boyfriend. Yep, I'm not looking her way at all... She says something in her friend's ear, then wanders off.

Ugh.

The Mad Hatter, in all his tall, dark, and tattooed glory, finally appears, seemingly unaffected by our previous interaction. I, on the other hand, try to ignore the heat of embarrassment rousing below my cheeks.

Bronson looks at the cake. "Fucking red velvet, that's my favourite!"

Max frowns as my eyes bounce away from his big brother. My lips tighten, smothering a nervous smile.

Max moves over to me and folds his arms over his thick chest. "Explain."

Gawd, I'm so transparent. Peering up at him, his stoic expression firmly in place, I cover my smile with my palm and talk against it. "I kinda walked in on Bronson. That's all."

"No big deal," Bronson states, leaning in and running a tattooed finger along the frosting. "I was fucking..." He pauses, staring out into space. "What was her name?"

"Laura!" I say, smacking his hand away from the channel he's just created in the icing.

He holds his hands up. "*Sorry*. Yeah, the lovely Laura. Cassidy walked into the wrong room."

Max growls, but his face is somewhat amused. "Fuck's sake, Bronson."

"What's he done now?" Xander asks, walking towards us. He puts his arms around his big brother. "Happy Birthday, mate." The Mad Hatter and The Joker embrace, patting each other's backs and it makes for a really funny visual. Imagining the shenanigans those two characters would get up to on-screen, I giggle to myself.

After releasing each other, Xander nods hello at Max. Max scowls at Xander and then looks at me, his eyes dropping to my belly for a split second. The tension around the two brothers feels like a brewing storm. Eventually, it will either pass with time or explode into chaos. My heart falls when Max turns his back on his little brother and walks across the room to stand with his friends again.

I purse my lips while studying Xander's now tight face. "Are you and Max okay?" The words just fall out. And it must be the pregnancy because I would never usually involve myself in anything between them. Knowing Max like I do, he would be bludgeoning his fists on a boxing bag during a conversation like this. But I want to know. "Things seem..."

He clears his throat. "Tense." Reaching for a bottle of vodka, he pulls the cap off and gulps it straight from the neck.

Bronson stays cavalier, but there is a flicker of a flame in his opal-blue eyes. Of disapproval. Of warning. "Slow down, dickhead."

Xander takes the bottle and disappears into the crowd.

With that, I quickly fix the cake, light the candles, and then attempt to embarrass Bronson by singing him "Happy Birthday".

I should have known... nothing embarrasses that man.

Max joins me, and we move outside to where Toni, Flick, Stacey, and some other people are all chatting and drinking. While everyone laughs and jokes around us, I pull my attention away from them and move closer to the man beside me. He lifts his arm and I cuddle his side. My wings create a little separation between everyone else and us. I peer up at this titan of a man and see pain in his eyes. I want to ask about Xander. About this rift. It must be affecting him; I can see it right now, a kind of resentment barely masked in his grey irises.

Realising I haven't seen Xander since he disappeared with the vodka bottle, I gaze across the vast property: over the alfresco, out across the lawn, and to the boat moored on the canal. He's nowhere to be seen, causing a strange feeling to play around in my belly. I breathe in the air, which is laced with cigarette smoke, menthol, and a musky wet smell from the river. It's a warm night, but nothing is as warming as Max's arms around me.

Instead of asking questions, I just hold him and breathe deep.

CHAPTER FOURTEEN

cassidy

THE PARTY IS STILL in full swing when Flick and I attempt to get a bit of peace and quiet. A girl dressed as Dracula's wife stops me on our way outside. "Cassidy." She touches my shoulder. "Where's the bathroom?"

I beam at her as if she's just told me how beautiful I am or how good Max and I look together. All the sweets... "Under the stairs"—I point—"is a powder room."

She grins. "Thanks. Great party, by the way."

Eeeee!

Flick eyes me, shaking her head in disbelief. "You're ridiculous."

"She knew my name," I squeak. "And that I'd know where the bathroom is."

"Everyone knows your name. They did well before Max Butcher, I might add."

"Sure... still." I giggle.

Carter follows us as we wander down the grass hill towards the edge of the canals. The murmur of guests dwindles the further we go. It's nice to get some quiet.

The canals run all the way down to Stormy River and out to sea. Looking out over them, I take the moment in. This is my favourite kind of weather. The breeze is warm, and the air is dry with a slight crispness to it. As the gentle wind hits the canals, it sweeps the earthy scent up the banks and sways my hair around my shoulders. Searching the horizon, I can make out the silhouettes of houses on the opposite side.

We stop at the grass mound just before the water and sit down. I wait patiently for Flick to talk, knowing she needs to express herself. I lean back, placing my hands on the grass, squeezing the blades between my fingers.

She sighs and places her hand over mine. "You seem really happy."

I smile at that. "That's because I am."

"You need to go see Mum more." She lifts her chin. "Her little girl has moved out and is having a baby thug. She needs to see you more."

Maybe I should get defensive, but that just makes me giggle. "Can you get me a onesie with 'baby thug' written on it, please?"

"I like him, you know." She stares straight ahead. "I do."

"That sounded convincing."

She looks at my face. "No. I do. He's a complete dickhead sometimes. Borderline psychotic. But... the other day, I saw a picture of you two on Twitter. The caption said, 'Get your-selves a man who looks at you like Max Butcher looks at Cassidy Slater.' Not the most original of captions, but it suited the image. He worships you. It is so plain to see." She pauses for a moment with her thoughts. "You can change him."

I stiffen. "I don't want to change him. I just want to be there for him and—"

My eyes snap around at the sound of a glass smashing

against something hard. Carter is already beside me, not concerned with the ruckus, only with me. I hear muffled growls and grunts. I climb to my feet.

"Stay here," I whisper to Flick before walking back up the bank and around the front of the house. Carter speaks into his chest microphone, ordering for backup. He's in my shadow. His feet basically hit mine as I walk, he is that close. Which should warn me to be cautious, but I want to know what's going on.

Rounding the side of the building, I find Xander pinning another man to the floor, pummelling his head into the aggregate driveway. The man swings back. As I catapult forward, intent on pulling Xander away, I'm swept backwards by strong arms around my middle.

"That would be a very silly idea, Miss Slater," Carter states, carrying me back a few steps. "I will take care of this."

Two guards appear beside me, another on the other side of the driveway. I hear a female growling and turn to see a man holding Stacey back from entering the fight. She is ready to dive in to protect her best friend.

Carter walks towards Xander as he rolls around on the floor. He's now on his back with the other man on top. Casually, a guard blocks the front door while another stands staunchly near the side entry, ushering away a few prying guests.

Carter stops beside the boys as they fight. "That's enough, Xander." He grabs hold of the black-haired man on top, lifting him easily and throwing him away.

The man collects himself. Wipes his bloody jaw. "You're fucking insane."

I take a step closer, my hands shaking for some reason. "What happened?"

"You!" He points at me and I step backwards instinctively. "You're the fucking problem. They have all gone mad. I just said that you're cute and he fucking started swinging at me."

My breath catches. "What?"

Xander stumbles to his feet. His costume makeup is all smeared around his face, making his expression seem crazed. He dives towards the man again, but when Carter catches the back of his shirt, he whirls around and starts swinging at him instead. I stare, my mouth agape. My back and neck suddenly turn rigid and uncomfortable, like a twisted rope.

Carter fends off Xander's advances, blocking his punches with his palms.

The youngest Butcher boy stops abruptly. Sways in place.

Holding out his arms, he shouts, "Isn't this what they want, Carter?" Advancing on him again, his fist connects with Carter's jaw. Carter steps back, allowing the attack but blocking most of what's thrown his way. I'm sure he could push Xander to the ground if he chose to. But he doesn't.

Xander stumbles again, seemingly getting tired.

Suddenly, his tempestuous blue eyes lock on my wide, concerned ones.

"I am sorry, Cassidy," he cries, the tremble in his voice reaching right inside my chest and squeezing my franticly beating heart. "I am so sorry. I fucked up." He stumbles towards me, sloppy in his movements. As he reaches out to me, Max charges into him, ploughing his little brother to the floor.

I jump as the air is smashed from Xander's chest. He heaves. Whines. And then he ignites. He punches his brother's chest. Again and again. Max takes the hits as if they are just rain smacking the pavement. He glares down at his brother, searching. Confused. *Pained.* There is so much hurt in both sets of eyes right now. I want to scream at them to stop.

Stop!

"Isn't this what you wanted, Max?" Xander grits out between sobs. "The brother you want! One that can hack a guy's head off and sleep soundly at night!"

All of a sudden, breathing becomes hard. I suck at the air, trying to draw it in, but it seems dense and boiling hot. I force Xander's words down. *Down.* They have no place in my life or in my mind and I won't analyse them.

Xander breaks, bursting into tears, but he still swings at him—weak, lazy swings that barely affect Max at all. My pooled eyes study Max's face. His jaw muscles pulse in time with his little brother's hits. Not from the pain, as I am sure there is very little, but from the emotion driving Xander's fists forward.

He doesn't retaliate. He waits for Xander to lose momentum, to lose energy.

Slowly, Xander's fists stop. He buries his face in bloodied hands, sobbing into them without restraint.

I never thought I'd see a Butcher boy cry. It makes me weak with sadness. Tears slide down my cheeks, over my top lip, and fall onto the driveway.

Is this my fault? What did I do?

Leaning forward, Max pulls his brother's shaking body into his arms, holding him against his chest and rocking him back and forth. "It's okay, buddy. It's okay."

"*Max*! I'm sorry." He cries into Max's shirt, his face distorted, crumbling.

"No," Max states tersely. "I am. Now stop this."

Two large bodies now stand beside me—Carter and Bronson. But I'm unable to pull my eyes off Xander falling apart on the driveway. Then it dawns on me. This is about the auction. About what happened to me. I step forward and kneel down beside Max and Xander, surprised when no one stops me.

Xander releases his hold on Max and reaches for me. Twisting his torso, he pulls me into his desperate and quivering embrace. Max leans back on his heels, allowing our interaction.

"I should have killed him," he mutters into my shoulder as the smell of vodka from his breath drifts around us. "Right then. Right there. It's what Max would have done. Bronson. I let them down. I let *you* down."

My throat locks onto the words I wish to say, the heat from my tears like steam expanding inside me. The salty drops track down my face and fall onto him. His onto me. I shake my head slowly in the tense crook of his neck.

"I don't blame you," I manage to say. "I never have." Cupping his cheeks, I lift his face up to meet mine. "Let this go." Pleading with my expression, I look up at Max. "You too. Let it go... *I have*."

CHAPTER FIFTEEN

JIMMY GAVE me two fucking weeks to help Cassidy adjust to her new world with me. Two weeks without chasing little shits down for money. Without sorting through tender after tender with Clay and Xander. Without working on Clay's campaign. Without meetings. Now though, my time of playing house with her is up and it's back to business as fucking usual. Except now that I have finished my dissertation, Jimmy has me working throughout the day as well as at night.

The glowing display in the Rover fucks with me as the time clicks past midnight. I had every intention of getting home earlier, but things took a turn at the last minute when I was forced to make an example of a Croatian arsehole who'd forgotten his bargain with the District Boss. We part-fund their tuna fisheries in South Australia, and they supply our markets. Pretty straightforward arrangement really. In fact, it's been the easiest fucking deal up until today when one of our associates saw crates and crates of imported tuna heading for our docks. So, of course, I called a meeting at their favourite strip club to find out where the fucking Aussie catch was going and why we know nothing about it. Needless to say, I broke a few noses.

I pull into the garage and make my way inside, but as I peer towards the entertainment room, I'm suddenly eager for another whiskey. Heading down the hallway, I growl at the stench of perfume and sweat on my clothes. It's from the skanks that were crawling all over me tonight. I have never indulged in the affections of women. Their place in my life was one of simplicity. An exchange of pleasure. Nothing more.

Until my little ballerina.

I won't hurt her. Won't be cheating. But I should still shower before lying in bed with her.

Moving into the room, I pour a Jameson's, throw it back, and then pour another.

Turning to make my way upstairs with it, I'm stilled by the sight of pink-blonde hair and smooth white skin. Too much skin. Skin that needs a good slap for being out of our room, wearing only silky hot-pink pyjama shorts that arch up at the sides and a silk camisole that showcases a perfect, trim stomach and ... *perky tits.*

I bite my fist.

A blush hits her cheeks and that's the exact colour I should paint her arse for not listening to me about what's appropriate to wear around the house. Around my brothers. Guards. *Fuck.*

"I fucking hate repeating myself, Little One," I state, looking at that smooth, freckle-laced skin.

Her sleepy eyes lengthen as she smiles. "It's hot." She yawns. "Why are you so late?"

The countless number of whiskeys I've had at the club, plus the one I just threw back, suddenly create havoc in my mind. When I narrow my eyes on her, she shuffles nervously.

"Menace?"

I set the whiskey down on the edge of the bar.

As I step slowly towards her, she holds her breath. I don't stop until my shoes graze her bare little toes, forcing her to arch her neck to keep my gaze.

I want to fucking eat her.

She swallows hard. My eyes drop to watch her mouth open and suck in air. Her chest beats harder in response. I lick my lips when I see her little nipples tighten. My hands tic with need. Need to touch those nipples. Twist them until she can feel the sensation rushing deep inside her pussy.

I raise my hand and place it over her chest. Her frenzied little heart beats away against it. I slide my hand up the column of her throat and band it, feeling the roll of her swallow against my palm. I squeeze to let her know she's mine. *Fuck.* I think I'm losing my restraint to that fucking whiskey.

Hazel eyes, speckled with gold and amber, peer up at me. "*Max.*" My name is spoken like she's praying to me. Her voice is husky and desperate, deliciously so.

My cock swells at the sight before me and the scent seeping from her flesh. I grin when she places her little hand over mine, gently coaxing it away from her throat.

I let her.

She slowly turns to face the door and lifts her shaky little fingers, locking it tight. Staring at it, at her escape, she takes a big breath in. I still intimidate the little thing. My perfect little piece of purity. Barefoot. Near naked.

I walk up behind her. Pressing my body to her back, the feel of her uneven breaths the ultimate turn-on, I cage her against the door. Her hands slide up, fingers flexing around the wood by her head. Lowering my nose, I inhale her. That sweet, aroused scent resonates in my cock, and I want to fuck her right here against the door.

As I drag the tips of my fingers down her sides, she tremors and squirms. My cock throbs. When I reach the seam of her tiny little shorts, I grip flesh, provoking little whimpers from her. I knead my hands up her sides, caressing the outline of her hips and the definition of her delicate ribs. Reaching her hands, I entwine our fingers and rub my cock against her arse, up and down the seam. The stimulation, although through fabric, drives me out of my fucking mind.

Her head drops back to my chest.

Little whimper-mixed pants spill from her.

One of my hands breaks away from hers, slides down her stomach, and into her shorts. I caress her smooth hairless pussy before I cup her, stroking my index finger along her perfect lips. Spreading them, I push inside and slide all the way in. She is slick with desire. I lick my lips, wanting that silky juice on my tongue, in my mouth, every-fucking-where.

My finger slides in and out, twisting and rubbing against the muscles enveloping them. Her broken pants get louder. Rocking her hips into my inward thrusts, she finds a rhythm with me.

"*Max*," she moans, her chin to the ceiling, her lips open wide.

"Do you like it when I touch you inside, Little One?" I whisper in her ear.

She moans, and it's sweet and husky and just, *fuck me*. "*Yes*."

I pick up pace, and she begins to pant so hard her breath leaves little steam marks on the door I have her pressed against. "You're beautiful. I'm sorry I'm late." When her thighs clench around my hand, I know she's moments away.

But I want her orgasms rubbed out around my cock tonight, so I pull my finger from inside her. She curls in as if chasing the sensation I've just abruptly taken away from her. I grin even though she can't see it. My little piece of purity, desperate to be finger fucked by me. Lifting my velvety slick finger to my mouth, I run it over my lips before sucking her off me. *Fuck.* As I lick my finger and then my lips, I rub my swollen cock against the silk of her pyjama shorts, wishing there was no fabric between us.

When arousal hits my forehead like a fucking bat, I spin her to face me, pick her up, wrap her legs around my back, and walk her to the billiard table. She's pliable and weightless. I can deadlift four times my ballerina. Placing her down on the green felt, she spreads her legs wide to welcome my hips.

She runs her hands up my chest, fingers spread wide, touching as much of me as she can. She caresses each muscle, indulging in the feel of me as I contract under her gentle worshipful strokes.

But then she stops abruptly, her eyes trained on my chest.

I glance down, scowling at the red stains on my shirt.

Croatian noses spill like a bitch.

My teeth lock together, enclosing all the words, excuses, and lies inside them. I don't want to bullshit her. Waiting for her to say something, I silently curse Jimmy and Butch and everyone else who taints these moments with her. In that vein, I curse myself too.

Pressing my forehead to hers, I breathe roughly, wishing away this life for her. And yet, I will never fucking let her go. I swallow down the evening, a shitty evening with dirtbags and sluts.

Rolling my head against hers, I groan the tension away.

She slides her hands up and, with shaky fingers, starts to open my shirt. Button by button. I lift my head to find her face filled with emotion as she slides my shirt off my shoulders. Tugs it free from my arms. Drops it gently to the floorboards.

"Now it's all gone, Max," she whispers, and my guts fucking twist like someone just drove a corkscrew into them. Too much. She affects me too much.

I take her mouth, stealing her air as she exhales. My lips move hungrily around her face, her jawline, nipping and tasting her sweet, soft skin. Perfection. I lick her. I've never licked a girl like this before. Like I want to fucking *consume* her.

While my hands work on removing my pants, hers stroke the length of my now bare abdominals. Nails lightly graze my taut skin. I drop my pants and boxers, kicking them away. Her shorts come off next.

I stare at her pussy, which is glistening from my touch and parted just enough to showcase her pretty pink centre. I lick my lips in hunger to taste her insides. And now I can't stop the throbbing in my cock. It's excruciating. Can't wait.

Feeding my hands under her arse, I lift her pelvis up and slide her towards me. Clenching my teeth, I bury myself deep inside her. Her sweet tightness is nearly too much to bear. I can't imagine what it's like for her to take me. She gasps for air when I'm balls deep. Lowering her down again, I start to fuck her on the table. I shield her whole little body with one arm, my bicep twitching with the need to have her close—engulfed. Unreachable. *Mine.* The other, I feed down the seam of her backside, clamping onto her arse, forcing her to meet my thrusts.

I start to fuck her hard.

As hard as I can. Quick thrusts. I keep myself buried deep.

And she's so tight, holding me like a satin vice, like a fucking velvet fist.

"You feel so good. So good," I praise because she should know. Should know how good she takes me. When I'm like this—*relentless*.

She starts to tremble around me, legs seizing up behind my back.

I don't let up.

Not for a second.

Needing my release and hers. Craving it.

"*Max. Max. Max.*" My name is chanted through choppy, pleasured breaths. Her hands go into my hair. She has a death grip around the strands as she bucks, fucks me back, then fucking comes with a scream.

And that *sound*.

Fuck me.

It's *beautiful*. I groan loudly in return—long and excruciating—as I chase my release. It's there, scorching a trail up the underside of my cock. I lean back and mash my mouth to hers, bruise her lips with mine, and then, *fuck*, I shoot hard inside her. My hips move fast to rub the sensation out within her clenching little cunt. The release is so good, so needed. I continue to roll into her, wringing the final pulses out until they subside. I slowly stop moving but stay deep.

We come down together. Her lips move on mine softly, wanting to show me her affections.

Ineffable.

That's what this is.

This thing of ours.

It's fucking ineffable.

CHAPTER SIXTEEN

"THIS WILL BE COLD, HONEY," the sonographer says as she squeezes the jelly-like substance onto my lower belly. I'm on my back, my white tee-shirt rolled up to below my breasts and my jeans unbuttoned at the top.

Pressing the handheld ultrasound to my skin, she begins to spread the gel around. She slides the camera with ease through the viscous fluid.

Max towers over us, his stare unreadable as it's completely fixed on the camera. Not the monitor. The camera. The lady's hand as she presses into my belly, searching for a sign of life. We wait, and with every second, with every tick of the clock in front of me, my pulse increases. Max clenches his jaw. The silence is uncomfortable and filled with fear that the test was wrong, that I had already lost him, that—

"Oh, there it is," she says, stopping just above my left hip. I drag a big breath in. Max's eyes snap up to the monitor. I follow his locked stare and then we hear... a clock ticking underwater—the beating of a little heart. And I could dance a million performances, visit hundreds of cities, gorge on endless fine foods, and none would compare to this moment. I wasn't prepared for it—the second I realised it's possible to love someone I've never met. So completely. With all my pieces.

Studying the display, I see a little circle, where inside is a blob, and inside that blob is a pulsing cell—a heart. I swallow a lump so big it squeezes my throat all the way down to the pit of my stomach. I can't look away. A sob breaks from me before my tears even release. And then the tears come on like a sprinkler shooting from my eyes.

"Oh my God," I whisper. "*Hi.*"

Max's hand moves up to my face, wiping away the tears. He would usually kiss them, but he's struggling to look away from the screen as well. His hand freezes on my cheek. I rip my gaze away from that little heart and watch the man I love, the emotionally guarded Max Butcher, stare, eyes misting over, at the blob we made.

"Max, you okay?" I ask, reaching up and entwining our fingers.

"Hm." Is all I get from him, which only makes me smile and cry a little harder.

The sonographer starts to talk about the different parts: the sack, the heart. She draws lines across the screen, measuring the different black and white and grey shapes. Because that is what they are... *shapes*. Circle. Shading. Blob. Beating dot.

It is all done within fifteen minutes. The lady gives me a picture: black and white and nothing much to look at at all. The name at the top: Cassidy Slater.

Me.

That is my blob. The picture itself is fine, a cute token.

That sloshing beat though... The heart that represents the love Max and I share is my new favourite sound.

As we leave, I'm overwhelmed with emotion. Leaving the room where I got to see and hear him, evokes a little sadness. Now, as we move out into the shopping centre, we enter a world he's not a part of yet, not really.

Max pulls me to his side in a possessive, firm hold that I adore. While we walk past the shop fronts, not going anywhere in particular, Max stays silent. He's usually broody, but this is more aloof than broody. A strange kind of emotional fatigue has settled around him. Like he's done for the day. He has nothing left to give. Maybe for him that was like climbing a mountain. He needs to rest at the peak for a while before he descends or he might hurt himself—break something. More like break someone.

He looks out of place, as usual. Even in his casual attire—jeans and a black shirt—he still seems larger than life. Too large to mix with commoners as they browse the discount clothing racks for a new outfit or pick the best oranges from the fruit stands.

We wander through the sliding doors and out into the piazza district. The warm wind hits me, bringing with it the smell from some of the nicest restaurants in Connolly. Garlic hits me first, and I immediately crave Italian food.

It's lunchtime and there are people everywhere, but my line of sight is snatched by the children playing with the water and light show. A blue and cream floor mosaic shoots illuminated water high into the air while the children rush through it.

I smile.

I really want to do that.

The arm around me pulls me in tighter as the number of people around us increases.

I place my hand against his chest, peering up at him. He glances down, catching my gaze. His eyes, like the first time I ever truly stared into them, tunnel beneath my layers. Searching. Owning me. Chaotic emotions are strangled and buried deep inside their grey-blue depths. Beautiful. They are beautiful.

His eyes narrow and he stops walking. "What is it?"

"You're beautiful."

Raising his gaze, he continues walking. "Are you hungry?"

I giggle. "Subtle transition."

"Did you expect anything else?"

Shaking my head at him, I talk through a smile. "No, Master of the Subtle Transition. And yes, I'm hungry."

He steers me into a little Italian restaurant, the kind with mismatched chairs and tables, the Italian flag over a beautiful wooden bar, and a ceramic Mother Mary by the cash register. It's full of patrons.

As we enter, all eyes flick in our direction, bouncing away almost immediately as if the sight of us has scorched their irises. A man behind the bar smiles widely, but his lips are also pursed. The greeting was both friendly and somehow not.

"Let me guess," I whisper as Max guides me into a red cushioned booth. "Jimmy owns this place."

He slides in beside me and opens a menu. He always sits next to me, not opposite me. "Bite your tongue. Jimmy is Sicilian and they hate being called Italian."

Turning towards him, I cross my legs and hook my foot around his calf. A young brunette girl is suddenly beside us, pulling a pad from her apron and preparing herself to take our order. She looks younger than me. Maybe sixteen. The pen shakes in her hand, its tip bouncing on the sheet of paper. She beams at Max, making me realise that her nervous energy isn't a result of fear or intimidation—she's flustered.

Her cheeks glow the way mine still do when I see him. The way they did a few nights ago when he came home past midnight and I could smell the whiskey on his breath. See the hunger in his eyes. There was a lingering scent of perfume that night as well, which only made me want to show him why he had become monogamous. Made me want to connect us in a way only we fit together. More than sex. I'm his strength when he's vulnerable. I lighten the hold the darkness has on him.

Max looks at me. "What do you feel like, Little One?"

I peer up when the bartender appears beside our table and ushers the girl away. When her smile turns to a pout, I can't help but stifle a giggle.

The man takes a big breath. "*Ciao,* Max. What can I get for you? Anything. It's on the house."

Max smirks, his eyes scanning the menu. "Stop sucking up, Giuseppe. I'm just here for lunch."

He shuffles. "*Ti devo delle scuse*. I've been meaning to—"

"*Stop*," Max drawls. "Look beside me." Giuseppe glances at me, swallowing hard. I bite my bottom lip and smile awkwardly up at him. "Make her something special. If she fucking *loves* it, I'll credit this month." Max finally raises his amused gaze to Giuseppe, a provocative curve to his lips. "Generous, right?"

Ugh, he's such a menace.

Giuseppe brightens. "*E per il tuo piatto principale?*"

Max closes his menu and slides it to the other side of the table. "Gnocchi and a Jameson's neat. For Cassidy, no unpasteurized cheese. Cook everything thoroughly. No alcohol!"

He nods knowingly. "Anything to drink, Miss?"

"Champagne," I state teasingly and then grin at Max, who is now scowling at me. "*Kidding*. Orange juice, please."

Giuseppe rushes away, his demeanour more relaxed than when he approached. Max spins to face me, hanging his arm over the headrest. His grey-blue eyes rake over my face... They are like a vacuum or a tornado or a tsunami, akin in both beauty and destruction. Whenever they focus on me, sense, rationality, and, well, my knickers fly away... I clear my throat. Clear my thoughts.

His lips pull to the side. "Did that bother you?"

I shrug nonchalantly. "What? The baby scan or the weird interaction I just witnessed?"

His hand encloses the curve of my neck, his fingers stroking my skin affectionately. "You have just saved him thousands of dollars, Little One."

Trying to remain cavalier, I say, "What if I don't like the food?"

He grins wider, his left cheek indenting with a dimple that I just can't resist.

I raise my finger, poking the little divot. "Boop."

He shakes his head, veiling a chuckle despite his serious mood. "You will."

I trace the outline of his unshaven jawline. "Can we talk about the baby?"

He nods, staring over my shoulder at his hand on my neck. "Sure."

When my skin ignites under his feather-light caress, I roll my shoulder up to squeeze his hand against my cheek. I sigh and say, "What was that like for you? The scan?"

His eyes meet mine again. "I don't have the words."

I lift a blonde brow at him, thinking he's copping out of answering. "Is Max Butcher speechless?"

He deadpans. "That's what I said."

Oh my God, he's serious.

He's speechless... My heart pirouettes. "Would you like me to give you some words?" I ask.

Before he can answer or I can tell him anyway, a middle-aged waitress arrives at our table with a tray. She sets down an ice bucket, an empty tumbler, an entire bottle of Jameson's, and an orange juice in a highball on the table. She then nods and quickly leaves.

Max prepares his own drink, adding the ice and then pouring the whiskey. He encloses the glass in his hand but doesn't drink any. "Go ahead."

I stare at my orange juice in contemplation before murmuring through a smile, "Magical. Privileged. Thankful. Real. Love."

His finger taps at his whiskey glass. "Love?"

"Of course. I'm in love with him. I didn't think it was possible to love a strang..." I trail off when Max's face tightens.

He presses the glass to his mouth, looking at me over the rim before draining it entirely. He sets it down, his eyes still trained on me. They narrow, suppressing something too strong for him to show. It's an intense stare that is veiled with pride and guarded with warning. "Is he going to take you away from me?"

My breath catches and I falter. "No. No, Max. Never." It dawns on me in this moment that I may be the only female who has ever truly loved him. For all his pieces—good and bad. Sharing my love with another, just as important, might truly distress him.

It's a different kind of love.

Of course, I know that. But how could he possibly know? How could he know that when he's never felt the love of a mother? My heart breaks for him. Like it always does when I think about that kind of emotional neglect.

"It's a different kind of love, Max." Pressing my hands to his cheeks, I bring my lips to his. His are stiff with defiance at first, so I coax them with mine. Coax the concern from them. From him. His hand drops to the lowest part of my back, pushing me closer as he accepts my kiss. My mouth moves over his lovingly. My tongue sweeps out to massage his. I can feel his frown on my forehead. Feel his rough exhales against my chest. The longer we kiss, the looser his body becomes, the steadier his breaths. He succumbs to our affections — submits to them.

Like I do.

Our food arrives and Max growls quietly at the interruption. We break our connection, and I stare down at creamy chicken and mushroom risotto with freshly grated parmesan cheese, lemon, and truffle. I immediately salivate. I smile at Max. "I think he gets his credit."

After I finish all of my risotto and a piece of garlic bread, we exit the restaurant. Max's arm is draped over my shoulder but in no way relaxed on it.

I notice Carter from across the piazza and smile, but then my face falls at his expression. I follow his piercing stare. An elderly Italian lady is suddenly blocking our path, bowed slightly with her hands clasped together in a prayer-like position.

When she reaches for Max's arm, he forces me behind him, blocking me with his tall, strong body. Her fingers cling to him with desperation, as if he is the only thing tethering her to earth. Twisting his free arm behind his back, he touches the gun I know is tucked down his jeans. I nearly lunge to stop him, but he's not drawing it out. Just tapping it with his finger.

This little lady must be in her eighties. Speaking in Italian and English, her words are expelled between sobs and whimpers.

She wails. "Please! Please. *Tis to implorando.* Where is my Marco?" She won't look Max directly in the eyes, instead gazing at his shoes. As if he *were* God and *could* actually smite her down. "*Lui e un bravo ragazzo!*"

I shuffle backwards. Max tries to gently shake her off, but then Carter is upon her, dragging her away. Her fingers slip from Max's arm. The tether broken. She reaches out for him with desperation, her gaze rising to meet his. Her face crumbles and with trembling fingers, she makes the sign of the cross over her chest before clasping her hands together again.

My heart races.

My breath stops abruptly in my throat when she glances past Max and spears me with her bloodshot eyes. "*Please,*" she cries. "*Tis to implorando.*"

I suck at the thick hot air as tears flood my face. Wanting to rush to her, to hold her, to help her, I dig my heels into the pavement to stop them from moving. Max whirls around to face me, grips me by the elbow and steers me in the opposite direction.

My eyes are torn from hers.

But I can still hear her.

Hear her wailing with absolute heartbreak behind me. "*Mafioso. Mafioso.*"

Mafioso.

CHAPTER SEVENTEEN

MAX DRAGS me to a nearby car. A man I've never seen before is sitting in the driver's seat.

"Get in," Max orders, opening the door and guiding me onto the squeaky black seats. He leans across me, buckling my seatbelt in, and I'm so glad he did because I'm not sure my trembling hands would have managed. The driver's eyes shift around, but when they meet mine, they cut back to the road ahead. "Keep your fucking eyes off her. Drive her straight home. Walk her inside. Bronson will be there."

My shoulders rise and fall as I draw in shaky, shallow breaths.

Max goes to leave, so I lunge for him and wrap my fingers around his forearm. "Come with me," I beg.

"I'll be home soon." He leans back into the car, placing his hand on the leather seat to my side. That scent of his, whiskey and man and Max, soothes me. I know how I should feel. My concern should be with that woman, and it is, yet, it's Max's heart—his darkness—I am committed to understanding. To lightening.

As I raise my chin to accept his lips, he freezes and scowls over my head. His whole mien turns steel-like. He crushes his teeth together and exhales angrily through his nose. He squeezes the seat, the leather protesting within his white-knuckled grip.

My pulse beats hard in my throat. Beats in my ears. Head. I twist around, following his death stare out the passenger side window to a parked black SUV. Two men sit inside, both sets of eyes drilling holes through our vehicle. Are they policemen? Jimmy's men?

"Fuck," he bites out, then glares at his driver. "You have never been given a more important job. Get her home." As I reach for Max again, he closes the door.

The absence of him sinks my heart. Is he in danger? I sit up as the car pulls away and watch as Max walks back towards the restaurant. I look down at my fingers, now scrunched into fists, shaking in my lap.

Trees and cars start to blur as we pass them, becoming formless streams of colour. The man driving does as he was instructed—never once peering back at me. I shuffle my feet around. Shift my weight. Pick at my nail polish.

Breathing methodically, I try to settle my nerves.

Closing my eyes, I take a big breath in. But then I'm fraught with the image of that elderly lady's face. I open my eyes again and my leg starts to jiggle. What exactly just happened? That lady was looking for someone. His name is on my tongue and yet, I can't seem to push it out. I remember her referring to him as hers—my ...someone. A missing boy, perhaps. She was elderly, so if this person is her son, then he would be older than Max and more than capable of looking after himself. I find comfort in that thought.

I'm not sure why, but I nod. As if I'm compiling a case in

my mind. A case for why I shouldn't be concerned. But... Max's response to her presence... So cold. So defensive. He shook her off like an insect climbing on his arm. And Carter, my gentle giant, pulled her away without hesitation. Where is he now? Where is Max now? He wouldn't hurt her, would he? Surely not. And with that, I hold on to his words. I hold onto them with absolute desperation: he doesn't hurt people like me, only people like him.

My fear for that lady lessens as I believe those words to be true.

max

"E TU SÌ *sicuru ca erunu vàddia?"* Jimmy's voice booms through the speakerphone, his accent so thick I can't decipher a fucking word. He must be pissed.

Forcing my way into the right lane, I flatten my foot to the pedal and pick up speed.

"Jimmy, speak English. I can't understand you," I state curtly.

"My boy. Work on your Sicilian. It is your mother tongue." Jimmy tsks. "Are you sure that they were officers?"

Frowning at the other cars on the road as they cruise without urgency or care, I confirm, "Yes. I recognised one of them."

"And this... *nonna*?" Jimmy asks, reminding me about the bitch who scared Cassidy.

She had the fucking balls to approach me in public, not to mention to then address Cassidy directly and beg her for help. I fist the wheel. Glancing at the white roses lying on my passenger seat, I cringe. The domesticated man, Max Butcher. The man who brings flowers home to coax his girl into forgetting what she saw and heard. My arms twitch with the need to throw them from the car. Not that she doesn't deserve flowers... *Fuck*. "She made a scene."

"They will think her *pazzu*, se? Mad." He laughs loudly and states, "Either way, I will get one of my men to pay her a visit. You believe her to be Paul and Marco's mother?"

He is far too jovial to not either be halfway through a bottle of whiskey or be staring at an open pussy he's about to whip. I hesitate on the yes, knowing what this means for the old woman and her family. "I believe so."

"Leave it with me," he states. I go to hang up, not wanting any part in what happens moving forward. "Ah, my boy, before you go, I believe congratulations are in order, se?" I tense, my finger stroking the cancel call icon. "I thought this might be the case when you told me your *bedda* girl-friend had moved in with you. I've been waiting for you to settle down. I suppose I won't have to read about you in the paper anymore with, how do you say it politely, an array of ... *conquests*?"

"I won't be fucking around," I rumble, trying to stifle the growing agitation inside me. I just want to get home, check on my girl, and reassure her. Not talk about cheating on her because that sure as hell will never happen. If I ever do that. Ever hurt her. Disrespect her. In that way... I'm content with the knowledge that both Xander and Bronson will cut me up.

"Ah, young love. I am very pleased with that," Jimmy coos, and it's never an agreeable tone for me to hear. In fact, I despise it. I don't need or want his approval. "Inconspicuous, my boy. That is all I ask. That is what I want for you. And she is a fine, upstanding citizen from a very influential family. An honourable family. The District loves Ben Slater. I know this. And we have Cassidy now. She is, well... she is famous for her sweet nature. People think little birds dress her in the morning, se? You have done well. This is good for our reputation. For Clay."

Red.

I see red.

His cheerful words singe a hot trail from my ears to my eyes and I don't hear anything past 'we have Cassidy now.' The bones in my hands shift and ache as I try to crush the steering wheel. I have Cassidy! She isn't an asset or a mutual possession; she's fucking mine.

I hit the cancel call button.

AS I WALK SLOWLY down the hallway towards our new room, I notice the glow of light under the door—a possible indicator that she's awake. I stop just before entering and stare down at the flowers in my clenched fist. I note the illuminated 12:20 a.m. on my wrist. She should be curled on her side, deep in slumber, dreaming about the good in this world. The soft things. I should buy her a puppy, not flowers. So she can cuddle her at night when I have to leave. I breathe out loudly, physically trying to dowse all the anger bubbling near the surface.

When I push the door open and walk inside, I'm stilled by her little body seated on the edge of the bed. Her knees are drawn up to below her chin and her arms make a band around them. She lifts her head, her glossy hazel eyes finding mine in the low light. Springing to her feet, she runs to me. I drop the flowers when she jumps into my arms. Catching her, I envelop her tightly.

And she's fine. I'm not sure what I had expected when I saw her.

Not this.

My anger vanishes.

Her hands thrust up into my hair before clawing down the nape of my neck. The desperate and needy grate of her nails against my skin awakens my cock. Squeezing my waist with her toned thighs, she secures herself to me. She slams her mouth onto mine. I groan as she loses herself in the kiss. Sliding my hands down the length of her spine, I palm her soft, perfectly round arse.

"I love you, Max," she whispers into our kiss.

A shiver rushes through me as those words fuck with my head. I devour her sweet-talking lips, fucking eat her mouth, sucking and tonguing her, wanting to taste every inch of the place those words came from. Claim every inch. It's just a fucking word, but when it sounds like a purr—husky and soft and breaking with sentimentality—it makes a damn fool out of me.

Because I'm starting to believe in it. The more a part of my life and world she becomes, the more I expect her to turn and run, but she never does. She stays by my side. My pillar of goodness. If that isn't what the word means, then I don't know what.

I didn't choose this last name, this legacy to uphold. An empire to help my family build and protect. To help my brother one day rule. But I have chosen Cassidy. The one thing that I'll keep for myself in amongst all this grit and shit.

I may not be able to give her the fairy-tale.

But she gives me a break from this nightmare.

And I'm a selfish bastard, so I'll fucking take it.

I climb onto the bed with her wrapped around me.

I fuck her slowly all night.

CHAPTER NINETEEN

SEEING that my studio is now a thirty-minute drive from my new home, I don't spend as much time within its mirror-covered walls. But when I finish early at ballet, I steal a few hours to dance in my own space and at my own pace.

Just for the love of it.

Mafioso.

I shake my head as if to physically prevent that word from settling for too long in one place. After having successfully drowned that thought with fatigue all day, I don't intend on stopping now.

Slinging my backpack to the floor, I begin to remove my shirt and shorts until I'm left in my leotard. Carter sits on a stool beside my little kitchen, looking strangely comfortable when any other man might feel awkward. He makes the spot he's sitting in his place. It's true confidence. A wonderful quality.

Mafioso. Was the missing boy confident? Wonderfully so?

"I'm glad you came inside today," I say to Carter, ignoring the slight spike in my pulse.

"I'm grateful to be here, Miss Slater," he states.

Maybe I'll dance something specifically for him. Maybe something with mystery and darkness and an epic battle scene. I put my ballet compilation on shuffle and move over to the barre to warm up. Aram Khachaturian sounds through the speakers, filling my heart with that freedom I feel when I dance. It pulls at me. Each note plucks at the threads that hold me together, unravelling me and revealing my soul. Much like my love for Max Butcher does. He bares me down and I think—I hope—I bare him down too.

The music suddenly consumes me. Smiling as a tear falls down my cheek, I place my hand gently on the barre and begin my exercises. Even though I am already warmed up and pretty exhausted, it is a routine I can't break.

After a thirty-minute barre session, I move into the centre of the room.

"Would you like me to dance something for you?"

"I would, yes. What would you suggest?"

Pondering on that, I peer around my studio for inspiration. My eyes land on an image of the Black Swan. That choreography would be suitable to a life lived hard.

It is haunting.

Much like the voice of that elderly Italian lady.

Mafioso.

My throat thickens with discomfort, causing me to force a swallow.

Force my mind back to the present. To ballet.

Hanging across the length of one wall are photos from my thirteen years of dancing. Cast photos. Accolades. Newspaper articles. In one of the black frames is the newspaper clip celebrating the first time I was cast as Clara—the youngest Clara in the history of my academy. Beside it is a new wooden frame. Curious, I wander over and stop before it. My dad must have had it framed and hung like he always does. More tears slide from my eyes. For some reason, my stomach sinks.

There I am, foot up on the barre, smiling widely. The article heading is *Golden Girl Cassidy Slater Our Sugar Plum Fairy.* That feels like a lifetime ago...

"Miss Slater, are you okay? Have you eaten enough?"

I wipe my moist eyes and nose with my wrist. "Yes." I pull myself away from the frame. Walking back into the centre of the room, I'm determined to dance my little heart out. My emotions out. *Mafioso* out. "I'm just hormonal. I'm not sad. I've been so lucky."

"It's not luck. It's hard work. You're a very special young lady," he says with a smile.

All the tears inside me suddenly erupt even though I'm shaking my head in defiance against them. They make no sense. And I don't have time for them. Covering my face with my palms, I sob into them for no reason at all. Carter is in front of me now, wrapping his arms around my head and shoulders. Feeling as though I am being comforted by my dad, I lower my hands and lean into him without reservation.

"I don't know why I'm crying," I admit. "This is so embarrassing."

"You're pregnant and you have been dancing since eight a.m. Go easy on yourself."

Breathing in strength, I break our embrace. "I'm sorry. I'm a silly girl."

He tilts my chin with his finger. "You listen to me. There is nothing silly about crying."

Collecting myself, I take a deep breath. "I love my life. I love Max. I love our blob."

He nods. "I know you do."

"I'm not unhappy."

"You have already said that."

My eyes bounce around my studio. "It just all happened so fast."

"Life does that sometimes. Would you change anything if you could?"

The late nights alone in bed.

The bloodied shirts.

Bruises that can't be explained.

Mafioso.

But then I think about dark-brown hair, conflicted grey-blue eyes, and big warm hands. I think about the way my heart flutters when he's nearby. When I can feel him tracking me around a room. I think about how vulnerable he can be when he allows himself to seek comfort in my arms. Sighing, I admit, "If changing something meant not having Max, then no."

His smile widens. "That's good to hear."

I crane my neck to stare straight at Carter, feeling such comfort even though he's practically a stranger. And I see past his scars. They don't shock me anymore. I stare at them, waves upon waves of craters and valleys. "Tell me something about yourself. We spend nearly every second together and I know nothing about you."

"My story isn't a happy one," he states, clasping his hands in front of him.

"How did you get your scars?" I whisper, the question just tumbling out.

He smiles at me, but it doesn't meet his eyes. "In a fire."

That makes sense; his face does look like it's melted. "What happened?"

When his lips form a thin line, I wish I never asked.

Shaking my head, I start to say, "Forget I asked—" when he begins to talk...

"When I was your age, I was a smoke parachuter. Many years ago, before you were even born, there was a huge fire in the District. It cut through half the city. When I made the drop, I miscalculated it and went down into the inferno."

I gasp. "Oh my God..." Filled with instant pride, I smile at him in awe. "You're a real-life hero... I always thought—" I clear my throat. "Sorry, I *presumed* it had something to do with, ya know, working for Max."

He moves over to the kitchen, sitting back down on the stool. "Most of the people in the neighbourhood lost something or someone over those months. As a community, we were on fire. And it was arson that started it."

I can't believe I didn't know about this. "Did they catch him?"

"They did." He nods once. "He got ten years but was out on parole after four."

My ears burn. "Four!"

"Yes," he confirms calmly, but his eyes lose a bit of vibrancy. A strange kind of detachment moves over him. And while this whole time he's been fixed on me, now Carter is suddenly missing from inside his own gaze.

I swallow hard and take a step towards him. "How many people died?"

"One hundred and thirty"

I exhale loudly. "*God*..." Words clog up my throat, making both breathing and speaking hard. I have to force the question out, choking on the fact that I shouldn't ask but doing it anyway. "Anyone you knew?"

For a split second, he gazes past me. "My wife and son."

My heart aches.

No.

Smiling at me sadly, Carter appears to be back inside his eyes. Beneath his burnt skin. That strong, resilient muscle. "Don't cry for me, Miss Slater. It was a long time ago."

It doesn't matter how long ago it was; I cry for him. Covering my face, I let more tears fall through the gaps between my fingers. Tears for my friend and the family he lost while protecting others.

After spending every day with him for weeks, I wish he would resign. Wish he would stop protecting people and find love again. Wish he would—could—move on. It is like he's stalling, caught in a gear he can't get out of. Unable to let go of the past. He's so locked in his need to protect and serve... *Oh my God...* He helped raise little Xander. My heart crumbles all over again as realisation takes hold of me. A surrogate son, I imagine. A little man he could watch over, watch grow...

I fight back more tears.

"Carter." I lower my hands and look at him through pooling irises and wet lashes. "Thank you for looking out for me."

His smile widens. "There is no greater honour."

Feeling Carter's story deep in my bones, in my marrow, in my heart, I decide to offer him an alternative story. It is the ending that I want for him. For Max and me. For the boys.

The fairy-tale.

It isn't mysterious. Or dark. Carter doesn't need to see my interpretation of his pain or fury—he's lived it. So instead, my dance is full of hope for his future—for all of ours—for love, contentment, peace, and placemats.

It is full of upbeat swooping movements that culminate in a happy ending.

The dance we all deserve.

CHAPTER TWENTY

I MAKE my way upstairs to my dad's office, leaving Carter to make a few phone calls—which I think means he needs to check in with Max. I hope my dad isn't swamped with work, and he's in a talkative kind of mood.

As I move through the second-storey corridor, I have to admit to myself that I somewhat miss my family home. It's still a huge house just like Max's, but it was built in the 19th-Century, and while it's been renovated a few times, it still holds its old-world charm.

When I walk past Konnor's room, something catches the corner of my eye. Taking a step backwards so that I am in the open-door jam, my face lights up at the sight of my beautiful big brother on the bed. With his deep emerald eyes downcast and focused on something in his hand, he hasn't noticed me. As I study him, a smile plays on my lips. With those eyes, the double dimples he often throws my way, and the strong lean physique of an athletic, he's just such a beautiful man.

Troubled at times, though. Despite being on the path to recovery from alcoholism, Konnor still seems to be suffering from a kind of post-traumatic stress disorder, although never clinically diagnosed.

"I never received a congratulations from you," I say with a knowing smirk because it's no secret that my brother does not like The Butcher Boys and most definitely doesn't approve of Max Butcher sweeping his little sister away.

His head shoots up. "Pipsqueak. I wasn't expecting to see you." He holds a hand up. "I'm happy to see you though."

I grin. "You're the one who lives hours away, not me. You should have told me you were in town; I would have come to see you." I glance around, squinting at him as he lowers his gaze to the small photo in his hand. "Where is Blesk?" I ask.

"She's shopping with Elise." His gaze rises to mine. "You remember Blesk's best friend, Elise?"

Chuckling at that, I say, "Who could forget Elise? She's like my spirit animal."

"Yeah," he mutters, moving his attention back to the photo, an action that might be rude coming from anyone else, but Konnor gets lost in his thoughts more than anyone I've ever met.

"What is it?" I make my way towards him and sit on the edge of his bed. Leaning closer, I stare down at an old photo of some people about my age. "Who are they?" I ask just as my eyes snag on the handsome face of our father. "Oh my God! Look at him. He's *so* cute."

"I'll take your word for it."

"What are you doing with this?"

He points to a pretty girl with light-brown hair. Offering me his attention, I stare into perfect green irises that hint at trouble and pain beneath their sheer layers. "She's my biological mother."

"Oh." I swallow hard before focusing on the woman who

raised my brother until he was four. Until he was taken from her. Only for her to die a few years after...

Perhaps she died of a broken heart.

I shield my lower belly with my palm, heat hitting the back of my eyes. He looks so much like her. As I study the image, I remember the night my father told us that he was friends with her in high school. Told us that he loved her. Told us some of the District's secrets. About the Mafia. About Jimmy. Max. The conversation still sits heavily in my stomach.

"She's pretty," I say.

Despite needing to visit my father before Carter takes me home, the pull of my brother's discomfort keeps me rooted to the edge of his bed. I put my hand on his tanned one. "What's going on, Konnor?"

He twists to face me, dropping his gaze to where my hand spans my stomach. "You're going to be a mother."

I blink at him and take a deep breath before folding my hands in my lap. "Yeah."

Locking his jaw, he speaks through a slow shake of his head. "I was fucking furious when I found out he'd knocked you up, Cass. I'm not gonna lie. I was on the verge of driving all the way here and choking him with my bare hands.

"Blesk stopped me, of course. She wouldn't let me call you either. I had the phone in my fist and was ready to, but... She settled me down. And then, a few days after that, I got thinking about *my* mother. And how I'll never know her. And..." He sighs, eyes deep with emotion. "I don't know. Now I'm a little jealous. I just wish I had someone in my life, anyone, who shares my blood with me. Someone I can spot similarities in. *Sorry*." He nods as a genuine but sad smile touches his mouth. "You're going to be an *amazing* mother."

The backs of my eyes begin to prickle. "You don't need to

share my blood. You know this. You're my brother, and you're his uncle."

His blond-brown eyebrows rise. "His?"

"Well, according to Max's dad, there hasn't been a female-born Butcher in over three generations, so I just call him a boy. He probably will be."

Konnor groans as he all but spits out the word, "*Butcher*". He curls his nose up. Thrusting his hands through his hair, he then pulls them back down his face. "Can't he be a Slater?"

I glance around dubiously before fixing him with an apologetic smile. "No, Konnor. He can't."

Before he can reply, my phone vibrates. Konnor nods at me to take it, so I pull it out of my pocket.

Carter: I have to get you home soon.

Frowning at the screen, I text back a reply.

Cassidy: Why?

Carter: Max.

One word that somehow delivers an entire explanation.

Cassidy: Ten minutes.

"Fuck, he's a controlling prick. Tell him you're with your family," Konnor snaps, glowering down at my phone.

I bite my lip and blacken the screen. "He worries, that's all. Sorry, big brother, I have to go. I love you." I cuddle him quickly and then wander from his room.

At the end of the corridor, I tap my knuckles softly on Dad's office door.

Before I can announce myself, I hear his gentlemanly voice say, "Come in."

Pushing open the door, I step inside, my arms opening wide. "Guess who?"

He jumps to his feet and rounds his desk, moving quickly to scoop me up into a tight embrace. "I've missed you." He pushes me out in front of him as he eyes me thoroughly. "How do you feel? I've wanted to be nosy and visit, but I was trying to pretend that I understand you're a grown woman and that I don't need my little girl anymore."

"Don't you mean, that I'm a grown woman who doesn't need her dad anymore?"

"No. I meant what I said."

I giggle a little at that. "I will always need my dad."

"Good," he states, gesturing to a seat. "Sit. To what do I owe the pleasure of my favourite person?"

Walking over to the spot opposite his desk while he moves back to his chair, I mull over how to delicately have this conversation. Resting my hands in my lap, I smile at him and inhale a breath of courage.

Mafioso.

When that word taunts me again, I decide to just get it all out. All my questions. Show all my cards.

"I want to ask you what you know about Max's family. About the Mafia. About Jimmy Storm. I want to know how to ignore what you know... about them. Because I've seen things. And I'm wrestling to keep my concerns suppressed. I'll never let go of Max. No matter what you say or what I see." I pause for a moment, always having known those words to be true but never having said them aloud before. Clearing my throat, I continue, "I just... want to know how you handle it."

He stands up slowly and then heads straight for his cabinet, pulling out a bottle of scotch. He pours himself a drink before making his way back to his seat. Instead of drinking it, he entwines his fingers in front of him. "What have you seen, Cassidy?"

A man die by my own hands.

A woman looking at my boyfriend with true fear.

Blood and bruises and secrets so terrifying I don't even ask for them to be shared with me, afraid of what I may hear and the apathy attached to the way I may hear it.

I drop my gaze to my fingers and pick at my nail polish.

"He is not a bad man," my dad says. He nods as if convincing himself too. "I wouldn't call him a good man either, but I'm not sure there is such a creature... Women are good. Men are... apes in shoes. We all do what we must to protect our own." He reaches for the glass, sipping the harsh liquor a few times before setting it down again. "I don't ignore it, Cassidy... But I don't know enough to make judgements. For a long time now, I have trusted in his ability to make the right decisions. He's clever. And he stands beside Jimmy Storm."

I wrinkle my nose in confusion, having thought he was talking about Jimmy all along. "Wait, who?"

"Luca Butcher... " He pauses with his thoughts, rubbing his hands down his cheeks and entwining his fingers at his chin. "How do I explain this to you? Do you know what the District was like before Jimmy Storm flew in from Sicily?"

I shake my head. "No."

"Drugs." He leans back in his chair. "Poverty. High unemployment. We are far away from the capital, and the Eastern States didn't care enough to aid in infrastructure or pay us many dues. Ninety percent of the mines employed fly-in-fly-out workers from other countries or the other side of Australia. We had a tiny budget for public servants—police, nurses. No one wanted to work here, so we had poor trades and poor doctors. There was so much violence in the streets. Bashings. Breaking and entering."

My body feels strange, like my heart can't decide whether to beat uncomfortably fast or slow down. I have known for a while that the District is built on corruption; stitched into the lining of most prosperous families' pockets is that truth. It just sounds so concrete coming from my dad's mouth. "But there is still violence," I say. "Lots of it."

He smiles tightly. "Not on our streets. Not in our homes. Can you imagine if people started breaking into houses under Jimmy's watch?"

That elderly lady's distraught face flashes behind my eyes. Her harrowing cries ring in my ears. And a name—his name—finally claws out from the depths of my subconscious. *Marco.*

"People die under his watch," I blurt out, feeling my face pale as the truth whirls around me like a frosty breeze.

Marco is dead.

This man is dead, and he has people like me that love him—miss him. Max's cold stare bores into my mind, his impatient dismissal when all along he had known... had maybe even done the deed himself. *"The brother you want!"* Xander's words blister my ears, demanding my attention. *"One that can hack a guy's head off and sleep soundly at night!"*

My lungs strain for air, but I try to hide it, sneaking in long, vibrating breaths.

Is Max capable of such an act?

"Not our people," my dad states. "Remember that. Not honest, hardworking people. Our employment rates are the best in the country. Jimmy secured our residents a huge tender for employment on the mines. He cleaned up the streets. He has given us wealth. Safety. I decided a while ago that I would accept the good in that man until I saw the devil in him."

So Marco wasn't an honest, hardworking person? Is that what I am to believe and hold on to like a fricking lifeline? I let that sink in, move through my body, and expand my chest, filling it with fresh air.

Blinking at my dad, I ask, "So what do I do?"

"I suggest you do the same. I didn't want this life for you. I fought very hard to keep you out of it. But you fell in love and the rest is history. I know love, and I'd never deny it for you nor push you away from it."

Remembering how sensitive my father is, I project a smile. "You're such a softy."

He shrugs. "Yeah."

I leave my father's office with my mind and body in a state of absolute exhaustion. The need to choose whose side I'm on seeps through me like dye, spreading out and changing the very essence of me. My heart. *My morals.* I accepted the gun. Accepted that in his line of work he hurts people. But can I accept that he's capable of real brutality?

Walking out onto the veranda, I stare across at Carter, who is leaning patiently by his car. He's a good man. And he works for Max. Max doesn't hurt people like me... And he's a great judge of character... Blinking a few times, I realise it's not a hard decision.

I trust Max. Always. Blindly or not, I do.

Nodding at Carter, I climb into the car.

CHAPTER TWENTY-ONE

I PUSH open the bedroom door, and Cassidy sits up in our bed, batting her eyelashes as though they are made of solid lead. Carter wasn't wrong. She *is* exhausted. She's been pushing herself with ballet. With fighting the urge to sleep just to be awake for when I get home. I can't allow this.

"What time is it?" she murmurs, wiping at her half-mast eyes.

I don't answer.

Instead, I walk towards her and stop just shy of the bed. As I trace her naked little tits and smooth stomach with my gaze, my cock stirs within the confinements of my pants.

Tucking my hands into my pockets, I frown at her. "You should be asleep."

"I worry about you."

Well fuck. I try to soften my expression. Not cocky or smug, just gentle and reassuring. "You don't need to, Little One."

Rolling her shoulder up, she looks down at my spot on

the bed. "I *miss* you." I stare at her for a moment, stare at this sweet little girl in my bed wanting me. Needing me.

Climbing onto her hands and knees, she crawls towards me. Her pink-blonde hair hangs down her back and plunges over her shoulders. Her petite but curvy, naked body moves provocatively to the edge of the bed. She takes a big breath in before arching her neck to meet my narrowed eyes. Her lips are set into a coy little curve and her hazel eyes, glossy with fatigue, gaze up at me through thick heavy lashes.

What does my little ballerina want?

To suck my dick?

My cock fills quickly with all the blood now pumping fiercely from my heart, causing it to span out across my thigh. Reaching down, I stroke her hair and then drag my thumb along her lower lip. I run my gaze down between her shoulder blades, to her little back, and over the crease of her backside. She leans up on her heels, and now I'm staring at those perfect, pert little mounds on her chest and the lips of her pussy. I reach for my belt and slowly unbuckle it, not taking my eyes off her.

Throwing it into the corner of my room, I ask, "Do you want to suck my dick?"

She nods, a glow hitting her cheeks. She licks her lips and, with shaky hands, reaches to unbutton my pants and draw down my zipper. When she pulls me out, she inhales quickly. I follow the roll of her throat as she swallows.

Her eyes bat heavily again—sleepily.

She's too tied to suck me. So before the temptation to force those lovely bow-shaped lips around my cock grows too great, I brush my fingers through the soft, satin-like strands at her crown. "Little One, you're tired." I take a step backwards. "Lay down on your stomach."

My erection knocks on my shirt as I wait for her to move back into the centre of the mattress and lay down.

She twists her head to the side, blinking at me sleepily. "But I want you."

Leisurely, I remove all my clothes—shoes, pants, shirt, tie, boxers—as I caress her physique with my eyes. She starts to pant as if she can really feel my gaze. I crawl towards her little body, sliding over her legs and burying my face between her arse cheeks.

"*Oh God*," she murmurs as I lick her arsehole. When she pulses against my tongue, I dip inside her and then mouth the tight muscles around her rim. She bucks, so I pin her down with my body. "*Max.*"

She's too good to me. She lets me pervert her. I want every part of her. Want to eat every inch of her. As my tongue fucks her arse, my lips and teeth mark everywhere else. I palm her cheeks, and she wriggles around beneath me. I fuck the mattress with my hips, groaning at the thought of what she lets me do to her. Sensation suddenly draws my balls up. I could eat her arse all day. But I want to come. Fill her.

Breaking away, I move up to hover over her. She twists her head. When I scroll my eyes over her pinkened cheek, the sweat tracing her freckle-dotted nose, and her open panting mouth, I grin. Bracing her thighs together with my legs, I lean on one elbow and reach down to stroke her pussy lips with my fingers. *Fuck.* She's dripping. I position the crown of my cock below the seam of her arse, rubbing the sensitive outer folds. I groan, needing my release. But I'm so fucking turned on, if I go too hard and fast, I'll come too quick.

Pressing her flat to the mattress with my body, I begin to slide into her. Slow, shallow thrusts that tease us both. She moans, lifting into me, her greedy little pussy wanting more. I growl. Unable to deny her silent demand, I give her what she wants, sinking in until I can feel the end of her and then pushing harder still.

She cries out as I start to thrust.

When I rear up onto my hands, I press one palm between her shoulder blades, holding her chest to the mattress. Her arse instantly rises up. I fuck her fast and deep, rolling against her lax arse until I hit her cervix, then drawing out to the feel of every one of those internal muscles begging me to stay deep. All that responsive flesh grasps me.

The bed starts to rock. I want to be inside every fucking part of her. Bury myself in her body. Find solace. My release. My peace. She fists the sheets and mewls around, her frantic movements surging heat into my abdomen. I crunch my stomach together hard, fending off the sensation; it's too soon.

Locking her thighs between mine, I restrict her from further movement. "Relax, Little One. Let me take your sweet little body."

She begins to vibrate, her legs and thighs contract, twitch, and squeeze together between mine, narrowing the smooth delta I'm currently fucking like my life depends on it.

"*Cassidy*," I hiss.

Grunting through gritted teeth, I move faster, my muscles scorching hot with adrenaline. She screams into the pillow as I fuck her through her orgasm.

At the sound of her sweet, uneven cry, I completely lose it. My veins suddenly ignite, forcing a wave of fire throughout my body. To every inch. My muscles tremble. And I explode. Letting out a broken groan, I grip her hip with one hand and continue to beat into her, feeling my cum pour down the sides of my shaft and out from between her legs.

She's still moaning softly by the time I slow down. When I let go of her hip, her pelvis flattens to the mattress. Resting on my elbows, I'm careful not to put too much of my body weight on her. I pant out that phenomenal orgasm, pressing my forehead into her hair.

Lifting my head, I fan her hair with my heavy, laboured breaths. "Don't wait up for me anymore."

With her head twisted to the side, I can see a sweet sleepy smile tugging at her lips. "And miss out on that?"

I frown. "Do as you're told, Little One."

Her expression grows even more content as she breathes out, "Yes, *Max*."

Which I know really means: 'I'll do exactly what I want.'

SINCE THE MOMENT she passed out—and she did fucking pass straight out—my mind has been churning with agitation. I toss and turn, completely unsettled by her level of exhaustion. Her lack of taking care of herself. Frowning at the dark ceiling, I decide it's no use trying to sleep in this tense state. Carefully, I slide from the bed and head downstairs to mull it over while beating the boxing bag in our gym.

Jab.

I know she cried in her studio today.

Jab jab.

Know she was on the go for nearly ten hours and barely ate a fucking thing.

I fucking lay into the bag.

When I return to our room, I sit down on the couch opposite the bed. The newly rising sun drills colour into the sky beside me. With my elbows on my knees and my fists under my chin, I watch Cassidy deep in sleep. She's on her stomach, cheek to the pillow, arms above her head—naked.

She's in the exact position I left her in, completely dead to the world.

I rub the stubble on my jaw.

I'm careless. Selfish. I shouldn't have fucked her on her stomach. If she loses this baby because I can't control myself with her, it'll be another thing that I've let happen to her. I shouldn't be home so late. Should be home to have dinner with her—make sure she fucking has dinner. *Fuck*, she used to love food. I guess the baby is messing with her appetite. I should eat her out and put her to bed nice and early while she's in a delicate condition. Should be here... I pull my new phone out and type a quick message to Carter

> Max: book an ultrasound for tomorrow around lunchtime.

I need to know that the beat of his heart is still strong so I can let that concern lay to rest. She *loves* him. Already. My jaw suddenly aches, but I didn't even realise I was clenching my teeth. *He* didn't have to earn her love or prove anything; she just loves him. It's still a concept I find hard to swallow, but despite that, if she loves him, then I will protect him with my goddamn life. That kid is a Butcher.

Closing my eyes, I exhale roughly.

My blood...

He is a part of this life now.

My eyes find her again. *So is she.*

And Jimmy all but said that he plans on using her to influence our public image. Use her to gain favour with Ben. With the more conservative members of the city. Like she is a fucking personal relations strategy.

And I did nothing.

Said nothing.

I am just a fucking pawn with no need other than to

decapitate and slice and fuck my way to a prized asset. *Fuck that.* My fists tighten until both of my arms shake violently.

Thirteen years! I have been knee-deep in Jimmy's fucking dirt for thirteen fucking years. I've never asked for a goddamn thing and yet, he still thinks he can claim what's mine. The only thing I want. Like hell he can! I stifle a growl.

I won't be sharing her to suit his or anyone else's agenda.

Next time, when I say she is out, she. Is. Out.

And I expect those words to ring between his ears every time he thinks about Cassidy.

Thinks about using her.

She is mine.

CHAPTER TWENTY-TWO

STILL AGITATED, I shower, dress, and head downstairs to start my day but not before switching Cassidy's phone off. She will sleep for as long as her body tells her she needs to. Fuck ballet. Fuck anyone who wants to talk to her.

As I take the staircase down to the first floor, I look through the windows over the open balustrade. Connolly. It's my city. Jimmy's too. But it's not Cassidy's. She loves quaint urban Brussman and yet, she's never once complained about dropping her whole life there. Her family. To be with me. To be in my room every night—alone.

Fuck.

The sight of Butch in his navy, tailored two-piece suit, sipping his espresso and reading the paper at the kitchen island, stills my previous thoughts.

Staring at him, I feel my forehead tighten. "You're here a lot these days."

When he peers over at me, I catch a hint of disappointment in his eyes. "Morning, son. How's your girl?"

I smirk, knowing he's here to spend his morning with

Cassidy. He has no idea that I know he has breakfast with her before she goes to ballet and he goes to Jimmy's. She has Butch completely smitten, wrapped snugly around her sweet little finger. What a soppy motherfucker. "So, do you want to be called Pop, Grandad, or *Nànnu?"*

A cocky-arse grin hits his lips. "Caught me."

Moving towards the fridge, I say, "She won't be down for a while. She needs to sleep..." I sigh angrily. "You probably speak to her more than I do at the moment, anyway."

As I make myself a protein shake, he watches me silently, his sceptical eyes following me around the kitchen.

I freeze, scowling at him. "What?"

He doesn't jump to answer me, seemingly contemplative. Then he states, "Every man has two options in life: either be the man she needs you to be or move out of the line."

I sneer, setting my glass down on the island bench. "I'll torch the fucking line."

He smiles, leaning forward on his heavy arms. "I believe you would. Love is maddening. Hasn't watching your brother all these years not taught you this?"

Scoffing, I say, "Bronson was mad before Shoshanna."

His brows draw in and he sips his coffee. This is Butch in an emotional mood. It's a rarity, and I have no doubt it has to do with Cassidy. "Your brother always leans towards the theatrics," he says, placing his empty espresso cup down. "He's more like your grandfather than me. You, you're so much like me."

His words settle in my stomach, like hunger or sickness, causing me to shift my weight. Was it a compliment or a dig? To know which, I would have to know exactly what Butch thought about himself. And that, I don't know. The discomfort in my stomach is soon fuelled by the realisation that I am like him, annoyingly so. Home late. Cold. Impatient.

"And just like you, I don't get home until after midnight and have no time for my family."

He leans back, folding those weapons of arms over his chest. My words rush off him like water. "I nearly gave up the life once."

That takes me by surprise. "I didn't think Victoria cared."

"She never did," he states adamantly and then I catch a glimpse of something in his stern eyes, a moment where they nearly reveal a secret. A truth buried deep. Something painful. "I didn't nearly give up for her."

Perhaps in other families that kind of statement would warrant a follow-up question, but we are not like other families. His business is his, and I have always taken exactly what he has offered me and never more. It's called respect in our world. Respect for a man's silence. "What would he have you do?"

Butch frowns. "Who?"

"Jimmy."

Butch's arms unfold, and he makes a fist, cracking his knuckles. "Do you think of me as Jimmy's property? That's never been the case. Don't mistake my quiet for compliance."

Shaking my head with contempt, I say, "So you'd see me leave my brothers?"

He scoffs and it pisses me right off. "Max, let's talk plainly here. Xander won't be collecting and reinforcing. He's more important to Jimmy than that."

And although he's the youngest, it's not Xander I'm worried about. I know he'll be working behind the scenes soon enough. It's my reckless, emotional big brother. "And Bronson?"

Butch lets out a long sigh. "He wouldn't have it any other way."

I tighten my jaw. "He'll get himself killed."

"You underestimate him; he's made for that life—the frontline work."

"He's not," I state curtly. "He has just given up on any other!"

"And you never did," he bites back. "So why are you still treating your legacy like a goddamn burden instead of finding a place amongst it that suits your interests as well as the Family's?"

It wasn't a fucking question that required an answer.

Fuck.

He's fucking right. I snarl to myself, thinking about the way everyone views me as the uninterested Butcher. The bored one. Out of all my brothers, I'm the one who just finds the whole organisation not worthy of my time. What a bloody insult that must be to my family. To the Family in Sicily.

Bronson seems to revel in the intimidation. Xander can't hack it emotionally, but that's fine. He's now motivated to study law and use his big fucking Einstein brain to keep us safe in his own way. Clay has embraced it, using it to his advantage. He's slowly been manipulating the entire Cosa Nostra mould to suit his endeavours, but me... What the fuck have I done to make this life my own?

When Butch stands up and turns to leave, I find myself interested in his business even though I know I should keep my goddamn mouth shut. *Respect, remember?* "Who was she?" I ask.

With his back still to me, he mutters gravelly, "It doesn't matter. She's gone."

As he leaves, I drink my shake. The front door clicks shut, and I stare through the alfresco windows to the canals.

The fucking bored Butcher...

Palming my tight jaw, I press down hard and release

some tension. It has never been a case of accepting the role on the ground with Bronson or disowning it.

I accepted it.

But I never wanted it.

I'm reminded of our first ever job, back when we were twelve. Bronson took that fucking cigar like it was a loaded MK37; the ash and embers, the bullets, the power and allure were just as dangerous. I never wanted the cigar or what it signified—loss of control. Loss of free will. That is what working for the Family has always felt like to me. And I never wanted to arm myself with their power. I'd prefer to beat a man on the field using my own hard-earned skills and strength.

That has never been an option.

I'm in.

I've seen too much. Done too much.

And I would never leave my brothers.

But for Cassidy, I'll step up and make my own way. Even if that means cementing myself to the Family. Involving myself in deep corruption. Managing it.

I text Clay and Jimmy, requesting a meeting this afternoon.

Placing my phone on the bench, I exhale loudly. I rub the tension that has returned to my jaw. There will be no going back from this. But it'll be on my goddamn terms. With my power. My resources. My specific skill set. Jimmy isn't nearly as educated as he believes himself to be—not even close.

I'll no longer be just Butch's son.

I'll be an earner.

An associate.

I'll control the means of producing so much fucking profit for the Family that Jimmy will be accepting my goddamn cigar. I find myself smirking at the prospect.

WHEN I STRIDE into Jimmy's boardroom, Clay is leaning on the bar, a drink clasped in his hand. Standing beside him, Jimmy laughs—a throaty laugh that he only does when in the presence of his son-in-law. That cheerful intonation makes my jaw tic. It speaks of a bond that goes beyond Clay having married Aurora.

Jimmy isn't his fucking family.

Always the fucking professionals, both men are dressed in dark suits and ties. I've only ever seen Jimmy a handful of times in anything else. They turn to acknowledge me, smiling easily.

"*Max*." Jimmy walks towards me, arms wide. "Clay, get your brother a drink. We should celebrate his future arrival."

I force a smile and embrace him. "Whiskey," I say, giving Clay a nod of acknowledgment over Jimmy's shoulder.

Pouring me a shot, Clay says, "I will drink to that." He moves over to me and I wrap my arms around him. "We don't see enough of each other," he says into my ear.

I release him and accept the drink he presents me. "I agree."

My big brother is all business these days. I can't remember the last time I had a casual drink with him. At his wedding, perhaps. I wonder how often Jimmy sees him, but as soon as I do, I bury that thought. Along with the resentment attached.

We drink for a while by the bar, keeping things on the lighter side. But after fifteen minutes of small talk, the tic in my jaw tells me I've hit my quota for sharing and receiving bullshit. We move towards the boardroom table and sit.

I relax opposite Clay while Jimmy positions himself on

my right, at the head. I text my guy and then hear a knock vibrate through the door.

"Come in," I say before Jimmy can, and it makes me want to smirk. My guy enters and passes me the documents, then leaves straight away. I slide one over to each of them.

Clay flips it over and then back again before flicking through to the last few pages—the summary pages. He begins to read as Jimmy opens the first page, skimming the text.

"What is this?" Jimmy asks, seemingly too impatient to read it.

Resting my elbows on the table, I clasp my hands together under my chin. "It's an introductory framework for a new commercial construction, design, and planning compliance policy. Once complete, it will detail a new scheme implementing more city-obligated approvals for high-value commercial projects or projects in dense areas or above a certain engineering margin. Basically put, all future construction projects under this scheme will undergo a string of design approvals, covenants, code checks... It's a bitch to navigate and interpret."

Jimmy raises a black brow at me. "And?"

I look at Clay, who is still skimming the summary, a subtle smirk pulling at his lips. "Next year, when Clay gets nominated as a councillor, he's going to introduce this new scheme and get it agreed to for a twenty-four-month trial. He'll bring me in as a contractor to help interpret the document and implement the changes. With this policy, the City Architect will have the final say on every new commercial construction in the District."

Clay clears his throat, closes the document, and leans his arms on the table. "Our city architect is fifty-nine. He won't like it."

I grin. "He'll fucking hate it, and it'll make him look due for retirement."

"And then?" Clay asks, tilting his head. The glimmer of satisfaction in his blue eyes and the sideways curve of his lips show me he knows exactly what *then*.

"And then you put my name forward for the position of City Architect after I've had time to win people over from the inside."

Clay looks at Jimmy, and they share a meaningful exchange. My brother taps the document with his finger and says, "How do I sell this new policy to the city?"

"It's a fucking elegant scheme," I state adamantly. Although it's all true, I hate having to convince others. I would much rather be running across a field than working in an office, but this is what it is. Business. A means to give Cassidy the fairy-tale. "On the surface, it focuses on space and environment. User experience and energy efficiency. It'll modernise the District. Innovate it. They'll lap it up. You won't need to sell it, brother."

Clay picks up his whiskey and unlike our last meeting, he actually drinks it. "You can't work for the city with your current reputation. The papers will eat me alive."

Jimmy chuckles. "You'll need to actually smile at people on the street, my boy."

I open my arms wide. "I'll smile. Cassidy will smile." I smirk and lean back in my seat. "Our son will fucking giggle."

Jimmy laughs that throaty laugh and this time it's directed at me. "You remind me of Clay toda—"

"I want something from you," I cut in because his warmth feels like a blade peeling my stomach.

He deadpans, his brown eyes narrowing on me. "*Se?*"

I fix my jaw but try to keep my voice steady and impassive. "Last time I spoke to you about this, I disrespected you and our Family. Which is why I understand how you missed what I had said. So this time, and the last time, I'm going to make myself clear." I lean closer to him. "*We* do not have Cassidy. *I* have Cassidy. She is out of this. I don't want her hands touching anything dirty. And whatever plans you have that deal with Ben Slater are to be discussed with me—I have the final say. I represent that family in our business. And I won't be collecting, so besides full Family affairs, I don't want to be disturbed at night. " I pause and let him absorb what I have just said. Let the trace of aggression that is simmering at the surface of my tongue dwindle. I exhale, eyes still trained on him. "Finally, when the moment is right, I want Dustin. I want to deal with him. My way. If you agree to that, under this scheme, we will have so much control over industry in the District that not even a little fucking cafe renovation will be able to get through approvals without our stamp and cut."

A slow smile spreads across Jimmy's lips, which means he's either going to fucking shoot me or kiss me—sometimes he'll do both. Relaxing into his chair, he swivels it to the side and rests his ankle on his opposite knee. He pulls the document to his lap and begins to read the first few pages. I doubt he has a clue what he's reading, but it doesn't matter. All the fucking fluff and flowers are right there in the introduction. He chuckles to himself and shakes his head as he mouths a few words. Then he slaps the document down on the boardroom table. "When can you have this policy finished?"

"Six months."

He nods slowly and then, without taking his eyes off me, reaches into his pocket and retrieves his cigar tin. He folds back the paper sheet and pulls one out. Wedging the cigar between his teeth, he draws the smoke in, the ember glowing with more vibrancy as he puffs and puffs.

When he slides the tin over to me, I stop it with my hand.

He blows out a cloud of white. "Have a cigar with me, Max."

I close the tin. "So we have a deal then?"

A rough sigh leaves him as he stares straight at me. Lies are easy for dishonourable men to tell. But Jimmy is a man of his word, so although I can see the agreement on his face, his tongue is having trouble sealing the deal. I just need to be confident that this proposition is worth more to him than his pride, more than Dustin, and more than whatever he has planned for Ben Slater, because I will surely say no when the time comes to use him.

"I couldn't run a scheme like this without Max. And we can't trust anyone else with this either," Clay states plainly.

I stifle a grin, burying my cocky fucking nature deep for a moment.

Jimmy removes the cigar from his lips, pinching it between his thumb and forefinger. "You, my boy,"—he points, waving the cigar—"*Facìsti n'affare.*"

Deal.

CHAPTER TWENTY-THREE

FLOATING on my back in the canal just outside of casa Butcher, I make water angels with my arms, moving the water forward and back to keep myself stationary. There is no current here, but it's deep enough to allow large boats through. Toni and I tried to dive to the bottom a few times, but I couldn't touch the sand, and the water is green and dark and slightly murky. It's clean though, or so I've been told.

I glance down at my bathing suit to look for grime, but there's none to be found. A smile curls my lips. I'm wearing the same pink one-piece I wore the first time Max and I ever spoke without the added delirium of alcohol. Pink. High riding at the hips. Arching at the buttocks. I like them. They are both modest and somehow not...

As the sun's warmth hits my cheeks in a lovely, soft way, I listen to the water swishing against my ears. Combined with the slow, relaxed beat of my heart, it reminds me of my blob. Having only heard his heartbeat a few hours ago, I can honestly say it's such a similar sound.

I have no idea why Max booked me in for another ultrasound so soon. It wasn't necessary until twelve weeks gestation. Maybe, it has something to do with his caveman decision to switch my fricking phone off and have me sleep until fricking ten am. Yeah, maybe it has something to do with that.

Fricking controlling butthead.

So my later-than-ideal start, combined with a spontaneous midday ultrasound appointment, basically wrote off today for me. When I feel fingers thread through mine, I grin over at Toni, who is now floating beside me. I drop my legs beneath me and begin to tread water so I can talk to him.

Water beads on his bronzed skin and dark lashes. "How does he even know my screen-lock pattern?" I ask.

He rolls his brown eyes. "Firstly, you don't need to know someone's lock pattern to switch a phone off. Seriously, grandma? Secondly, are we still on this?"

"Yes!" I state, splashing him a little. "I'm pissed at him for making a decision like that for me. If he wanted me to have another ultrasound, he could have just asked. I would have said yes. I would do anything for him. I let him run every aspect of our lives but not my daily schedule. He is at work or the gym. I do my own thing. I'm... *ugh.* He's such a butthead."

Toni wiggles his brows. "Speaking of butts and head. You have to stop holding out on the details. So if you love it when he licks your arsehole, just say it."

My mouth drops open; I am once again floored. "How do you find a way to redirect every conversation to suit your agenda?"

He chuckles, tipping his shoulders in delight. "It's a talent of mine."

A cheeky grin forms across his face, provoking flashes of

last night to hit me in a rush. Max's tongue and teeth and... I press my thighs together, ignoring the pulsing between my legs. "Yes." I breathe the word. "I like it. Can we move on from that?"

His entire face is suddenly bright with mischief. "Well, yes, you can move on from that, but that would be letting him fuck your arse."

Ugh! "Not what I meant, obviously."

Unfazed by my tone, he sings, "You'll like it."

I'm surprised when I shake my head, cause, like, all of a sudden this is the topic of conversation. "It'll hurt."

"Actually, under the right conditions, it shouldn't," he states smugly. "I'm kind of the authority on this topic. No offence *waaaas*"—he quickly changes the direction the sentence was heading—"needed and Braidy still handcuffs me and takes me like I'm a convict.

I smile hard. "You just did it again."

"Yeah. Sorry," he says, swaying his arms in the water. "Anyway, I'm surprised you haven't already."

I sink down a little, my legs getting tired of kicking. "He's big, Toni. Like *big* and ... you know, thick."

He beams at me. "So it wasn't really a starter shaft?"

"Oh no," I say, wide-eyed, remembering the ache I felt the first few times he entered me. And still, even to this day, sometimes it's just too much. "It's definitely not an apprentice appendage."

His expression deadpans. "Not a rookie rod? Not a trainee tube?"

I cover my giggle, my cheeks burning. "More like an expert-level erection."

Toni smacks his lips in contemplation. "What's above an expert?"

I beam so hard my face hurts, remembering the first time

Max and I ever spoke. I thought he was *too* hot to be human and, therefore, must be a male witch...

A warlock.

"A warlock!" I state with a giggle.

He cracks up, his eyes thin, smiling lines. "Definitely a warlock wand then?" Toni pretends to wave a wand, chanting, "*Impregnace uterius.*"

I lose myself in laughter for like two whole minutes. It just takes over my body, my laughter on loop. I can't get the image of Max chanting *impregnace uterius* while waving his warlock wand at me out of my head. "*Oh my gawd.*"

Toni keeps egging my laughter on, waving an invisible wand and then stroking it and then waving it again.

"Stop it," I cry, laughing. I take a big breath in and exhale slowly. After which, I try to regain a sense of calm, coaxing myself with, *okay, pull yourself together, Cassidy.*

Toni, who can be laughing and serious all at once, suddenly squirms in the water. "I'm getting a semi talking about warlock wands. What are we saying now? Eight inches? Nine? Ten?"

With that, I steer the conversation back to where it started. "Thank you for the delightful detour, but can we get back on track and focus on the fact he switched my phone off?"

"Sure." He nods with feigned sincerity. "Fun police, I get it. Police are fun. Sorry. I'm done... You just need to tell him that you would have taken the day off if he asked. Talk to him like you want him to talk—"

"What the fuck are you doing?" Max's deep gravelly voice forces tingles through my whole body. I curl my toes under the water. Splashing around to face the bank, I find him striding down it, working fiercely to pull his tie and white shirt off. With all of those muscles now exposed and rippling, I'm somehow blinded from the other emotions I should be feeling right now. Arousal is holding the others under the water. Out of sight. Out of mind. *Oh my God*, he *is* a warlock... But I should be feeling something else...

What is it?

I blink at him—muscles...

Oh yeah!

What's *his* fricking problem?

Toni swims towards the jetty and chuckles, "And here is your chance."

"Get out of the fucking water!" Max barks before diving in with his black pants still on.

"What?" I mutter to no one, squinting at the ripples where Max just disappeared beneath the surface. My heart hits the back of my throat when something grabs me, and then Max reappears. I'm in his arms now as he powers through the water towards the jetty.

"Max, stop it!"

Once beside the ladder, one big, tattooed arm reaches to grab the railing, bicep contracting as he pulls us both up. Water rushes off us. As soon as we are on top of the wooden slates, he lowers me down, a fierce scowl etched onto his face.

"Big fucking boats speed down this fucking canal, Cassidy!"

Carter is suddenly nearby. "I've been keeping an eye—"

Max snaps his deadly stare to him and points. "I'll get to *you* in a fucking minute!"

His eyes hit me again. They snatch my breath straight from within my lungs. I try to stay firm, but he's making me tremble beneath the intensity of his near-black eyes. "Xander said you guys swim in it all the tim—"

"Xander isn't pregnant!"

My eyes well up. "Don't yell at me."

He turns around and grips the back of his neck with both hands, arms growing as they pulse beside his head. Turning back to face me, his expression has quelled in anger a bit. "Little One, you're pregnant. I feel like you're being fucking reckless."

I blink the tears out. "Swimming? I was just swimming."

He reaches to wipe my tears away and I step backwards, not wanting his comfort right now.

"Don't do that," he admonishes curtly.

I pant through my agitation. "You turned my phone off. You have no right."

"What?" His brows draw in tighter. "No right?" His body, big and powerful, looms over mine, the cords in his neck bulging, his jaw clenching. "Anything to do with you is my *right*."

My sudden need to settle the darkness in him replaces my agitation. So when he turns to leave, I reach for his arm. He stills with his back to me. Circling around his staunch frame, I position myself in front of him again.

"*Max*." I reach up to press my palm to his pulsing jaw. As he moves into my touch, he squeezes his eyes shut and sighs that rough sigh that is almost a growl.

I smile softly at him. "You just have to ask me, okay? Please, just ask me next time."

He opens his eyes, the black of his pupils slightly smaller, allowing a ring of that beautiful grey-blue colour to shine through. "Everything okay with the ultrasound?"

I breathe a little harder in response to the soft, confused edge to his voice. Why was he worried? I don't understand. "Yes. Everything is fine." Stroking the afternoon stubble on his jawline, I say, "Why did you book it?"

He lifts his head to look over my shoulder. I twist around

and relax slightly when I see Toni is out of earshot, chatting to Carter. I turn slowly back to the half-naked man-god in expensive black pants dripping canal water. "No one can hear us."

The look on his face tells me he doesn't want to share. "I fucked you on your stomach."

Warmth moves through me, and I try not to let my smile break my face because Max Butcher is irrationally concerned for our blob.

Yay.

And I have learned to accept his affections in the form of hints, tones, and actions. That is his way. And that is what he has just wordlessly told me.

"He's safe, Max. I promise." My fingers trace the tight cord in his neck. "It's not until the third trimester that they kind of run out of room, and we'll need to be careful."

The tension in him drops off like a lead belt and he wraps his big arms around my middle, arching my back, lifting me onto my tippy toes so he can kiss me deeply. The water on our skin causes our bodies to slide together. His tongue moves into my mouth, demanding mine. We breathe each other's breath. I cup his cheeks with both hands, feeling his jaw work as he loves me with his kiss.

His hands start to roam, kneading down the muscles of my back to cup my bum and lift me so I can straddle him.

"This suit," he groans, palming my cheeks. One of his hands slides lower, fingers dripping to tease me. "I wanted to tongue every part of your body when I first saw you in this."

The need behind his lips is devastating to my will. To my sense of self. To the space between us because we don't want any space. Want to be as connected as two people can possibly be. Moans crash loudly from me and into his mouth. He swallows my sounds as if they are his to claim, before shamelessly walking us up the bank towards the house.

I break away and, between laboured breaths, say, "Don't. Switch. Off. My phone."

His lips move to my jaw and neck, forceful in their pursuit to assert his words. "Don't overdo it!"

I hear Toni laugh as we move past him. "I guess I'll wait, like what? Twenty? Thirty minutes?"

"You're welcome to stay," Max declares just before his tongue chases my racing pulse up the length of my throat. "Settle in."

CHAPTER TWENTY-FOUR

TONI DIDN'T STICK AROUND, and I feel a little embarrassed, but I'm sure he was rather impressed with Max's stamina. If we'd been done in twenty minutes, he probably would have been disappointed.

"How are you home so early?" I ask and then stick my fingers in my ears and squeeze my eyes shut as one of the Butcher guards calls, "Pull." From across the yard, I watch Bronson cock the rifle and shoot at the flying target as it soars through the sky. That other worldly bang vibrates like a cymbal between my temples.

When I unplug my fingers, the sound of Max's laugh moves over me like a warm blanket —it's such a fricking amazing sound.

"Why did you close your eyes, Little One?" He laughs again.

I beam at him. "It's a reflex." My cheeks bunch high above my smile. "Is that even legal?" I ask, pointing at Bronson as he drops the gun, heading over towards a tree to retrieve whatever it was he was shooting at.

"Does it matter?" he says with a smirk.

I scoot in close to him on the outdoor lounge, my legs making a pyramid over his lap. I rake in his expression while he looks out over the yard. His grin is relaxed, eyes gentle. His fingers draw little circles on my legs. He's in such a good mood and after the concern he displayed towards our blob, I feel like maybe we can try to talk about the baby again. Last time it didn't go too well. Max seemed more suspicious of our blob's presence than excited by it. But right now, he's laughing at Bronson, and loving me with his eyes every time they meet mine. Maybe today he'll handle this conversation better. "Can we talk about the baby?"

His casual demeanour remains, but his brows tighten. "Sure."

Swallowing down my hesitation, I proceed despite that tiny show of resistance. "Have you thought about names?" I ask, even though I know he hasn't. I immediately feel like one of those girls who lead a conversation—manipulate one —and I hate it. I just... I just really want to talk about our blob. With him. I want to have this conversation with my best friend and my lover and the father of my unborn baby.

His eyes blink at the horizon and then he turns to meet my gaze. "You can name it."

It. My heart fractures, a few little pieces crumbling to the pits of my being. "I don't want to name *it* without you," I spit out, failing at stifling my growl. "I want *us* to name him."

He eyes me with uncertainty. When his narrowed stare moves to my belly, it is as if he is looking to our baby for answers on how to deal with its hormonal mother.

Max glances back at me and says, "Little One, I'm going to be here. For you. For him. But naming him is not some-thing I ...*Fuck.* It just doesn't matter. His name changes noth-ing. I'm sorry. That's just not me."

I divert my eyes from his because I have to. I have to hide my deep disappointment in him. Looking down at the fabric of the lounge, I whisper, "You named Xander."

"How did you know that—"

My own words make me angry. "At some point in your life, you cared enough about a name that you named him," I cut in, grimacing up at Max.

He shifts his weight, turning his whole body to face me. "I was five."

I stand, having to leave as heat hits the back of my eyes and my mind can't form anything nice to say. It's all aggressive. It's all antagonistic. And I'm not that. My mum has often said, 'If you can't say anything nice, don't say it at all.'

So I have to walk away while the pregnancy hormones make me want to yell at him.

Max catches my elbow, fingers clasping around me, freezing me in my tracks. "It takes imagining him to form the need to name him."

I swallow hard and he pulls me back down to the lounge. He releases my elbow and grabs my neck, forcing me to stare at him even as I try not to. My eyes reluctantly meet his... which are soft with that love he won't say aloud and scorching with that determination he has to show me through his actions.

"I can't afford to let my mind reach too far into the future," he says. "I've learned not to. It's dangerous in my world. I don't daydream our forever, Little One. I live it. In the now. Every second. I'm here. With you. I'm always right fucking in the present."

My heart collects all the pieces, some from him and some from me. I settle back down into the lounge and look across the yard at Bronson, who is now up the tree with a chainsaw. I tilt my head at him. Mad. They are all fricking mad.

Sighing, I turn back to my Max and acknowledge his truths. "I get it."

He grins, the corner of his mouth ticking, revealing the dimple in his left cheek. I lift my hand and poke it. I poke it in a form of defiance against his cuteness and mockery and emotional ambiguity. His chin jolts to the side, and I gasp as he presses his bared teeth into my finger, his eyes menacing. This is my favourite kind of Max Butcher.

I glare playfully, feigning aggression as I climb on top of him. Swinging my leg over his lap, I pretend he can't just throw me metres and metres away with little ease, pretend I am pinning his muscular body down as I poke his dimple over and over. He catches my wrists and pulls me until my cheek is pressed to his.

His lips meet my ear. "Put your fucking tongue in my mouth now."

I don't hesitate; my lips mash against his. His hands roam everywhere. Rolling on his lap, I cup his cheeks to deepen our connection, feeling him wanting me through the touch of his fingers and the demand behind his lips. Somehow, through the intoxicating sensation of his hands palming me and his tongue and mouth devouring me, I'm still drawn away by the feel of something vibrating in the back pocket of my denim shorts. And it isn't what I'd like to be vibrating back there.

I pull away from him to retrieve my phone. The word Konnor flashes at me from the display. Max groans when he sees it. Moving his big, tattooed arms to the sides of the outdoor lounge, he looks at me with exasperation.

I smile sickeningly sweet at him. "Sorry, I have to get this." He frowns at me. "Don't frown at me." I smooth the creases between his brown brows and lift the phone to my ear.

"Hi," I answer. "To what do I owe this pleasure?" I catch Max's scowl and giggle.

"Cock blocker," Max says loud enough for Konnor to hear.

"Fucking charming," Konnor snaps on the other end of the receiver.

"Don't fucking swear around your sister," Max growls.

I roll my eyes and attempt to climb off Max, but his palms come down on my thighs, locking me in position. "No," he admonishes gruffly.

Covering the speaker, I say, "Then play nice." I direct my attention to Konnor on the other end of the phone. "You okay, big brother?"

He pauses for a moment, but I can hear his sigh. "There is this charity thing in two weeks. And I'm going with Blesk and..." His voice trails off with uncertainty. "It's for me. *Fuck*. That sounds stupid. I mean, my bio mum created this charity for missing children... And I want to go. And I'd really like it if you—" He groans his displeasure. "And *Max*, I suppose, if he wants to, come with us. Dad bought us a table. It was something ridiculous, like, ten grand."

Excitement over my favourite person inviting me to an event overwhelms everything else. I bounce and squeal on Max's lap. "Yes! Of course. I'd love to."

I remember Dad telling us about this charity. Konnor's legacy. After he was kidnapped, his mother, Madeline, created this charity for young families who found themselves in the same situation...

I still.

I'm painfully aware of this stillness because the gentle brush of Max's fingers on my thighs now feels like glass scoring down my skin.

Blinking over Max's shoulder, I hardly even acknowledge

the way he is now scanning my expression. How the blue in his eyes is absorbed by his pitch-black pupils.

The charity... It's called... Nerrock Missing and Beyond... *Nerrock...*

My thoughts freeze.

My mouth opens to exhale the name.

Dustin Nerrock.

It's *his* charity. Konnor won't be safe. I won't be safe. I feel the frantic bat of my lashes before I even realise Max has taken my phone from my hand, hung up on Konnor, and stuffed it into the side pocket of his jeans.

Warm hands meet my cold cheeks. "What just happened?"

Max's voice finds me in my haze of panic. "It was Konnor. He wants to go to this... *charity event*. It's for missing children." I stare straight at Max. "It's Dustin Nerrock's charity."

Max's hands pulse against my cheeks at the mention of Dustin's name, but no other part of him seems to respond. He leans in and kisses the tip of my nose. I smile softly at him.

"It's not," he assures me. "It's his dead wife's charity. He isn't even in the District right now, and from what I've seen and heard, Dustin has zero involvement in it."

"Konnor wants me to go," I breathe out the words, trying to ground myself, to draw myself back to the now. "I'm not sure I can though, not when Dustin has any association—"

Annoyance flares in Max's eyes. "It does things to me, knowing you are still afraid of him. I will know the exact moment Dustin arrives back in town. I have eyes on his every move, Little One. That bastard can't shit without knowing about it."

I didn't expect that.

Swallowing hard, I say, "This is a really big step for

Konnor. He's never shown any interest in his biological mother before. Always kept her memory at arm's length. But when he found out I was pregnant, he told me he was jealous. I think that by going to this charity, he's really embracing his past. Finding a connection to her. I should be there for him." *I should be there for him!* "And you're sure he has nothing to do with this charity?" I confirm, seeking further reassurance.

Max frowns at that. "Nothing. Trust me."

I nod to myself. "I should be there for Konnor then."

"Your brother is a pain in the arse. He stresses you out." Max clenches his teeth. "I don't like that."

"If you just got to know him, you'd see just how wonderful he really is."

He lets out a long exhale and stares at me contemplatively. "Fine. You can go then. I'll go with you. *Get to know him.*"

My blonde brows rise. "You'll come? And, like, be nice?"

A gentle grin spreads across his lips. "When am I not, *like*, nice?"

I giggle at that. *Like all the time, Max.* "Menace. You're seriously coming to a family thing with me? With Konnor and Blesk?"

His grin transforms into a provocative curve. "I look fucking magnificent in a tuxedo."

CHAPTER TWENTY-FIVE

Grief defined in five words:
A child without a mother.

AS SOON AS we arrive at the Hyatt Hotel, it's apparent to me that this is the kind of event that will have its own spread in the District's social magazines and on their websites.

Carter opens the passenger door for us, and Max exits first, allowing me the sweet view of his backside. His black slacks are perfectly snug around him. Turning, he holds his hand out for me as I step out of the car. My six-inch gold, rhinestone-encrusted heels press into the red carpet, and my sheer skirt flows around my ankles, making me giddy.

I was so excited when I found this dress the other day. It's a new red Alamour design with a square neckline and sheer bodice banding just above my newly showing bump.

My underwear is covered both by a small sewn-in bra and mini skirt lining. It's a fricking beautiful dress!

Standing beside Max, I take a moment to appreciate him in his black tuxedo. I didn't really know the difference between a suit and a tuxedo until yesterday when Toni told me. It's in the satin details—satin lapels, lining down the slacks, and buttons. I lick my lips and then adjust Max's bow tie, envisioning him in only it. I can feel his eyes tunnelling into mine.

I blush without looking at him. When I finally gaze up, I find his stare devouring.

"How do you do that?" I ask, reaching up to stroke his freshly shaven jawline.

His smile is soft. "What?"

"Go from animalistic, rugged sex god, who spent most of this morning with his face between my thighs, to this power-ful-looking gentleman?"

He leans in close, a salacious curve to his lips that sends flutters down between my thighs. "I'm going to find a place tonight to shove my cock into your mouth for calling me a gentleman. Then I'm going to wash that word down your throat with my cum." My lips part and I swallow hard. He leans back until I can see that sexual appetite in his narrowed eyes. "Is that better?"

I nod and bite my bottom lip. "Much."

Cameras start flashing around us and I smile shyly at them. Max doesn't though, saving all those glances of emotion for me. But he does offer them a nod of acknowl-edgment, which in comparison to his usual scowl, is quite the game changer. Placing his hand on the small of my back, his fingers spanning out, the press of them apparent and possessive, he leads us up the carpet, towards the front door.

When we get to the entrance, Max grins at me and that

hint of menace makes me melt. We pause in front of the grand lobby. The chatter of the press surrounds us, the flash of their cameras evident, but we are in our own world. He lifts a finger to my chin, tilts my head up to meet his adoring eyes, and then plants a loving kiss on my lips for everyone to see and photograph. I almost moan but manage to quell it.

He's so good at playing the part; I suppose he's learned that over the years. The Butcher Boys are always being photographed. Max is usually less than impressed with the attention, but today he seems to be putting on a show for everyone. Showing me off. Showing *us* off. I absolutely adore the way that makes me feel—warmth in my stomach and chest, a softness to my stance and movements.

Walking up the staircase, we make our way inside the banquet hall. From across the room, I spot Konnor. He looks handsome in his tuxedo and grey bow tie. My jaw drops open at the sight of Blesk in her dusty-blue strapless column dress. She is a classic beauty, there is no doubt about that, and my brother can't keep his eyes off her.

I basically skip over to them, and then pull them both in for a hug.

"Jesus! Cassidy, you look stunning," Blesk coos.

Konnor's brows draw in. "Should you be bouncing like that in your condition?"

"Thank you," I hear Max say gruffly from over my shoulder. His fingers find my elbow, his touch shocking me with its authoritarian disposition. "No. She shouldn't be bouncing like that."

Konnor frowns at Max. "Max," he says, and that is apparently his greeting. "You fucking knocked up my sister. I should kick the crap out of you."

A pleased sigh breaks from Max. "And I thought this event was going to be boring."

"Remember where you are, Konnor," Blesk says softly.

"Right, that's enough testosterone-based bullshit," I hear a female voice say from behind me. I turn to see Blesk's best friend Elise approaching in a black fishtail gown, and my whole face lights up. I've only ever met her once, but she made an impression—the good kind. She is about my size—petite—and she has blue eyes and brown hair and mismatched nail polish.

Elise eyeballs Max. "I don't even know you, but you have trouble written all over your face." I nearly choke on a laugh. "And you." She points at Konnor. "This is a very important evening for you, so behave yourself appropriately." Then she is all smiles and weirdness when her eyes land on me. "Congratulations on the baby, Cassidy." She cuddles me hard. "Are you happy?"

We break our embrace, and I nod. Looking up at Max's weaved brows, I giggle. He is staring down at Elise like he has no idea how to handle her. Most people know him, so the fact that she doesn't is hilarious. I doubt anyone would usually talk to him like that.

I glance back at her. "I am very happy."

She shrugs at Konnor. "Then why are you all cranky-pants about the baby? She's happy. And he"—she looks at Max again—"is kinda scary but hot. I think he's happy too; are you happy too?"

He clears his throat. "I need a drink."

I cover my giggle. "*We* are very happy."

Max reaches for a waiter and pulls a beer off the serving tray before draining half the bottle. "Cassidy makes me happy," he states before grinning at her, that charming dimple setting into his masculine face. His mien is dangerous and sexy and smooth all at once. My heart expands at the sight of him trying to be sociable when I know he hates small talk.

She leans against me, muttering, "He's kinda intimidating. In like, a hot way. A scary way. Is he trouble? You can tell me."

"He's a right menace," I whisper through a silly smile. I touch Max's arm. "This is Elise, Blesk's best friend and—" My eyes are suddenly locked on Jaxon as he appears through the crowd with a glass of water in his hand. I jump up and down, squealing a little. "There's Jaxon." He is Konnor's best friend. They play rugby together, and by the way Jaxon is tilting his chin at Max, I suppose they know each other too. Jaxon is built like Max but shorter, so he looks quite stocky. He passes Konnor the glass of water before moving behind Elise. Wrapping his arms around her middle, he rests his head on top of hers.

I grin so hard my cheeks ache. "Hi. You two are so cute. When did this happen?"

Jaxon chuckles. "She finally wore me down."

"Wore *you* down?" Elise drawls. "You have been waiting for me outside of my dorm every day since we met in case *somehow,* between my room and the entrance to my *female-only* dormitory, I get hurt or trip or fall into someone's arms. He basically stalked me. I really should have just called the police."

I giggle.

Jaxon grins at me. "Little C, hear you're in the family way. Congrats. And ah"—he looks up at Max—"you too, mate. Congrats."

"Thank you," Max says, feigning a casual demeanour, his stance loose and easy, convincingly so. His jaw is set tight though; it's a small thing, but I notice it. I know that all this baby talk is grating on him, making him feel like someone is right in the middle of our business, riffling through it, having a say on it. And I imagine that it feels like fingernails scratching inside his brain because my lover is a private man who shares with only his family and me—and even then, I have to sweet-talk it out of him.

After downing the rest of his beer, Max places his hand on my lower back and leans toward me. His lips meet my ear. "I'm serious, Little One. Stop fucking jumping around or I'll do something to limit your movement."

I twist my head to meet him, a smile playing on a corner of my lips. "Like what?"

He lowers his voice further, adding a luscious growl to it that forces the air from me. "*Like* put a ball up your pretty little arsehole so every time you jump, it bounces inside you."

My cheeks burn and I giggle nervously through the next sentence. "I kinda want to jump even more now."

We chat amongst ourselves, but Max seems to know a lot of other guests and they keep approaching us. He introduces me each time though, making me feel wonderful and at ease even with the constant flow of women wanting his attention and asking about our relationship with insincere interest.

"So Max Butcher does have a type then," one girl says, twisting her strawberry-blonde hair around her finger.

"My type is Cassidy Slater," Max replies, and I swoon.

At the sound of the announcer, we make our way over to our lavishly set circular tables. We eat three courses and talk, keeping things light even though the whole night is about something so heavy and personal that it's hard to concentrate. Thanks to Elise, there is never a dull moment or a lap in conversation.

Nearly everyone at our table appears to be keeping their beverage intake virginal, and I suppose it is out of respect for my recently reformed big brother. Max, though, has been enjoying his beers with enthusiasm.

Konnor has barely said a word, but his double-dimpled smile has been on display all night. The one he often has around Blesk. I've been watching him intently, worrying about what this might be doing to him. Being here. I wonder if anyone knows who he is? If they do, they are all purposely leaving him alone.

Casually leaning back in his seat, Max drapes his arm across my chair, his fingers making little patterns on my neck and shoulder. Their course across my skin is claiming. Hot. Intense. They whisper a yearning. I feel a shiver rush through me. Turning, I catch him nailing me with a powerful stare. His touch no longer whispers but screams instead.

As my cheeks heat up, he brushes his knuckles down them. "You're blushing."

I glance across the table at Konnor but find him staring at his food, shuffling the pieces around, not conversing with anyone.

I twist to face my Max. "Want to make good on your promise? You wouldn't want me to mistake you for a gentleman again, now would you?"

"*Fuck*. Little One, you're a bad influence."

I giggle at that. "As if."

Over Max's shoulder, I am suddenly struck by the sight of Butch and a young lady sitting a few tables away. Max turns to follow my gaze, his brows drawing in together when they land on his finely dressed father.

I place my hand on his thigh. "What's your dad doing here?"

Max stares at them, his eyes scrutinising the pair. Sliding out from the table, he begins to stride towards them. I quickly fall into step beside him, not wanting to be left behind. He entwines our fingers and I smile, thankful he didn't tell me to go back to the table, thankful he didn't tell me this is none of my business.

"What's this I see?" Max laughs, eyeing Butch and his pretty guest.

Butch twists in his seat, doing a double-take when he sees us. "Well, well." He stands and pats his son on the shoulder. "How is smiling at people working out for you?"

Max smirks, seemingly amused by the comment. "Fuck, Clay has a big mouth."

Butch just grins, and for a moment, I see Max—older and more weathered, but the similarities are blatant. "He was impressed with your proposal, as was I." I blink at them, not sure exactly what's going on or why I somehow feel strange about it. Turning his attention to me, Butch's smile softens into a genuine curve that makes his chiselled masculine features somehow less so. "Cassidy, you look beautiful. How are you feeling?"

"Full. The duck was fricking amazeballs," I say and then catch the eyes of the brunette lady sitting beside Butch. She is circling the top of her whiskey glass with her finger and chewing on the inside of her lip. Smile lines beside her eyes and mouth denote both her age and her nature.

"Amazeballs?" Butch chuckles. "Did you hear that, Louise?" He turns to acknowledge her—*Louise*.

"I agree," she says, gazing brown eyes up at us. Her mien is gentle and humble. "*Amazeballs*."

I grin hard at her.

"This is Louise," Butch says. "Louise, this is my son, Max, and his far better half, Cassidy."

She nods, an almost demure and coy slant to her lips. "It's lovely to meet you both."

I wave awkwardly. "Hi."

"Where's Victoria?" Max teases. I shuffle uncomfortably and glance at the ground. I half expect crickets to sound but instead, Butch answers with little duress.

"She doesn't come to this event."

Before anyone can reply, the clapping of other guests draws our attention to the front. As the presenter takes the stage, the crowd quells their conversations.

The presenter taps on the microphone.

Butch sits back down. "We will talk after. Sit with us. My other guests left early." He motions to a few empty chairs. I glance over at Konnor as we sit, still worried about what this all means or doesn't mean to him. Maybe it's just too much to absorb. It feels that way to me. They literally created this charity in memory of him. He is silently and helplessly a part of it, and no one even knows. When the presenter begins to speak, I stare at the stage.

After introducing and thanking the main organisers, he then begins to thank the donors. "I'd like to pay a special tribute to Luca Butcher," he says.

My eyes widen and I turn to stare at Butch, who is casual and unaffected by the attention. Maybe even a little displeased by it?

"He has been attending this charity since its inception and to date—" he looks at a piece of paper—"has donated over five hundred thousand dollars."

The room erupts in applause. Once it quiets again, other donors are thanked. After a few minutes, the screen behind the presenter lights up with the image of a beautiful young woman—Konnor's biological mother. An acute ache moves through my chest and I find Konnor again. He is blinking at the screen, mouth parted, breathing heavily with emotion. Blesk has her hand on his shoulder.

The man on stage continues to talk, sharing Madeline's

story—Konnor's story. He details the night Konnor was taken from his bed. The nightmare Madeline endured trying to find him. He tells us about her single-mindedness, giving up everything else in her life to become solely a mother searching for her little boy. He tells us about her sudden illness.

Her death.

My lower lip quivers.

I can feel Max studying me. I can always feel him; our connection is that profound. He hangs his arm over my seat again, sliding the entire chair closer to him until I am pressed snugly against his body.

The presenter continues to talk. He tells us about the light at the end of this dastardly tale. They found the boy. Alive and, for the most part, well. He was given a new life and a new beginning. I know this better than most because it was with us. With me. The presenter clears his throat, pauses, and then looks straight at Konnor.

I smother my outward gasp.

"We have a very special guest with us today," he says, his voice hesitant. "I only just realised this myself, and I have been wrestling with what to do about it. I wanted to leave him his anonymity. But I also wanted more than anything to shake his hand. To pat him on the back. To share my deepest respect and admiration. Madeline's boy is here today."

A high-pitched crack breaks the quiet beside me. Glancing over, I see Butch holding a shattered glass in his fist, blood leaking out from between his fingers. No one outside of our table has noticed. He quickly grabs a white cloth napkin, wraps it around his hand, and excuses himself. I'm sure he forgets his own strength, just like Max does on occasion.

My gaze is pulled back to Konnor, who is struggling to

keep his composure while everyone looks at him in awe. He breathes in deeply and then slowly stands. When everyone applauds him, I can no longer hold back my tears of joy. For the first time in his life, he's close to having a relationship with her. He's right there, standing opposite her image, being referred to as her son. As the clapping continues, the genuine nature of the applause becomes apparent, and Konnor's face transforms from tight with discomfort to soft with emotion.

I wipe at my tears, rolling my eyes, when I notice the smudge of black mascara on the side of my finger. "He's so brave."

Konnor's eyes find mine for a moment and his well up too.

He mouths, "I love you."

And my throat tightens further. "I love you too."

CHAPTER TWENTY-SIX

I HIT shuffle on my after-dinner mix, letting the mellow tunes hum through the car. We cruise down the empty, dimly lit coastal road with the river to our right and the hills to our left. I lower the rear passenger window to feel the crisp night-time breeze stroke my face, to smell the fresh ocean air. I close my eyes and inhale it, thinking about tonight. About Konnor's closure. About the glistening of his eyes. I'm glad I went.

The sound of a bass guitar fills the Chrysler. Hypnotic, sad, and passionate, "Nothing's Gonna Hurt You, Baby" by Cigarettes After Sex rolls from the speakers, and my heart expands. This song can pluck you from the earth. Defy gravity. Lift you into the clouds so that you can view yourself from above. It is state altering. The lyrics start and I flush a little. This song reminds me of Max. A smile hits my lips and I turn to find him grinning at me, his hair messy, his top buttons open, his legs spread casually in his black satin-lined trousers.

Twisting towards me, he slides his hand across my red

dress, fingers grazing the floral embroidery. He stops at my neck, circling the arch with his warm palm. "This is an interesting song." His thumb follows the roll of my throat down and then up.

The title is the basis of the song's story, so Max probably suspects that it reminds me of his promise to never let anyone hurt me again, but he'd be wrong. Nothing is going to hurt *him*. A month ago, when I heard this song for the first time, it filled me with this urge to protect him— protect that rare, fragile gentleness he hides from everyone other than me. Protect that fiercely guarded heart with my life.

I try to stay strong beneath his burrowing stare. "It reminds me of this guy I like."

"Do I need to kill him or is that guy me?"

I giggle. "You don't know him."

His brows draw a straight line above his serious expression. "Not funny, Little One."

Leaning in close, I kiss his stern face until it softens. Pulling back, I find him now contemplative with a thought but hesitant to share it.

He finally says, "I'm going to work for Clay at the council. How do you feel about that?"

Blinking at him, I say, "What does that mean?"

"I'll be using my degree. It'll be nine-to-five."

I nod, unsure why he's looking at me as if he's waiting for approval. "But you'll hate working in an office." I glance around the back carriage. *No. No.* "You'll hate it. Why can't you play rugby?"

His face pulls in tight, teeth locking, eyes defensive. "I thought you'd be happy."

"You can go pro, Max," I say. "You can—"

"Leave my brothers. The District!" he snaps. Sighing with

strained breath, he bites down his anger. "Sorry. But that's never going to happen."

I understand family loyalty. *Frick*, my whole life has revolved around Konnor, but I want more for Max. He's so talented. "But they have their own lives—"

Max clears his throat. "On weekends."

The words have no context and I'm left staring wide-eyed at his angry expression—an expression that is smothering a kind of uneasiness. "What?"

"You said the fairy-tale would be nine-to-five and rugby on the weekends. I can give you that now."

Still confused, I say, "What?"

He leans back in his seat. Closed off, he looks out of the window with anger snapping at the heels of casual dismissal. "Forget it." I imagine in any other situation, he would have left me to punch the bag already in an attempt to release his anger.

"No." I straighten. "Wait... are you trying to give me the *fairy-tale*?"

"Apparently not," he mutters tersely as if the whole conversation has left acid in his mouth.

I'm taken aback, feeling my level of agitation rise as he shuts me out. The space he's put between us sends a shiver up my spine. No! I'm not letting him block me out like this. No way.

"I'm *so* sorry that I want the best for you, Max Butcher! But you won't be happy in an office! It'll drive you crazy. Why can't you have what you want? Rugby? I could come see—"

He growls. "I have what I want sitting next to me being a pain in the fucking arse!"

A wave of happiness hits me, crashing into my heart and splashing up my body. I beam. I'm the pain in the arse... *that's me*. He wants me. Twisting forward in my seat, I glance at Carter in the rear-view mirror, but he's pretending to hear nothing, just staring at the road.

I unbuckle my seat belt, kick off my heels, and hike my red dress up my thighs before swinging my leg over Max's lap to straddle him. I pretend to pin him beneath me. "Listen to me, Max Butcher, I love you, you menace." I kiss his tight lips. When he doesn't respond, I lick the defiant flesh of his lower lip, coaxing him. He lets out a pained groan. Loosens. I lean back on his thighs and match him stare for stare. Match him intensity for intensity. "If it's what you want, then I'm your girl."

Two big hands slide up my thighs to my waist and back, massaging with a possessiveness I only understand because I feel the same way when I touch him. "You're my girl either way."

I smile at that. "*Yes.*"

The feel of his touch over the soft sheer material of my dress sends tingles throughout my body. Awakening every cell to him. To us.

As his eyes caress my face, studying and memorising, he sighs roughly. "Look at that face." Tension visibly leaves him. "How do you feel after tonight, Little One?"

I blink at him, my lashes heavier with the weight of mascara—something I don't often wear. "I feel... content. Like, I got some kind of closure tonight as well." I nod to myself as that truth seeps in. "I've always worried about Konnor. I think, maybe, I was a little obsessed with wanting happiness for him. I was only five when my parents adopted him. And I was the baby. I had all the attention. Then I didn't. He challenged us, ya know?"

I pull my hands into my lap, staring at my nude-coloured nail polish, feeling guilty for what I'm finally admitting. I was gifted a brother—this amazing little boy who deserves the world after what he went through. I should be grateful. "This broken kid became my brother," I say to my fingers.

Max lifts my chin up and I meet his narrowed eyes, which hint at concern. I stare at the swirling sheer layers of blue in his irises and they ground me, whispering acceptance in a way I've never felt before. Like, this is my safe place. With him. I can tell him anything. Even admissions I'm not proud of.

"I would do anything to make Konnor smile. Even then, at five. I remember feeling that way. Flick was older. She had her own life and friends and didn't get dragged into it as much, but I still needed Mum's and Dad's attention a lot, but it was often directed at Konnor. So to not be left alone, I took on that role too, in a way. None of this makes sense. I'm being silly—"

"It makes complete sense," he states, sliding my backside a little further up his thighs until I can feel the heat from his body radiating beneath mine. With the music humming and the car rolling, the darkness outside and the dim in, I feel so much right now. For Max.

My love for him burns too strong. Too bright. But no words of sentimentality will ever do that feeling justice. It's like when I try to take a photo of fireworks and it just doesn't come out right. It's because some things aren't meant to be captured or titled.

They are just for us.

Like this, it's our thing.

"Do you remember the first time we met?" I ask, presuming that he doesn't.

He searches my face. "When we first spoke at your birthday? Or when I first saw you in that fucking pink leotard, I wanted to rip straight off your body?"

"Neither." I smile at the memory. "We met years ago.

Like, ten years ago."

He frowns. "Do tell."

I shuffle up a little on his lap. "Konnor has a problem with his anger. He found out that a kid across the street stole my yo-yo, so he went to get it back. I didn't care too much. I was a bit upset, but I didn't want him to get into a fight over it. I chased after him. He took a swing at the kid who took it. But he had a bat. He started wailing on Konnor. Is any of this ringing a bell?"

"Nope."

Smiling at him now because I had a feeling this was a casual encounter for him, I continue, "I was screaming. Konnor was bleeding. I remember, seriously thinking, that he was going to die. Then this boy appeared." I lift my hand to his cheek, feeling the way Max's jaw tightens beneath it as he swallows. "*You.* You looked a bit bigger than Konnor; I thought you were like fifteen or something. You jogged casually across the lawn towards the fight, grabbed the kid attacking Konnor, and nailed him with a precision that looked effortless. You laid him out across the lawn, grabbed my yo-yo, and approached me. I remember it as clear as looking at you right now. You reached for my hand. Barely touching me, you placed the yo-yo in my palm. I said nothing. You said nothing. But you looked straight into my eyes. I remember your eyes, Max. Then you walked off like nothing had even happened."

Something like realisation crosses his face. "That was you?"

"You were like a superhero to me," I admit without shame because he's my safe place, and I don't need to be cool or coy or protective over my heart. I can wear it on my sleeve. Hell, I'd thrust it right into his chest if I could so his and mine could beat at the same cadence forever. Max Butcher is the love of my life. And I'm his. "You saved my brother. My precious, sensitive, broken brother. You're my hero, Max Butcher."

He winces a little at that, so I smother his discomfort with my lips, cupping his smooth jawline as I take his mouth lovingly. I lift my other hand and feed my fingers back through his brown hair, knotting the strands in tight because I can't get close enough to him. Can't connect us enough.

Just as our lips move together, a loud siren breaks through our world. I'm jerked backwards as Carter slows the vehicle. Max catches me, his fingers spanning my spine protectively.

"Boss," Carter warns, his tone filled with urgency.

Red and blue lights glow through the rear window. Chasing us. Were we speeding? Is it because I didn't have a seat belt on? Everything inside the car shifts in an instant— the energy, the air, our connection.

Max slides me from his lap.

I hear Carter cock his gun.

My heart stops.

The black Chrysler pulls up along the coastal road. Carter winds my window up and yet, even through the reinforced glass, I can still hear the sound of the ocean smashing on the shore. Can still hear it through the wailing of sirens. It is like a force that has nothing above it. Nothing to still it. Silence it.

I shudder. I lean back in my seat, willing myself to stay calm. Don't over analyse. It is probably just a routine breath check. Max pulls out his phone, and punches in a message. He's all business.

As three police cars roll to a stop behind us, their sirens deadening to silence, the blinking, whirling blue and red lights still filling the spaces around me, my world tilts. This isn't routine. My belt. This is my fault.

My belt.

Reaching for the belt and tugging on it, I whimper, "I need to get this on—"

Max leans across me and belts me in, a quick movement that probably makes little sense to him but one I needed. And he knew it. His head snaps up, watching over my shoulder. Black shadows cross us. His stern, territorial gaze drops to my belly for a split second.

And the look in his *eyes...*

My heart splinters.

He stares up at my face and now I can't breathe because he's not Max. He's blank. The grey-blue irises I know and love are pitch-black. "Don't move from this seat. No matter what." He tugs on the belt. "Leave this on."

"Max Butcher," I hear a man state, formal and authoritarian. "Please step from the vehicle with your hands up."

"Hands on the dashboard, Carter," another states.

My eyes widen.

What? What is happening?

Then I blink. It's too long. A long blink. Must be.

Because that's all it takes.

One second.

One blink.

And I don't catch my lover's expression before he steps from the vehicle.

The door slams behind him. It's a haunting sound. A separating sound. A sound that cuts the connection between us physically and emotionally. And I'm sure he has taken parts of me out there with him because my heart feels *wrong.* Fractured.

"Carter!" I yell, irrationality taking hold of me like an entity all its own. Like a snake wrapping itself around my body, suffocating me. "HELP HIM!"

I hear a click and realise Carter has locked me in the car. "Stay, Miss Slater. It'll be okay. Stay calm."

Max raises his hands above his head as he steps into the middle of the road. It is then that I see that they have their weapons drawn, pointing straight. At. Max.

No. At *my* Max.

NO!

I can't breathe. "Carter!" I wail, squeezing the door handle, tugging at it, hearing the *click click click* as I draw it back desperately, over and over. I need out. "Let me out!"

The Chrysler's headlights illuminate Max as he walks forward.

I start to suck at the air, as if it is somehow thick and sparse and I have to fight for it.

I will fight.

Pressing my palms to the door, I lean against the glass. Several uniformed bodies now surround my dangerous tall lover. The waves crash hard against the rocks. I inhale that salty air—that's the ocean. Wild. Free. Uncontainable. Like Max.

Helpless to do anything, I press one of my hands to my lower belly. "Daddy will be okay. He will. Nothing can keep him from us."

I watch as the officers approach him with caution.

As Max threads his fingers together behind his head.

As it takes three of them to kick his knees out and force him to the ground.

As they kneel between his shoulder blades, pinning him.

As they handcuff his wrists behind his back.

"Max Butcher, you are under arrest for the murder of Marco Cappelli. You have the right to remain silent. Anything you say can and will be used against you in a court of law. You have the right to an attorney..."

CHAPTER TWENTY-SEVEN

Everyone is made up of little contradictory pieces, and you should never judge another person's decisions because you don't know the pieces they have to choose from.

"I SHOULD GO and check on him," Xander says, standing up quickly as something shatters. The sound of Bronson in the gym is riotous even from the couch I'm perched on in the living room. His roar is animalistic, raw, and pained, and I'm being drawn to it. It matches my insides. I want to go in there and hold him close. Have him hold me. Share our pain and anger and helplessness. But I'm just not sure that's a good idea. I've never seen him angry before, and this is more like a manic blind rage. A flicked switch in his head. I wince when I hear a howl of fury, followed by a smash and a hiss of pain.

Stacey touches Xander's forearm, subtly persuading him to sit back down beside her and wait. In any other situation, she would arm herself and join his cause or... *I don't know.* But tonight, she isn't. I've never seen her so... *passive.*

"Leave him," Clay orders, leaning back into the single recliner. Aurora sits quietly on the armrest beside him. She is usually such a big personality; her lack of comments feel uncomfortable. I blink at her. At her appearance. She has just been dragged from her bed at one a.m. and still looks like CEO Barbie. With her long dark hair pinned back neatly and her black column dress somehow wrinkle free, she looks like she is on her way to an executive job in the city. She must be a witch.

"Leave your brother. He needs to blow off steam. You know what happens when he doesn't," Butch states, positioning himself on the chair opposite mine, offering me all his attention. "You should get some sleep, Cassidy." Leaning forward onto his knees, he says, "It's nearly two. You don't need to be here when Jimmy arrives."

"I'm staying right here," I mutter, my eyes downcast, hiding the blatant accusation in them. A feeling I can't drown. It is all their fault. It's Butch's fault for sharing his sons as if they were commodities. It's Jimmy's fault for existing.

I want Max.

Pulling my knees up onto the couch, I hold them in close and rest my cheek on top. Forcing a kind of mindlessness, I will myself to focus exclusively on my breaths in and out. I attempt not to let my mind wander to a future without Max. Where I raise this baby with his family and mine but without him.

Frick. Good attempt, Cassidy.

A single tear rolls down my cheek, settling into the red fabric of my dress. For every moment he is locked away, imprisoned in a cell that lacks warmth and softness and me.

I'm fearful that his gentleness will die and the dark will take hold. Dig its claws in deep and pierce his heart and mine. I'll feel that cold room when I place my hand on his empty side of the bed. When shivers rush the length of his spine, they will also find mine.

I swear I can feel them now.

When Bronson stops hurling things around the gym, the house is left in a chilling state of quiet. The clock ticks intrusively and mockingly loud. While we may all want to fill the space and time with conversation, talking is exhausting. And the silence is noisy enough.

I shoot up with a start as the tall, tightly wound form of Bronson Butcher appears, his face flushed from exertion, his chest weighted with heavy breaths. As he clenches his fists, my eyes drop to the ripped skin at his knuckles. My core twists.

Max.

I'm reminded of Max and how much he needed me a month ago—his knuckles and face bludgeoned from boxing. How I'd turned him away. How the nights between this one and the next time I see him, he'll be dealing with his darkness alone. Just like that night. I cover my mouth quickly, forcing a sob down my throat.

I'm on my feet before I realise I'm moving. Dragging Bronson over to the kitchen sink, I pull his hands under the faucet and begin cleaning them. I focus on the butcher bird tattoo on his hand, scrubbing it over and over again. *Max.*

Grabbing the first aid box that I made and left beneath the sink when I moved in, I then wrap both his fists in gauze. Sighing, I slowly gaze up at him, silently sharing with him my pain and need to help Max when I'm helpless and unable to. He shows nothing, projecting only a steel-like expression that would've scared the frick out of me if I didn't know him.

He pulls me against his chest, and I welcome his embrace, throwing my arms around his waist and letting another single tear slide out.

"It should have been me," he whispers hoarsely for only me to hear. I don't analyse that statement as I already know that Max has something to do with Marco's disappearance. What settles like a boulder in the pit of my belly is how very little I care. It's heavy, that truth —I don't care. I don't know what pieces Max had to choose from when he made that decision. Whatever the decision.

I don't care.

All I want now is Max in my bed and in my arms so that I can hold him tonight. And every other night of his life, even when he has to choose the pieces that pull him into dark places and make him do bad things—*especially then.*

My breathing shudders out. "It shouldn't be either of you."

The front door suddenly swings open and the formidable presence of Jimmy Storm appears, flanked by two other men, one clearly a guard and the other a tall, slim, nervous looking man with a briefcase. I let go of Bronson and take a step towards them, my eyes barking questions while my lips purse to stop from verbalising them.

Jimmy surveys the room quickly, taking us all in.

"What have you found out?" Butch addresses the bean-pole of a man.

He rubs at his sleepy eyes. "I am going to see him tomorrow—"

"They have nothing," Jimmy says dismissively.

"Then why did they take him?" I bite out, rendering the entire room silent. Butch and Clay both rise to their feet and *oh God,* I probably shouldn't have said that. Or like, maybe should've used a different tone or sent a text or maybe a polite email... I sink back and hit Bronson's chest just as big, colourfully inked arms go around my shoulders protectively. When Jimmy turns his gaze on me, my heart starts to thrash around between my ribs. These dangerous men are all unreadable, easily hiding their agendas. Their loyalties.

"Cassidy." Jimmy's polite, yet disembodied tone seizes my spine. "They took him because they have mistaken him for someone else."

Liar.

Liar. Liar. Liar. My eyes must chant that word because a twitch hits Jimmy's lip. I don't know what that twitch means. That I should stay quiet like Stacey and Aurora, perhaps? Or maybe he likes my strength? He used to like me. I remember months ago not being able to fathom how a girl like me could cross a man like Jimmy Storm, but now I know exactly how to. And I'd happily cross him if I thought it would free the pieces of me locked away in that jail cell. I know what Jimmy Storm is.

He is no politician.

No philanthropist.

Mafioso.

I can still hear that old lady's grief-stricken voice crying out for 'her Marco' and I don't blame Max. No. I blame Jimmy Storm. And this must be the pregnancy hormones—must be—because these are unsafe thoughts to have. I curl my lips together to stop from saying anything further, but I'm scared he can read the threat etched onto my tight foolish features. I glance at my feet. And I think if Bronson wasn't holding me, I might actually tremble so hard my knees gave out.

"Take her to her room," Clay orders Xander.

No.

"She'll leave when she's ready," Bronson states smoothly.

Clay's jaw muscles pulse as he squeezes his teeth together. A tangible energy crackles between the two eldest Butcher brothers.

"That's enough from both of you," Butch snaps. "Listen more and talk less!"

"Clay, there is no need for that, my boy," Jimmy says, his voice calm and yet dominant. "She represents Max." He fixes me with a stare, his narrowed brown eyes boring into mine with a message. *Be careful. Be smart.* "Don't you?"

Swallowing, I nod. "*Yes.*"

"The, the issue is"—the nervous guy cuts straight in, perhaps trying to blanket the embers flying across the room from one glare to another—"that he had a handgun on his person. That is going to be a problem. I will go see him tomorrow morning to discuss his options. Needless to say, we will get him out on bail while he awaits his trial, but I imagine the bail will be substantial. He has the means and could leave the country."

All I hear is that Max will be out on bail soon.

I hold on to that like it is my last breath.

CHAPTER TWENTY-EIGHT

THE ENSUING days are like one big hallucination. I'm not sure when the first day ends and the next one starts because I'm emotionally fatigued and have the curtains drawn shut to avoid the prying eyes of The District News. With our very public displays of affection at the gala and then Max's arrest mere hours later, the media are having a field day.

Who doesn't like a romantic tragedy?

Not me. And nothing is set in stone yet, so I refuse to fall into a heap until I know what we—Max and I—are dealing with. If I let myself fall, I'm not sure I'll be able to claw my way back up again. So I just can't fricking fall, no matter how drastic the earth feels like it is tilting beneath my feet. Every day. Every second. That I am without him...

So I only allow myself a few hours at night to cry. It's when I feel closest to Max, knowing he's probably lying on his back, feeling the absence of me as I feel the absence of him. The rest of the time, I put up a façade for Butch and the boys.

As I hold my tears for the fifth day, I call Toni.

"I can't leave the house," I say as soon as he picks up. Clutching the handset to my cheek, I peek behind the heavy fabric at the news crew parked up across the street. "I mean, how boring is the District these days that they can afford to station a van out there night and day?"

"Well, I'm thoroughly engrossed in your epic love tale. The Ballerina and The Butcher Boy. I especially like it when Bronson goes to get the mail in the morning and forgets to put clothes on."

He doesn't *forget.* I scoff. "Yeah. I bet every girl in the fricking District is enjoying those posts. Clay had a heart attack when he saw the photos. It's really bad press."

"*Erm,* a naked Bronson Butcher is not bad press. Also, gotta tell you something, darlin', you are going to have to start saying fuck not frick. Your baby daddy is in jail now—"

"He's getting out soon," I state firmly with a nod of my head, ignoring the light-hearted teasing, not really feeling like I want innuendos and humour and silly retorts right now. "Yeah, really soon. Maybe tomorrow. Then it'll all be over."

"Oh," he says, his tone pitching higher. "So you've spoken to him then?"

"Nope." I yank the curtain shut and move back to my spot on the floor beside the Nintendo controller that has been my distraction for the past few painfully long and lonely days. "It's been five days and Butch has spoken to him, Bronson has spoken to him, Xander has spoken to him, and the maids have probably spoken to him. I don't know, have you spoken to him? You probably have." I slump with a sigh, ceasing my petty comments and jealousy and *ugh.*

"I just need him to be out soon. That place can't be good for him." I want to say it can't be good for his darkness. A place like that feeds toxic masculinity. It stokes it. Fuels it. But I don't let that concern leave my lips.

"Golden Girl, come on." He lets out a slow breath. "He probably can't talk to you because he doesn't want to get a boner in case he ends up all Shawshank Redemption-*ed*."

I smirk in condescension. "I'd like to see anyone try."

Toni smacks his lips. "You think he'd be the giver then?"

Ugh! "I'm hanging up no—"

"I'm lightening the mood, darlin'." He speaks gently as if he can tell I'm a few stupid comments away from either bursting into tears or hissing like an alley cat. "You know why he hasn't spoken to you."

"No, no, I don't."

"He's ashamed."

I roll my eyes even though he can't witness my silent display of derision. "Max doesn't get ashamed."

"*Okay.* Then he's probably just trying to keep his head in the game—"

"If you make a head job reference!"

"I wasn't going to." He chuckles quietly because maybe now he wants to. "I was going to say, you know he needs to stay tough in there. You're all gooey and sugary and he can't have that right now... I get that."

"Yeah." I nod sadly, imagining how exhausting it must be to continuously feel defensive and on high alert. To lack the luxury of honest expression, unable to show any form of vulnerability. "I get it too. And that is totally him." I hesitate on the next question, not really wanting to extort my best friend's boyfriend... Still, the need for information outweighs my uncertainties. "Have you spoken to Braidy about it?"

"Yes, of course," he states straight away, and if I could kiss him for that, I would. "The first thing I did was get all up in his grill, but he's local control, darlin'. He told me this is in Australian Federal Police jurisdiction."

"Miss Slater," Carter's voice comes through the bedroom door, followed by a light tapping sound. "May I come in?"

"I gotta go," I say to Toni as I end our call and stand up. Staring down at my yoga pants and Max's oversized shirt, I cringe a little. There are Cheeto stains on my chest and a wet patch on my shoulder that I'm pretty sure is drool—maybe orange juice. Using my hands to brush the crumbs off, I mutter angrily to myself, "Pull yourself together, Cassidy."

When I look less like a depressed little pregnant girl who has been sprawled out on her couch for the past few days, drowning her sorrows in Skyrim and junk food, I make my way over to the bedroom door. Opening it, I am immediately greeted by Carter.

I crane my neck to smile up at him. "Hi."

His eyes drop to Max's shirt and then to my bare feet. I wiggle my toes instinctively when his gaze touches them. "Put shoes on. I am taking you for a drive."

I roll my head around my shoulders a little in protest. "I just want to wait here for Max. Maybe he'll be back soon."

Carter's starkly beautiful eyes beg me to listen and accept. "Just a little drive to get you out of the house, hey?"

Sighing in defeat, I nod. "Okay. I'm just going to change my shirt."

I move back into the room and pull on my own shirt, missing the smell of Max as soon as I do, and a pair of ballet flats. We exit through the back door to avoid the press, and as we pull around the house to leave, I duck low in my seat even though the windows are tinted dark and no one can see me. They snap pictures of the car and Carter.

"I feel like I should talk to them, ya know? Give them their story. Maybe they will leave if I do. What do you think?"

"I highly doubt that, Miss. Luca has already spoken to them. They are waiting to interview Max upon his arrival."

I exhale loudly, feeling a pang of anger and resentment that people can't just leave us alone. They want a piece of him. My Max. They can't have it because it isn't available. I am slapping a 'zero vacant spots' sticker up. I don't even have enough of him right now.

Frowning at the media, I wonder how long that has been going on for. I know the boys have been headliners most of their lives, and I know Max hates it, but I've never experienced anything like this before. We are going through something hard and personal and... Max is going through something—something life-changing—and he doesn't need this... this... *shit*. Yep, shit. And *fuck them*. So... *yeah*. My baby daddy is in jail, so I can say that now, thank you, Toni.

I stare out the window, scowling silently as the world passes by. After about fifteen minutes, we pass over into Brussman and I feel a flitter of happiness move through me, being in my own city again. A quiet city. The car pulls onto a street and I sit up, staring at the beautiful old houses on the big country lots. This part of Brussman was developed first. It has a rural feel and look, but it's only fifteen minutes from the city centre. As we roll along, the speed bumps keeping us at a slow pace, I realise that I recognise this suburb. It's about fifteen minutes from my home—funnily enough, both my old home and my new one.

Right in the middle, actually.

When Carter slows to a stop, I frown questioningly at him in the rear-view mirror. "Why have we stopped?" I see his eyes smile.

Warmth rushes through me, heating up every cell in my body.

In my soul.

My heart leaps when the realisation hits me. "Is he here?"
He's here!

Flying from the car, I search the street and properties, body spinning, eyes bouncing around. *Nothing.* Beside me is a big empty block of land covered in long green weeds that have surely been there for a while. There is a steep incline and— My heart pirouettes and aches, and I let myself cry when I see Max standing at the top. With his hands in his pockets, casual stance, and thick muscular body, there isn't a woman alive that wouldn't feel his presence like a flutter settling right between their thighs.

I rush to him, laughing through my tears when I see him scowl at me as I run.

"Stop fucking running," he barks. But he's not angry. Not at all.

Controlling butthead.

My feet can't take me fast enough and then I catapult into his arms. He catches me behind the thighs, moulding me around him until my legs band his waist and our bodies press so tightly that they almost fuse together. I wish they would.

Our noses touch. Lips connect. His tongue moves inside me with aggression, licking, devouring, claiming. My palms cup his cheeks and I accept it, accept the need. The yearning. It's the best sensation ever. I can feel his heart's pounding rhythm, a sure sign of his passionate, desperate, longing response to seeing me. Holding me. Mine matches his as we kiss breathlessly, with a frenzied possessiveness that isn't safe and guarded but instead dangerous and utterly vulnerable.

"When did you get out?" I pant against his lips.

"This morning."

I freeze, pushing away from his chest to stare into his

penetrating stormy-blue eyes. "This morning? I've been waiting for you. I've been worried. I've been... kinda messy."

A hint of a grin draws his lips out. "Messy?"

"Yes," I admit through a light smile. "Why didn't you come straight home?"

"I had a few things to sort out." He holds me effortlessly with one hand under my backside and feeds his other up through my hair. His brows bunch for a second, and then he pulls a Cheeto out from my knotted strawberry-blonde strands. My cheeks ignite with shame. I cover my blushing face, which is already wet from my tears and hot from my embarrassment.

I grin into my palms. "Oh my gawd. *Kill me.*"

He laughs, deep and real, and the sound touches my heart. Lowering my hands, I find his gaze caressing my face. Then he grins at me and eats the Cheeto.

My mouth drops open.

"You're feral," I say, with a soft giggle, briefly forgetting where he has been for the past few days and letting myself relax against him. "That could have been from yesterday."

He laughs again and holds me close. Then he sets me down on the ground. The thick, lush grass feels like a sponge under my ballet flats. I grip his forearms and rake his body thoroughly—inspect him—searching for hints of trauma or turbulence within his presence.

"Did they hurt you?" I mutter as I catch his eyes, but I'm met with only cool, calm, menacing Max. No shadows are hidden within his irises. There is sadness though, and it hurts my stomach.

I touch the stubble at his jawline, and he closes his eyes, moving into my palm, chasing comfort in a subtle way. "I'm sorry, Little One," he says, his voice stern, hoarse, rough, as if he's been shouting or yelling all night long. And I wouldn't know..."Did what happen scare you?"

Clenching my jaw, I draw breath in through my nose. Quick, short breaths. I remember the feeling of having him ripped away. Of my world tilting. Spinning. "*Yes.* Yes, of course it did, Max. I was scared for you."

He exhales slowly, shaking his head. "Don't be scared for me."

"That's a stupid thing to say," I state, glancing away from him, over his shoulder at the vast block of land we're standing on. "What happened to you?" I mutter without offering him my gaze, my voice hesitant and breathy. "Were they nice to you?"

He straightens, causing my palm to slip from his cheek. A big warm hand grips the curve of my neck. His thumb pushes my chin up, demanding my gaze meet his. "Little One, don't do that."

I fight the well of tears. I fight it, but it happens anyway. "It *kills* me to think about you in that dark place... Behind bars. You're so much more fragile than—"

His hand tightens on the arch of my throat. "Little One, stop it."

"You could lose yourself in there, Max," I say in barely a whisper. An echo. "God, I can't lose you." I grip at his fore-arm, fingers kneading him with a kind of desperation.

Cradling my head with his hands, he leans in closer and says, "You won't."

I stare up at him, craning my neck to fix him with my passion and meaning. "In here, Max." Pressing my palm to his hard chest, I feel the muscles ripple below his shirt. "I know you think that's weak and silly. I know you want to cringe; you probably have the urge to just throw me down on your mattress and silence me with your mouth, but I am here for—"

"I always have the urge to throw you down on my mattress and silence y—"

"Those places can be rough. And, well, it's over anyway," I say weakly. "Right? So you don't need to be strong anymore. I want you to be able to tell me what that was like for you. I don't want you to have this life-changing event and not share it with me. I don't—"

"Cassidy, I need you to stop talking." He presses his lips to mine, their warmth and gentleness coercing me to be quiet. I close my eyes and let his mouth consume me, silencing the questions and thoughts. I lock them away for now to enjoy the peace and contentment of our world. We hum into our kiss, a strange kind of sadness behind the motion of his lips and tongue. A gentleness that isn't hopeful but painful, and I try to ignore it.

Our kiss is broken when Carter clears his throat beside us.

Max frowns at the interruption.

"Sorry, boss. The sun will be down soon." He hands Max a black headset of some kind. "Here you go."

Max looks at my wide-eyed expression. "Turn around and face the block, Little One."

A nervous giggle leaves me. "What are you doing?"

"I want to show you something."

He positions me in front of him with my shoulders and head pressed to his hard broad chest. He slides the headset over my eyes, and I'm immediately staring at a black abyss.

"I'm nervous," I say, shuffling on the grass.

A little fizzle sounds by my ear as Max flicks the headset on. Then an image of a beautiful house appears on the empty lot. I cover my gasp. It looks so real, as though I could walk straight up through the portico and open the double doors. It is two storeys high with carved trimmings around the roofline, a gable, and exposed eaves. There is a veranda on the base level, adorned with low fencing. It is a modern representation of a 19th-century-style home. It's fricking beautiful. I beam with pride. Max has designed this house; I just know it.

I twist my head and the house stays stationary as if it is really cemented to the earth. "Is this VR?"

"Yes." His voice makes me jump a little as he sounds far away, my eyes and ears not experiencing the same environment. It's quite jarring.

"What do you think?"

I grin. "It's cool."

He chuckles. "Of the house, Little One. Not the VR."

"Oh." I smile hard and wonder if he's looking at my face. "Well I think it's just lovely."

I take it all in, noticing a building set back behind the house, offset slightly to the left. "What is that?" I point as if he can see what I can.

"That's a dance studio."

My heart skips a beat, possibly an entire chorus. I pull the headset down, and the block is empty again, shadowed by the low light of the newly setting sun. I spin to face him, blinking fast. "What?"

He sighs roughly, searching my flushed features. "It's for us."

I squeal with excitement. My heart jetes and fouettés and piques and does a silly dance. "Really?"

He nods, a pleased smile hitting the corner of his mouth. "If you want. I know this is your city. This is where I want you to be."

Wrapping my arms around his middle, I squeeze him tight. "Thank you."

He pushes me out in front of him and I notice his eyes have glossed over. I do a double-take, not quite understanding the sadness I see within their depths. Not wanting to...

My throat tightens.

"You're my life, Cassidy Slater," he says, trailing his fingers down my cheeks. "Now, with your perfect face. While you're so beautiful it fucking hurts. And when your belly is swollen with my babies and you're grumpy and a pain in the arse, then too. And when you're old and grey and for some fucking reason still putting up with all my shit. You're my life."

I can't breathe.

I can't think. I don't want to hear any of this. Not liking the break in his throat, the shudder in his voice, I shake my head slowly. "Why are you saying this?"

He grits his teeth, fighting back emotion, his face lightly veiling so much pain. "I'm going away."

My lip trembles uncontrollably. "Where are we going?" Spinning away from him, I cover my face, tears bursting out too fast to control. *No.*

"Don't do that." He twists me back to face him, his jaw pulsing when he sees my tears. "Hold on to the feeling from before. Don't cry. They want me to plead guilty for possession of an illegal firearm and assault on an officer."

"You didn't assault anyone!" I cry.

"Actually... *I did*." He nods with a show of regret. "They can't get me for anything else. Jimmy made sure of that. We are hoping for thirty-six months, out on parole at twenty-four."

No. No.

"*No. No. No*," I chant, shaking my head violently, feeling dizzy, feeling my world fall to pieces. My legs give out from under me, and my knees hit the grass, giving up. I'm giving up.

He grips my shoulders, pulling me to my feet. "Listen to me, Little One."

"No."

"Listen," he growls, but he's not angry. It is aggression manifesting from passion, and I understand it all too well.

I want to scream.

Shriek.

I ball my hands into fists.

"While I'm in, I need you to be the bravest you have ever been. Don't disappear in here." He presses his big, warm hands to my cheeks, tapping one of his forefingers on my temple. "Be you. Bubbly. A silly little girl. Soften my brothers' lives."

I can't see him now, not through the tears.

So many tears.

"I can't do this without you!" I cry.

"Do what?

I gasp for air as sobs begin to cripple my body, anger disappearing into a melting pot of despair. "Anything! Live. *Breathe!*"

He kisses my lips quickly, our mouths coated in my tears. He pulls back and wipes at my face, thumbs moving under my eyes and around my cheeks, but more salty water rains down. I'm helpless to stop them.

Helpless to save him.

Us.

"Are you kidding me?" His brows draw in tight with severity. "You're the fucking boss, Cassidy. You run things for us now. You can do *anything* without me."

"No."

"Stop saying no."

I squeeze my eyes shut, holding them that way as I shake my head over and over. *No.*

"Look at me." He tries to pull me back to him, to a place where he breaks my heart. But I don't want to go. Don't want to hear it. Don't want to be a part of this conversation. "You're not just little Cassidy Slater anymore. I'm not sure you ever were... You're my girl. Strong. Fierce."

I open my eyes to find his are narrowed and locked on mine, ready to dive straight inside and drag me out and back to a place where I am whole.

I blink tears out. "But... *I. Need. You,*" I whisper, each one vibrating out of my heart-broken little body.

He swallows his emotions down again. "Do you know what I need?"

Sucking a big breath in, I try to steady my panic. "I don't know anything."

"I need you to be my wife."

What?

He kneels on the grass in front of me.

Oh my God, what is he doing?

I cover my mouth with both hands, blinking tears over the top of them.

"I need your last name to be Butcher, so everyone knows you're mine." When he reaches into his pocket and pulls out a ring box, I completely stop breathing. No, no, I don't stop breathing. The air doesn't exist anymore; this moment is so monumental that the atmosphere around us is thick with emotion. So thick that I can't find the oxygen between the fibres of our feelings. He flicks the box open and my eyes widen further.

"It's not a diamond. I didn't think you'd want a diamond

after—" He clears his throat. "And I don't want anything dirty touching your perfect fucking hands. It's a ruby. A really rare ruby. I paid for this with clean money, Little One.

"Look at the block. That house will take eighteen months, maybe two years, to build. By the time I get out, it'll be ready for us. Ready for us to start our life together."

My heart is being wrenched around, aching with absolute sadness, flipping with so much love. I want to say something. Want to respond. I don't have the words though—they're lost in my mind, smothered by confusion. Am I happy? Sad? Both? Every fricking emotion at once? I can't ... can't think straight.

"You know who I am," he says with a seriousness and sternness that knots my stomach up with conflicting truths. I love him. More than life. More than anything. But I know who he is... *Yes.* "You know what I do. It'll always be a part of me. What I need to know is... are you in this with me anyway?"

I find myself nodding. Because I am. I always have been. Then I move my hands away and breathe out, "*Yes.*"

He takes the ring from its satin mould. "Is that a yes to being Cassidy Butcher?"

"*Yes.*"

Standing up, he grazes his finger from my thigh to my wrist. Pulling my little hand out between us, he slides the ring onto my finger. I gape at it. It's big. A deep-red teardrop with sheer cut facets that shine pink, purple, and claret. The band is a white metal—white gold or platinum.

I breathe in deep, the air returning to my lungs like a gift of possibility. Of hope. The wind whirls around me as I stand on our block with his baby in my belly and his promise on my finger. I lift my head up to meet his eyes and can't help myself. I leap into his arms and we pepper kisses all over each other's faces.

And even though he broke my heart today...

He tied it back together again with the promise of our future.

It just has to wait. I can wait for him.

Mrs Cassidy Butcher.

CHAPTER TWENTY-NINE

Three days, seventeen hours, and thirty-four minutes left.

ACROSS FROM WHERE I'm sitting on the outdoor sofa, nursing my whiskey neat and pretending I don't know the minutes until I am forced to leave her, I watch as my brothers, Ben Slater, and Konnor attempt a game of rugby. Too bad they can't get through ten minutes without arguing over the fundamentals of 'holding the ball.' It's *in* the name, dickheads. But Bronson just hates letting that fucker go. He's shit at following the rules in sports; such a trait applies to all aspects of his life.

I fix my eyes on Toni, Aurora, Felicity, and Stacey as they stand by the grassed area, watching the men play. There might as well be four women up there with the way Toni carries on. I like the guy. I don't pretend to understand him, but I like the way he adores Cassidy.

"Let's let Konnor make the calls, hey? He's the only

professional on the grass." Xander yells out to me, "The other is sitting on his arse."

I scoff, taking a sip of my whiskey.

Konnor glares at me and I grin at him, tempted to call him my brother-in-law just to watch him squirm. He'll never like me. Not that I blame him. If Cassidy was my little sister, I wouldn't like me either. I would have ripped my arms off by now, but Konnor plays at being tough when he's actually just as big of a pussy as his father.

To my left, Victoria natters to Renae Slater. The two women are worlds apart in every aspect. Fuck knows what they have to talk about. My son, perhaps. I clench my teeth, well aware I'm not good at sharing and yet being forced to learn how to every day.

Renae projects a smile as Victoria drawls on about something. I find myself wanting to rescue Cassidy's sweet mother from the claws of the woman who birthed me, but I don't. If Renae is anything like her daughter, she can handle her own. What must she think of me, having stolen her baby girl away and made her mine in every way?

My wife... I feel fire in my chest when I say that word—wife. I never knew how much I would enjoy the way it rumbles with authority from my tongue. *My wife.*

My wife giggles with Blesk, wearing the same pretty white dress that she wore three hours ago when she became my most precious possession. Most girls would hate being referred to as a possession, but not my wife. She knows it's a damn fact.

I am hers.

She is mine.

My face feels tight as I scan the backyard. White fairy lights drip from every tree. The sun hits the canal, creating ribbons of silver on the rippling surface. I woke this morning wanting to spend most of the day in bed. Inside my wife. Instead, I was coaxed by her lovely lips to have a small reception. "For our family," she begged. Then pouted. Then dropped to her knees and sucked me so good I would have said yes to just about anything she asked.

At least she allowed me to keep her all to myself for the ceremony—us and a priest.

But if she wants to do it all again when I get out, a big wedding like she deserves, I'll do it. Then. Just not now. My time is short, and I don't want to waste it with my eyes on anyone else besides her. I need my fucking fill.

I set my whiskey down, aware that I'm being a fucking arsehole for not getting up and being charming. But the sight of our two families making a show of how it will work while I'm away feels a lot like a grater on my skin. I should like the view or appreciate it at the very least. I suppose I do.

But when I glare across at them, my awareness of my jealousy spreads through me like blood stains on a shirt. They have a future. In three days, seventeen hours, and thirty-one minutes, they will still be... *this*. Just as they fucking are. Unchanged. Unaffected.

And they'll have her.

They will be able to watch her mouth move when she speaks silly words. Watch her pick at her nail polish when she's nervous. Watch the blush of her cheeks when she's embarrassed.

They'll watch my son grow inside her.

Hold him the day he's born.

Growling, I push up from the outdoor sofa and move into the house. Move away from the scene of happiness being thrown in my fucking face.

"*Hey*." Cassidy's voice stills me. She rounds me until she is standing between me and the sliding door. Big, golden-hazel eyes gaze up at me with a question. I reach for her hand, lifting it to my lips and kissing her fingers.

"Are you okay?" she says as my lips touch her. I stare at the new rings on her hand. My territory tagged with these two platinum bands. Her engagement ring is a gem cut for royalty. Her petite, slender fingers appear even smaller beneath the size of that rock. While I'm away, I'll hold on to the vision of the way it sparkles as she strokes my cock.

"*Max*?"

I shift my gaze up to meet her eyes. "Do you like the ring?"

She smiles nervously. "Where are you right now?"

"Here."

Lifting onto her tippy toes, she kisses my neck, and it's such a gentle chaste show of affection, that it burns my chest.

I miss this already.

Clearing my throat, I place my palm on the soft white skin of her cheek and drag my thumb possessively along her pink lower lip. Following my thumb with my gaze, I watch as her tongue lightly touches the tip, watch as she draws in weighted breaths and—

My eyes snap to hers again. "Don't fucking touch anyone else with these lips."

She sucks a sharp breath in. "*Max.*"

I straighten. "I'm just getting another drink, Little One." I tap her little nose and she smiles softly in response. It is a sad little smile though, and it screws with my head. I fucking hate that I just said that. Hate that I felt the need to. Hate the bullshit inside me wreaking havoc with the constant reminder of how I won't be here to touch her, smell her, fuck her when she needs to come...

Keep her safe.

Walking past her, I keep my head high and move with purpose towards the billiard room to find Butch's Gold Label.

When I enter, I'm thrown by the scent of cigar smoke. Butch is sitting in the corner of the room, fixated on the translucent brown liquor in his glass as he swirls it around.

"I haven't seen you today," I mention gruffly, coming to a stop. "Aren't you going to celebrate with us?"

He doesn't look up. "My son is losing three years of his life. I don't feel much like celebrating."

I sigh jaggedly, but appreciating the bitter honesty. We really are so alike.

"I was so fucking close to giving her what she wants." I shake my head at the bullshit that just expelled from me, at myself for being pitiful. A man can either be powerful or pitiful, but he can never be both.

"Max, sit with me for a moment."

Frowning at him, I contemplate snatching the whiskey and heading back to my wife, smiling at her family, and kicking Konnor's arse in rugby. But I stroll over and position myself on the red leather chair opposite Butch instead, giving myself some time away from the false cheer.

Smoke fills the space between us, the cigar he just blunted out still snaking a line of grey into the air. Cracking his fists, he alleviates some of the ache. I know that his years of boxing have left him with arthritis in his knuckles. They have started to tremor, but I would never admit to noticing such deterioration. I wonder how much worse it'll be when I get out.

He leans forward onto his knees. "You're not alone in there, son."

Mashing my teeth together, I try not to feel *anything*.

He fixes me with his stern gaze, and the fucking pain in his eyes twists something deep inside me. They scream at me. Scream that he failed me. I see remorse and regret shadowing those worn blue irises. And it's a look so foreign, I barely recognise him.

"There are lots of our men in there," he states, his eyes telling. "And they will follow you. Keep your head in the moment. Don't let your guard down for anyone. Don't be loose with your temper. Save it. Save it for the right moments." He pauses and I try to relax my shoulders. "And son... you have to forget about Cassidy when you're in there. Her memory will only bring you torment and make you weak."

All true. Too true. I'm not prepared to admit to anyone, especially not my wife, that I have been preparing myself to enter the chaos since the moment I found out I was royally fucked. Prison isn't safe for anyone. Someone like me though, with my family name and reputation, it could be fatal. I know this. And by the darkness and despair in Butch's reddened blue eyes, he clearly fucking knows this too.

Looking down at my finger, the tattoo I have in lieu of an actual wedding band still raised and red, I'm reminded that I only need one thing to make it out intact. "Look after my wife," I murmur, my voice deep with self-loathing.

"Don't think about her right now."

"I said, look after my goddamn wife!" I roar, slapping the table with my palm and levelling him out with narrowed eyes.

He leans back in his chair, the leather protesting beneath his weight. "I will."

"No." I smile contemptuously, feeling fucking sick of the bullshit, wanting to rip the walls he put up between us down. The walls he built around himself and made us build around ourselves to keep us emotionally impenetrable. From being victims. From being gentle. Open and raw and fucking vulnerable. I want to take my fists to those walls. "Not like you look after Victoria. Not like you look after your own fucking sons. Goddamn it, Dad. Look. The fuck. After her!"

Dad.

He nods his head firmly. "You have my word, son."

In this moment, I want to tell him so much, but the words are so unnatural they don't even form in my mind. I reach for his cigars and draw one out, biting it and lighting it in quick succession. I breathe it in and lean back, focused on the movement of the smoke as it leaves the cinder. Butch's shoulders relax on a sigh and he joins me in contemplative silence.

Several minutes later, a knock interrupts us and I twist to see Konnor-fucking-Slater by the entry.

He leans his shoulder on the door frame. "I want to speak with you about Cassidy."

I smirk. "There is nothing you can say about Cassidy that I don't already know."

Twisting back to face Butch, I'm hit with a scowl and a pulsing jaw. Is he pissed I'm not playing nice with Cassidy's family? Him of all people? *Fuck that.* "What?" I snap.

Ignoring me, Butch stands and rubs his palms down his black pants. I glare over my shoulder to watch him stride towards Konnor.

"You play rugby too?" Butch asks, sizing Cassidy's brother up.

Konnor pushes his chest out and lifts his chin—a defensive stance for sure. And a commonly taken one when sharing space with Luca Butcher. A man so far removed from his own dad that I'm surprised they speak the same fucking language.

"Yeah," Konnor confirms, his narrowed green eyes flaring with distrust.

"You any good?" Butch asks, stopping just before him.

Konnor adjusts his footing, a tight line forming between his brows. "Yeah. I'm pretty good."

Butch tilts his head. "Ever boxed?"

"No," Konnor says, standing strong in the face of ... *whatever* the fuck Butch is doing. "I don't enjoy fighting. Unlike some people." He takes a dig at me and I just grin, taking this opportunity to lick my lips and think about his sister's pussy.

"You're competitive," Butch notes. "And boxing eases tension. My boys all box recreationally."

Chuckling, I say, "You know what else eases tension?"

Konnor runs a hand through his hair, ignoring me, and that pisses me right off. "What makes you say I'm competitive?"

My face tightens as I glare back and forth between them.

What the fuck is going on here?

"You're a man. That's all. We're all competitive...You should sit with us." Butch motions to the spot beside me. "What do you drink?"

"I don't," Konnor states curtly.

"Water then?" Butch presses.

"Here they are," Cassidy calls out, entering the billiard room with her dad trailing behind her. As her pink-blonde hair sways around her shoulders, I'm reminded how I should be inside her, wrapping that pretty hair around my fist. I find myself grinning when she raises her palms in the air and sings, "Bride in the house," but that feeling is short-lived. As soon as she catches sight of her brother, she lowers her hands and glances around the room with uncertainty. "Sorry, are we interrupting something?"

Something is definitely going on right now, and while I don't pretend to know what it is, I do know it better not disturb her day.

"*Ben*, what are you drinking?" Butch calls to Ben Slater, who looks like he has just walked in on his wife talking to his male lover. Butch walks over to the bar, and I watch as he pulls out two glasses, preparing multiple beverages.

"Nothing, Luca, thank you," Ben states, pacing over to his son and saying, "They're missing you out there, Konnor."

I watch my wife gauge the room before she steps cautiously towards her brother. "Yeah, now no one actually follows the rules," she says with a nervous giggle. I can read her like a fucking rugby field. She is wary of whatever it is she's just walked in on, immediately taking the defence to protect her precious Konnor—like Butch might break him.

Konnor turns to look at her. "I'll be back out in a minute."

"Let the boy stay," Butch states calmly, handing out drinks like a fucking butler. He moves back to his spot opposite me and throws back his whiskey. My eyes dart to my wife again, not liking the space between us.

Leaning back in my chair, I study these restless men as they share glances of significance. I'm reminded of the last time I saw them together. The day I found out about Cassidy's condition. These two share a fucking secret. It better not have anything to do with my wife. My brows tighten to an uncomfortable level. The Slaters are my business now, so whatever this is about-

"We planned on telling them tomorrow anyway, Ben," Butch says, his words stopping my thoughts. "And I won't lie to the boy. I can't exactly just stay away anymore. Your daughter has married my son."

Ben takes a step towards Butch. "Not like this. This is supposed to be a happy day."

"Happy?" Butch scoffs and I stare straight at my wife's face, catching the sadness washing over it. Heat hits my ears. "Don't be blind, Ben," Butch says. "Cassidy is about to lose

Max for years, and he is about to lose far more than that. Let's not play at this bullshit."

I growl loud enough for them all to hear. It is one fucking thing to see the bullshit; it is another thing entirely to point it out to my wife.

She blinks a few times before muttering, "Just tell us what this is all about so I can get back to my *silly* celebration." Her voice is strained, and my bicep twitches with the urge to knock Butch's teeth in. I glare at his profile, but he's too busy scrutinising Cassidy's brother to notice. I ball my hands into fists.

Butch uses his drink to motion towards Konnor. "You deserve to know."

Konnor frowns defensively. "Know what?"

Ben turns towards his son, looking panicked. "You can leave if you want."

"*Ben*," Butch drawls. "Tell him. Tell your boy the truth."

Ben motions politely to the seats beside me. "Does everyone want to sit down first? Maybe have—"

"Dad, what the fuck is this guy on about?" Konnor bites out. My sweet wife is beside him in a second, placing her hand on his forearm. She peers at me for the first time since she entered, her eyes pleading for help. If I get up, I'll be dragging her out.

Ben all but collapses beside Butch. Yep, he's never the impartial man in the room. His son does a far better job. At least he appears pissed off in lieu of weak. Ben looks down at the ground, his forehead indented with taut lines. He shakes his head slowly, and Cassidy's expressive blonde brows slump. My knuckles ache as I squeeze my fists tighter. She cares too much about everyone around her. I should lock her away, protect her from their drama.

"Konnor," Ben says, looking at his son. "Fourteen years

ago, you came into my care. But it wasn't a coincidence. It wasn't just because your mother was my first love and I felt the need to protect you... Your father asked me to take you in as my own. To keep you far away from the people who hurt you. Give you a good life. He entrusted me with his son."

"You mean *Dustin*," Cassidy whispers, articulating his name as if it were poison. And to her, it is. To me too. He's not getting within a mile of her ever again. Carter will make damn sure of it. He'll do whatever he needs to do to keep them apart while—While I can't.

"No, sweetheart," Ben says reluctantly as guilt flashes across his face. "I mean his biological father."

My wife's eyes gloss over, and the betrayal crouching within them boils my blood. It makes me want to beat the lies out of Ben Slater's mouth for her.

Konnor grips his water glass with white knuckles. "You told us you didn't know who my father was."

"I know I did." Ben shakes his head. "*Christ*, I *hate* that I did. I lied to you, son. After everything you endured, we just wanted peace for you. I thought this was the way."

Konnor sets his water down on the edge of the billiard table, seemingly wanting to hurl it into the wall. I get that. "We?"

Ben nods. "Yes. Luca and I."

What the fuck?

Butch drains the last dregs of his whiskey, stands up, and strides over to the bar again. I frown at him. Butch has never wasted his time on the likes of the Slaters before. Konnor isn't his fucking problem.

"I thought you'd be safer out of my world," Butch states gruffly. "I owed that to your mother. You have her eyes. Well, I suppose you have heard that many times from Ben." He turns to face Konnor and nods. "But when I look at you, it's like she's staring back at me. I would have died for that woman."

I'm on my feet now, pacing over to catch Cassidy as her cheeks lose colour. She jumps when my arms go around her, which only makes me tighten them. She takes a big breath in and leans back.

I got you, Little One.

"So the rumours are true," Konnor states, his voice a tremoring mess. "I'm not Dustin's biological son. You?" He stares at Butch, and Butch stares at Konnor.

What the fuck?

I cringe when I realise what they are fucking implying —confessing.

"You had an affair with my mother? I'm your... You're my..." Konnor trails off, clutching the side of the table to stop from toppling over.

Butch takes a mouthful of his newly poured drink. "You're a Butcher."

My teeth lock. "*Fuck.*"

CHAPTER THIRTY

KONNOR IS A BUTCHER BOY.

I cover my mouth with my palms, smothering the gasp that tries to escape. *Oh my God.* I think everyone in the room just stopped breathing. Max's arms tighten around me, enveloping me, grounding me.

Konnor immediately turns ashen, appearing to be flooded by nausea. "*Fuck.*"

Moving over to his spot on the lounge, Butch sits down slowly and leans forward, his arms resting on his knees. "Dustin must never find out. He'll want revenge and he'll come for my family. Made-men don't lie to made-men. It is a law. He'll come for Cassidy. He'll come for your brothers."

"*My brothers...*" Konnor grips his forehead, and when his knees buckle, he slides down to the floor. Leaning against the leg of the table, he stares straight ahead. "*Brothers.*"

"*Fuck,*" Max says louder this time.

Oh my God. I feel dizzy.

"There will be casualties on both sides if this gets back to him," Butch states empathically. "That is what we have been trying to avoid for over a decade."

"At my expense," Konnor mutters, outwardly trying to comprehend all this information.

"No." Butch stands and walks over to him, squatting down at his side. "*At mine.*"

Fingers peel my hand away from my mouth, allowing sweet air to rush into my lungs. I didn't even realise that I was holding my breath. I can't see Max's face, but I can feel his heart's hammering rhythm against my back.

Konnor is his brother.

Butch fixes Konnor with his serious, stern blue eyes. "Konnor, Ben gave you a far more peaceful life than I ever could. And that is what Madeline wanted. She begged me not to drag you into this world. I gave her my word that I would stay away. For her, I did... I'm actually surprised you stopped looking for *me*."

Konnor glares at him. "What do you mean?"

"A few months back," Butch says with a raise of his salt and pepper brows, "you were asking questions. I thought you'd find out. I'd even hoped you wou—"

"You told him!" Konnor barks at our dad. "You just ran right over here and—"

"I did no such thing, Konnor," Dad states defensively.

"You've got a temper on you." Butch chuckles easily. "You get that from your grandfather."

Konnor looks queasy again, his head doing a slight roll against the table leg. "How did you know that I was looking for answers?"

"One of my men told me," Butch states simply.

Anger flares in Konnor's eyes. "You have people watching me!"

"I have people watching *over* you," Butch corrects. "I have people watching over *all* my boys."

"Who?" Konnor demands. "Is it someone I know? A spy?"

Butch nods. "Your doorman—Adolf."

Konnor blinks over and over again. "What?"

"He was Madeline's captain of security." Butch straightens and takes a step backwards. "He was very fond of you as a boy. He is now too."

"This is too much." Konnor stares straight ahead at the wall, seemingly wanting to disappear into it. "I moved on. I gave up caring about you. You, you fucking didn't give a shit about—"

"*Rispettu!* Respect, son!" Butch barks, and I flinch. "In this household, we respect the head. I did *give a shit!* I wanted you and her more than anything. When I found out she was pregnant, I wanted to take my boys and her and leave the fucking country."

"What stopped you then?" Konnor sneers, locking eyes with him.

"Your goddamn life! Your safety. We'd always be looking over our shoulders."

Konnor scoffs. "But I wasn't safe."

"We didn't know what would happen," Butch says through a tight jaw. "Madeline thought Dustin would be a good father to you if he thought you were his. I gave him my son with that hope too."

"He found out I wasn't his," Konnor murmurs, his voice fracturing.

"Rumours in the District; it is like a plague... I should have never left her with him. He was blindly infatuated with her; he'd rather see her dead than in another man's arms. He said as much on several occasions. If I didn't have my own boys to protect...

choosing one over the other all this time has not been done without considerable pain. And if Dustin believed the rumours, then what happened to you could have been his doing."

But there is no proof. "But there is no proof," I find myself saying out loud. "That's the issue, right? That's why we can't touch him. He does all these terrible things, but no one can be sure it was him." My lower lip shakes uncontrollably.

"I want you to go outside," Max orders quietly.

"No," I breathe. "I want to be here."

"Do you want me to drag you out?" he threatens.

I squeeze his bicep. "Please, Max. Just keep hold of me."

His arms tense up, but luckily, he doesn't fight me on this. Yeah, luckily, because I wouldn't have retaliated if he had scooped me up and carried me to our room. I'm done pretending for the day, ignoring the lies in every smile. The pity in every congratulation.

I just want to be with my husband. Want to cry in his arms. For Konnor. For Butch. And for everyone who has been living with these secrets weighing them down like stones shackled to their ankles.

But I need to know the truth. So I will stay.

"That's right, Cassidy. We don't know anything for sure," Butch confirms as he rises and holds his hand out for Konnor to take. "And that is why we are telling you this now."

Konnor stares at Butch's hand as if its existence is a complete mystery to him. After several seconds, he swallows hard and accepts it, letting Butch pull him to his feet.

"Why?" Konnor shakes his head. "Why now?"

"Because Ben and I have a favour to ask." Butch exhales, seemingly regretful. When he turns to face us, my eyes widen. "Of Max." Feeling the earth tilt again, I lean further into my husband for support. *Please don't say the P-word.* Please don't remind me again that I'm losing him. That soon he will be gone. That I'm losing half of myself. The reality of our situation has been locked away in a dark pit inside of me, and no matter how many times it tugs at my nerve endings, sending shocks of sorrow through my entire being, I force the truth back down.

I fight it.

I fight it so that it doesn't creep into my chest, leaving nothing in its wake but a gaping hole where my heart used to pump.

Max's biceps contract around me, but he's warm and sturdy in every other way. Butch continues and his pained eyes physically hurt something raw and maternal within me. "It is something I shouldn't ask of my son. Not now. Not when he should serve his time and think of no one but himself while he is in there. But it might be our only chance and I know he'll do it." He spares a glance at Konnor. "He'll do it because you're his brother and nothing matters more to my boys than their blood."

"What is it?" Max asks tightly.

Butch sighs slowly. "There is a man in the maximum-security prison you will be sent to," he states, looking at Max firmly. "Donavon Knight. He is responsible for kidnapping Konnor. Holding him in a basement. He is a lying sack of shit, and the cops couldn't get a straight answer from him. He pleaded guilty all those years ago with no trial. He was more afraid to snitch than he was to do hard time. Max, I want you to find out why he took your brother." Butch grins ominously. "And *who* he's so fucking afraid of."

CHAPTER THIRTY-ONE

Fifteen hours and twenty-two minutes left.

I CROSS my legs up on the mattress. Staring at the floor plan of our new house in Brussman, I walk my finger down the hallway and into the master suite. It's an open-plan bedroom with a resort-style ensuite that is separated from the main area by white shutters. I imagine opening those shutters and touching myself in bed while I watch my husband shower. I picture him catching me, grinning menacingly, and running out to grab me, still dripping with water, leaving wet, size-eleven footprints on the carpet. He will carry me to the shower and make love to me under the flowing water.

We are not saying goodbye.

This is not a fantasy; this *will* happen. I have an entire house and yard to decorate. A baby to nurse and play with. Shaking my head, I smile with tears in my eyes. He did this so

258 · NICCI HARRIS

I'd be busy. Too busy to miss him, perhaps. He really does underestimate just how much I love him with every fibre of my being. In all the seconds. Not just the lonely ones.

I wipe the tears as they fall, having promised him we are not saying goodbye.

Max has asked two things of me, both of which are incredibly painful and impossibly hard.

Not to go to court tomorrow.

Not to visit him in prison.

I exhale a shaky breath, the two requests terrifying to think about. To accept. I understand them though, and that is why I will do what he has asked. Because no matter how hard I think this is for me, I know... *God*... I know it will forever haunt him. So I'll do what he needs me to do to get him through this. I know he can't be soft. Not in there.

I just pray—even though I'm not religious... I've never understood people who pray. I suppose, I have never felt so *powerless* that I needed a miracle. So unable to dig deep and fight my own way out of a situation.

Absolute helplessness.

So I pray. I pray that when he is released, he can find that gentleness again, dig it out from wherever he had to hide it, and shine a light on it... *for me.*

Max is downstairs right now with his brothers, sharing final moments of laughter and messages of wisdom that I am sure would break my heart to hear. They will be accompanying him tomorrow morning to court. Butch. Clay. Bronson. Xander.

Flick and Stacey will be here at nine to hold all the pieces of me together until the boys come home... come home... with one less person. I jump up from the bed and rush to the bathroom, wiping my eyes as the tears fall.

Quickly, I wash the sorrow away.

We are not saying goodbye.

Standing in front of the mirror now, I turn side on and trail my hand over the taut skin covering our blob. I hear the bedroom door open, so I walk slowly out to find Max sitting in the spot I was previously, looking at the house plans.

"Come here, Little One," he orders, placing the pieces of paper onto the floor.

I make my way towards him, crawling along the mattress until I am on his lap. He pulls me in closer, cradling me against him. I bury my face against his chest. As aligned with his heart as I can be, I listen to its beautiful beating cadence.

This is my other half.

The person I will grow old with. This is the sound of his life source.

I nuzzle in deep, the scent of his soap, sweat, and *him*, the ultimate aphrodisiac. Needing to be closer, as close as two individual people can be, I lift my head, cup his cheeks, and plant a devouring kiss on his lips. The heat between us ignites.

Max moves me around the mattress, flattening my back and mounting me. As his tongue strokes inside my mouth, I fumble with his jeans, the button, the zipper... *Get them off.* He kicks them from his ankles. His shirt comes off and flies across the room. Floors always look better with Max Butcher's clothes all over them. I trail my fingers down taut muscles covered in hot smooth skin, his washboard ridges contracting as I awaken them with my touch. My hands meet the seam of his white boxers, and then one dips beneath them in an attempt to band the large breadth of his penis. I fail to circle it all. Its form lengthens. Thickens. Pulses.

He growls, thrusting his hips into my palm. "*Fuck,* Cassidy. *My Cassidy.*"

Our mouths dance together. We share breath, unwilling

to break away. We would rather suffocate. I stroke him and we kiss passionately. I stick my tongue in his mouth and he sucks on it the way I know he likes. As I drag my hand up and down his expansive shaft, the tension and strength in it beats against my palm's rhythm.

"Make me come, Little One. *Good girl*." He growls when I speed up. Feeding his hand up the inside of my leg, he touches my knickers, then works them aside to stroke the lips between my thighs. A single finger trails the length of the valley between my folds, getting wetter and wetter, before pushing between them.

"Oh, *fuck*. I crave your little pussy, Cassidy. The way I have to convince you to let me in. The way you grip me like you never want me to leave." I arch my back on a tremor when his knuckles meet my entrance, feeling him beautifully deep. My mind wrestles between the sensations wanting to consume me and the gruff demand to make my husband come.

He drives his hips into my fist, doing all the work himself so that I can shamelessly chase my own high. Another finger pushes inside me, applying pressure to that perfect spot, too much pressure. I mewl against the onslaught. Heat rolls through my muscles, reaching a boiling point before crashing together at the tips of his skilled fingers. I moan and he eats my sounds of delight.

I release my grip on him, the rolling delight of my orgasm loosening me, making me feel as though the very connective tissue holding my muscles together has fallen apart. Melting into the mattress, I barely notice when he removes my knickers and camisole, leaving me bare to him. He stands up and gazes down at my naked body, emotion shadowing his grey-blue eyes, revealing a crack in his resolve.

It's gone almost as soon as I see it.

We are not saying goodbye.

He disappears into the bathroom but quickly returns, rubbing his erection, the smooth skin glistening with a kind of lotion or oil. Swallowing hard, I scoot backwards slightly as he stalks towards me. He is on me before I can think. His lips find mine, our breaths collide, but he doesn't kiss me. Grey-blue eyes gaze into my being. I hook my legs around his back, and he threads his arm between our sweat-slick bodies until he gets to a place that makes me suck in a sharp breath. Stroking my puckering hole, he uses the wetness all over my lips to ease passage inside me. I open my mouth. My eyes widen.

He doesn't kiss me.

He *stares* into me unapologetically because it *is* his right. I am his. "I want to watch you take me, Little One." He begins to move his finger inside and my eyes roll into the back of my head, forcing them shut. "You like this, Little One. Sometimes when I want to get you off again and again, all I need to do is stick my finger up your tight little arse and you come hard."

I don't understand it myself. The sensation is so erotic, I can barely control my own body. I squirm around as he moves his finger inside me, twisting and rolling... Then he stops. Pulls out. My eyes fly open when I feel the crown of his erection meeting that hole.

He drops onto one elbow, combing his fingers through my hair as his thumb strokes my pinkening cheek. His other hand moves from his erection to my hip, holding me still. His eyes soften, inches away, boring into mine.

I see vulnerability.

I see honesty.

No bares held emotion.

We are not saying goodbye.

"If you want me to stop, say it now."

"I don't want you to stop. *Please*, Max.

"I'll go slow." He starts to roll his hips in shallow dips, squeezing his erection between tight muscles. I inhale quickly, tensing up everywhere. The feel of him is impossible. Impossibly big. Forgetting how to exhale, I hold my breath.

I see the pleasure in Max's eyes as I squeeze against his penetration, the challenge to get inside me only spurring him on further.

And now I can't feel my lungs. Diaphragm. Any part of me that once understood the mechanics of breathing has been rendered useless.

"Breathe, Little One," Max whispers through a groan, pushing in slower. Unhurried. Inch by inch. "Keep breathing. You're doing so good. You're such a good girl. So good to me."

I am pinned down by his scorching hot gaze, loving me, lusting for me.

Our noses slide together.

I'm exquisitely stretched—impaled. I don't know how deep, but it's the only body part I can feel. The only part of me that exists. All my sensory cells, pain and pleasure, cling and convulse around his deepening plunge.

A sound comes from my throat. A whimper. A mewl. A whine.

When I feel his balls touch my backside, I know he's in fully.

Both hands meet the side of my head, holding me in a vice. "Relax. I'm going to move now. Relax and breathe deeply with me."

As he begins to draw out and push back in, my every sense now revolves around his penetration. I sink my fingers into his shoulders, gripping him as though he is the only thing keeping me from losing my sanity. Tears glide down my temples and puddle against his palms. The stimulation is shattering my nervous system.

He rubs the side of his nose along mine. "You're doing so good. Feel so good." He praises me over and over, broken whispers that flow straight into my mouth, rough exhales that heat my lips like flames licking out from a hearth.

Picking up pace, he curls my backside up with each roll of his hips against me. My entire world is channelled in my pelvis, my mind incapable of wandering.

No sadness.

Just him and me—*us.*

Releasing my face, he grabs my hand and slides it between our bodies, coaxing me to stroke my throbbing clit with my own fingers. I pulse against the pad of my forefinger. When I begin to masturbate, he moves faster inside me. Max's complete domination of my body throws me to a whole new level of arousal. Then, through the unparalleled pressure moving up into me, it happens. I feel pleasure bubbling. A shock of desire causes all the muscles inside me to jolt. Vibrate. Max groans long and loud in a guttural pitch like I have never heard from him before.

Like pain.

Too much pleasure.

"Come, Little One. Your little pussy is begging for it."

Or is that me? Pain. Too much pleasure. I convulse on that intense current, screaming out loud and shuddering with the aftershock of a savage orgasm.

My head rolls on the pillow as I moan.

"Good girl," he growls as he tenses up, his body losing its precise beat, becoming shaky and uncontrolled. His fingers knot in my hair, and we break eye contact when he squeezes his shut, coming with a fierce groan.

When my body drifts down from that consuming state, I brush my fingers up through his brown hair, holding his forehead to mine with hopelessness. I blink more tears out as our reality tumbles back on top of me. What time is it? How long do we have? I lift my chin to press my lips to his, move down his strong jawline, and across his throat.

"I don't want to sleep," I rasp out against his sweat-slick skin. "I'm going to stay awake all night."

My body is thrown to near climax when he shifts his weight to the side. His penis slips from inside me, still hot and semi-hard, the release of which is so sweet and yet any absence of him is unbearably sorrowful.

He spears me with an intense look. "We're going to shower. Eat. I'm going to lick your sweet pussy. And then I'm going to stare at this face"—he trails his knuckles down my cheek—"until I can't forget how it looks. How it moves."

We are not saying goodbye.

"Will you stay awake with me?" My voice trembles something awful.

"I'll stay awake *all* night, Little One," he promises, cradling me against him as he stands and strides into our ensuite.

We are not saying goodbye.

A WHINE.

Something wet slides across my cheek. I'm snatched from peaceful oblivion back to the waking world by a strange sound and that sensation. The sun glows behind my eyelids. Something touches my leg and I smile, curling to my side to cuddle—I shoot up. My eyes fly open. Startled by the sight before me, I nearly fall off the bed. Big brown eyes watch me.

A wet black nose meets my hand, nudging softly. She is a *big* puppy. Brown and black, probably a German Shepherd. She is on her belly, her tail swiping across the sheets with excitement.

"Hi. Who do you belong to?" I ask, ruffling her fluffy brown mane.

Smiling softly at her, I am suddenly hit with panic. What time is it? I fell asleep.

I fell asleep!

I dive from the bed, grabbing my robe and wrapping it around my body. I stumble through the bedroom door. My heart thrashes around inside me, its frantic thundering hurling me into a frenzy. No. No. No.

The puppy rushes after me, tumbling its chubby body into my heels. I take the staircase down, each step huge, one after the other, a never-ending decline. At the bottom of the stairs, I dart my gaze around, looking for a sign I am not alone. Anything at all.

He's just getting a drink.

What time is it? I hear a car engine and my head snaps towards the front door. I race over to it, opening it wide, before coming to a dead stop on the porch.

The Butcher Boys are climbing into a black car, all in dark suits as if they are going to a funeral. Max freezes when he sees me, his eyes piercing through mine. He stands with one foot in the passenger door, his tempestuous grey-blue eyes glistening in the gathering dawn.

I watch his throat roll. "She's yours."

Tears burst from the corners of my eyes, the heat and power of them burning my irises. I want to sink to my knees and cry hysterically. Scream at the pavement.

I don't though.

Instead, I lean down and scoop my puppy—*Clara*—into

my arms. Her tongue whips out to catch my tears as they flood down my face.

Are you scared, Max?

Don't lose your gentleness in there.

I shake my head through sobs of despair. "Weren't you ever going to tell me that you love me, Max?"

He smiles softly. "If I don't, will you still know?"

I laugh through a splutter of tears, nodding my head frantically. "*Yes.*"

"Good." He climbs into the car and I take a step closer, my body trembling with the need to race after him, to beg him to run away with me, to flee with me to Bali or New Zealand or anywhere. The place doesn't matter. Just leave the District. Change our names. Have babies and puppies and placemats and—

He shuts the passenger door.

My feet suddenly feel like lead.

The car rolls slowly down the driveway.

I can feel that my heart is still beating. But I'm stunned. Stunned it hasn't just decided to wilt and die.

I don't know who you'll be next time I see you, Max...

On shaky legs, I make my way back to our room. I softly close the door, locking myself away from everyone and everything. I stare across the empty space in a horrendously painful state of being. Lost. A chill moves down my spine, so I hold Clara tighter. My pooling gaze lands on his bedside table, on a pile of paper folded down the middle.

A letter.

I place Clara onto the floor and move over to stare at the paper. Twisting my wedding rings around my finger, I remind myself that he has promised me a future with him.

Cassidy Butcher

I unfold the sheets.

The salty droplets pouring from my eyes slap the white sheet, beading on top of the fresh red ink. I read the pages, the words blurring through my tears. I run my finger over the cursive writing. Then I reach for the pen that created these beautiful words, still with its cap off, and slash a red line straight through the first sentence.

One down.

CHAPTER THIRTY-TWO
max's letter

I love you. I love

you. I love you. I love you. I love you. I love
you. I love you. I love you. I love you. I love
you. I love you. I love you. I love you. I love
you. I love you. I love you. I love you. I love
you. I love you. I love you. I love you. I love
you. I love you. I love you. I love you. I love
you. I love you. I love you. I love you. I love
you. I love you. I love you. I love you. I love
you. I love you. I love you. I love you. I love
you. I love you. I love you. I love you. I love
you. I love you. I love you. I love you. I love
you. I love you. I love you. I love you. I love
you. I love you. I love you. I love you. I love
you. I love you. I love you. I love you. I love
you. I love you. I love you. I love you. I love
you. I love you. I love you. I love you. I love
you. I love you. I love you. I love you. I love
you. I love you. I love you. I love you. I love
you. I love you. I love you. I love you. I love
you. I love you. I love you. I love you. I love
you. I love you. I love you. I love you. I love
you. I love you. I love you. I love you. I love
you. I love you. I love you. I love you. I love
you. I love you. I love you. I love you. I love
you. I love you. I love you. I love you. I love
you. I love you. I love you. I love you. I love
you. I love you. I love you. I love you. I love

you. I love you. I love you. I love you. I love
you. I love you. I love you. I love you. I love
you. I love you. I love you. I love you. I love
you. I love you. I love you. I love you. I love
you. I love you. I love you. I love you. I love
you. I love you. I love you. I love you. I love
you. I love you. I love you. I love you. I love
you. I love you. I love you. I love you. I love
you. I love you. I love you. I love you. I love
you. I love you. I love you. I love you. I love
you. I love you. I love you. I love you. I love
you. I love you. I love you. I love you. I love
you. I love you. I love you. I love you. I love
you. I love you. I love you. I love you. I love
you. I love you. I love you. I love you. I love
you. I love you. I love you. I love you. I love
you. I love you. I love you. I love you. I love
you. I love you. I love you. I love you. I love
you. I love you. I love you. I love you. I love
you. I love you. I love you. I love you. I love
you. I love you. I love you. I love you. I love
you. I love you. I love you. I love you. I love
you. I love you. I love you. I love you. I love
you. I love you. I love you. I love you. I love
you. I love you. I love you. I love you. I love
you. I love you. I love you. I love you. I love
you. I love you. I love you. I love you. I love
you. I love you. I love you. I love you. I love

you. I love you. I love you. I love you. I love
you. I love you. I love you. I love you. I love
you. I love you. I love you. I love you. I love
you. I love you. I love you. I love you. I love
you. I love you. I love you. I love you. I love
you. I love you. I love you. I love you. I love
you. I love you. I love you. I love you. I love
you. I love you. I love you. I love you. I love
you. I love you. I love you. I love you. I love
you. I love you. I love you. I love you. I love
you. I love you. I love you. I love you. I love
you. I love you. I love you. I love you. I love
you. I love you. I love you. I love you. I love
you. I love you. I love you. I love you. I love
you. I love you. I love you. I love you. I love
you. I love you. I love you. I love you. I love
you. I love you. I love you. I love you. I love
you. I love you. I love you. I love you.

I love you. I love you. I love you. I love
you. I love you. I love you. I love you. I love
you. I love you. I love you. I love you. I love
you. I love you. I love you. I love you. I love
you. I love you. I love you. I love you. I love
you. I love you. I love you. I love you. I love
you. I love you. I love you. I love you. I love
you. I love you. I love you. I love you. I love
you. I love you. I love you. I love you. I love

you. I love you. I love you. I love you. I love
you. I love you. I love you. I love you. I love
you. I love you. I love you. I love you. I love
you. I love you. I love you. I love you. I love
you. I love you. I love you. I love you. I love
you. I love you. I love you. I love you. I love
you. I love you. I love you. I love you. I love
you. I love you. I love you. I love you. I love
you. I love you. I love you. I love you. I love
you. I love you. I love you. I love you. I love
you. I love you. I love you. I love you. I love
you. I love you. I love you. I love you. I love
you. I love you. I love you. I love you. I love
you. I love you. I love you. I love you. I love
you. I love you. I love you. I love you. I love
you. I love you. I love you. I love you. I love
you. I love you. I love you. I love you. I love
you. I love you. I love you. I love you. I love
you. I love you. I love you. I love you. I love
you. I love you. I love you. I love you. I love
you. I love you. I love you. I love you. I love
you. I love you. I love you. I love you. I love
you. I love you. I love you. I love you. I love
you. I love you. I love you. I love you. I love
you. I love you. I love you. I love you. I love
you. I love you. I love you. I love you. I love

you. I love you. I love you. I love you. I love
you. I love you. I love you. I love you. I love
you. I love you. I love you. I love you. I love
you. I love you. I love you. I love you. I love
you. I love you. I love you. I love you. I love
you. I love you. I love you. I love you. I love
you. I love you. I love you. I love you. I love
you. I love you. I love you. I love you. I love
you. I love you. I love you. I love you. I love
you. I love you. I love you. I love you. I love
you. I love you. I love you. I love you. I love
you. I love you. I love you. I love you. I love
you. I love you. I love you. I love you. I love
you. I love you. I love you. I love you. I love
you. I love you. I love you. I love you. I love
you. I love you. I love you. I love you. I love
you. I love you. I love you. I love you. I love
you. I love you. I love you. I love you. I love
you. I love you. I love you. I love you. I love
you. I love you. I love you. I love you. I love
you. I love you. I love you. I love you. I love
you. I love you. I love you. I love you. I love
you. I love you. I love you. I love you. I love
you. I love you. I love you. I love you. I love
you. I love you. I love you. I love you. I love
you. I love you. I love you. I love you. I love
you. I love you. I love you. I love you. I love
you. I love you. I love you. I love you. I love

you. I love you. I love you. I love you. I love
you. I love you. I love you. I love you. I love
you. I love you. I love you. I love you. I love
you. I love you. I love you. I love you. I love
you. I love you. I love you. I love you. I love
you. I love you. I love you. I love you. I love
you. I love you. I love you. I love you. I love
you. I love you. I love you. I love you. I love
you. I love you. I love you. I love you. I love
you. I love you. I love you. I love you. I love
you. I love you. I love you. I love you. I love
you. I love you. I love you. I love you. I love
you. I love you. I love you. I love you. I love
you. I love you. I love you. I love you. I love
you. I love you. I love you. I love you. I love
you. I love you. I love you. I love you. I love
you. I love you. I love you. I love you. I love
you. I love you. I love you. I love you. I love
you. I love you. I love you. I love you. I love
you. I love you. I love you. I love you. I love
you. I love you. I love you. I love you. I love
you. I love you. I love you. I love you. I love
you. I love you. I love you. I love you. I love
you. I love you. I love you. I love you.

I love you. I love you. I love you. I love
you. I love you. I love you. I love you. I love

you. I love you. I love you. I love you. I love
you. I love you. I love you. I love you. I love
you. I love you. I love you. I love you. I love
you. I love you. I love you. I love you. I love
you. I love you. I love you. I love you. I love
you. I love you. I love you. I love you. I love
you. I love you. I love you. I love you. I love
you. I love you. I love you. I love you. I love
you. I love you. I love you. I love you. I love
you. I love you. I love you. I love you. I love
you. I love you. I love you. I love you. I love
you. I love you. I love you. I love you. I love
you. I love you. I love you. I love you. I love
you. I love you. I love you. I love you. I love
you. I love you. I love you. I love you. I love
you. I love you. I love you. I love you. I love
you. I love you. I love you. I love you. I love
you. I love you. I love you. I love you. I love
you. I love you. I love you. I love you. I love
you. I love you. I love you. I love you. I love
you. I love you. I love you. I love you. I love
you. I love you. I love you. I love you. I love
you. I love you. I love you. I love you. I love
you. I love you. I love you. I love you. I love
you. I love you. I love you. I love you. I love
you. I love you. I love you. I love you. I love
you. I love you. I love you. I love you. I love

you. I love you. I love you. I love you. I love
you. I love you. I love you. I love you. I love
you. I love you. I love you. I love you. I love
you. I love you. I love you. I love you. I love
you. I love you. I love you. I love you. I love
you. I love you. I love you. I love you. I love
you. I love you. I love you. I love you. I love
you. I love you. I love you. I love you. I love
you. I love you. I love you. I love you. I love
you. I love you. I love you. I love you. I love
you. I love you. I love you. I love you. I love
you. I love you. I love you. I love you. I love
you. I love you. I love you. I love you. I love
you. I love you. I love you. I love you. I love
you. I love you. I love you. I love you. I love
you. I love you. I love you. I love you. I love
you. I love you. I love you. I love you. I love
you. I love you. I love you. I love you. I love
you. I love you. I love you. I love you. I love
you. I love you. I love you. I love you. I love
you. I love you. I love you. I love you. I love
you. I love you. I love you. I love you. I love
you. I love you. I love you. I love you. I love
you. I love you. I love you. I love you. I love
you. I love you. I love you. I love you. I love
you. I love you. I love you. I love you. I love
you. I love you. I love you. I love you. I love

you. I love you. I love you. I love you. I love
you. I love you. I love you. I love you. I love
you. I love you. I love you. I love you. I love
you. I love you. I love you. I love you. I love
you. I love you. I love you. I love you. I love
you. I love you. I love you. I love you. I love
you. I love you. I love you. I love you. I love
you. I love you. I love you. I love you. I love
you. I love you. I love you. I love you. I love
you. I love you. I love you. I love you. I love
you. I love you. I love you. I love you. I love
you. I love you. I love you. I love you. I love
you. I love you. I love you. I love you. I love
you. I love you. I love you. I love you. I love
you. I love you. I love you. I love you. I love
you. I love you. I love you. I love you. I love
you. I love you. I love you. I love you. I love
you. I love you. I love you. I love you. I love
you. I love you. I love you. I love you. I love
you. I love you. I love you. I love you. I love
you. I love you. I love you. I love you. I love
you. I love you. I love you. I love you. I love
you. I love you. I love you. I love you. I love
you. I love you. I love you. I love you. I love
you. I love you. I love you. I love you. I love
you. I love you. I love you. I love you. I love
you. I love you. I love you. I love you. I love

you. I love you. I love you. I love you. I love
you. I love you. I love you. I love you. I love
you. I love you. I love you. I love you. I love
you. I love you. I love you. I love you. I love
you. I love you. I love you. I love you.

One for every day I can't show you with
my actions.

I swear I'll never say it again, Little One.

M

CHAPTER THIRTY-THREE

Four months later

METAL DOORS SCRAP through metal tracks, revealing the red dirt yard and hundreds of incarcerated bastards with no one to impress but each other. That's a sad and dangerous fucking reality. The stale heat is thick as I stride through it. Some men glance my way with stiff nods while others cast their eyes low.

Some of them laugh and mock and beat their chests because there is fuck all else to do and it feels good to be noticed. They would never admit it, but it's the lingering feeling of neglect they feel behind these walls that slowly dissolves their person. It's the world of free people so fucking close their presence can be heard—their cars, their horns, their music. It's fucking psychological warfare. These 'badarse' men are reminded every day that they have been left behind.

"Don't let Butcher hear about him."

At the mention of my name, I stop in my tracks and narrow my eyes on the sack of shit who spoke. "Explain."

"New guy," Jones says, gesturing towards a slender rake-looking dickhead with his head hanging low. He's clearly weak as piss. I bet he's a snitch.

"Rat," Jones confirms, chewing on tobacco with his mouth open.

I crack my jaw, knowing that Jones just wants my permission to start a fight. "Anyone would think your last name is Butcher, Jonesy, with the way you fucking want vengeance for us. Do you wanna suck my dick? Is that what this is all about?"

The six men around him snigger. The belittling sounds make me smile. The lot of them sit casually around their table as though they are out for a drink with the lads after a hard day of making minimum wage. These guys call themselves The District Crew. They're all in here for crimes that took place under our management and orders, but that doesn't mean they matter to me anymore than the wife bashers, paedophiles, and snitches.

There are maybe four men in here that I would consider my friends, a handful that I have a use for, and the rest are lucky I want to get out on good behaviour.

All lucky, except one.

Jones's face falls, the cocky expression he usually throws around faltering. "Just don't like people ratting on us."

"Us?" I scoff with a shake of my head. There is no *us*, dickhead.

Scowling over at the new rat, I massage my fingers along my tense jaw. He's going to have a hard enough time guarding his virginity; he doesn't need a warning from me.

Catching sight of Lars from across the yard, I make my

way over to him. He's near my age, but we don't share facts like that. If we talk at all, it's to say something important. We both have a healthy respect for silence; watching and listening are far more powerful skills to foster.

I suppose most women would think Lars is a sharp-looking man despite the jagged gash running the length of his left eye. The iris is cloudy-blue and redundant, but that disability doesn't hold him back.

I stroll straight past him, and when he falls into step beside me, we navigate our way down the hall. The predictability of incarcerated life is treacherous for anyone who finds themselves with a target on their back. I can anticipate with great accuracy where half the pricks in here will be at any given time.

Which is how I know we have seven minutes to get the deed done from the moment we stride into the toilet block to the moment we leave.

My pulse quickens with the onset of adrenaline.

We pass one of the female guards, her cheeks pinkening when I grin at her. The door is in view, and like fucking clockwork, Mathews strolls out after his morning wank.

We step inside, ducking into a cubicle each. We wait. The pipes creak, the taps drip, the cleaning lady switches her vacuum on in the adjacent room, and I smile.

Reaching into my green scrubs, I draw out a plastic pen. It's red. I didn't notice the colour when I snatched and stashed it three weeks ago. There was a crazy search squad trying to find this fucking pen. For nearly seven days we were in lockdown, but then they found it. They found *a* pen. A black pen.

This one is red.

I love you.

Ripping off the plastic plug, I draw the ink tube out with

my teeth and thread it down the drain. I don't want it to be red. Now with only the clear plastic column, I squeeze it in my fist. The piece of shit we are stalking has one week left before his release, after serving nearly thirteen years of hard time. *Fuck*, he was so excited when he told me. "Heading straight out to find my little girl," he said. "She's a knockout."

I grin to myself.

We wait.

The door opens and we both jump out like fucking animals. I clasp my palm over Donavon's open mouth, silencing the break of his imminent howl. Lars grabs his arms, pinning them to his sides as he helps me manoeuvre the heavy bastard. Donavon's feet shuffle, trying to stay balanced, in control, upright. We drag him into a cubicle.

Lars presses his back to the door as I force Donavon to his knees. Slamming his cheek onto the lip of the bowl, I press him into position. A good position to get drained by a Butcher. Tilting his head down, I brace his neck with my grip and stab the plastic column an inch below his ear.

The whites of his eyes scream at me.

Stab.

His body convulses violently.

Blood pisses out and into the bowl.

Stab.

My arm vibrates as he thrashes around beneath it.

Stab.

I bend to his level, making damn sure he can hear my voice as I snarl, "Konnor Butcher says congratulations on getting parole."

Stab. Stab. Stab.

CHAPTER THIRTY-FOUR

803 I love yous later

I PAD down the hallway towards Bronson's room, shaking my head with a sigh. This happens more often than I can count. I still when I see Clara with her front paws up on the windowsill. I wander to stand beside her, placing my hand on her fluffy brown shoulder as we peer through the glass together. When she rears up on her back paws like this, she is at my height. I had her DNA tested last year. She is part Bernese Mountain Dog and part German Shepherd—both big dogs. Clara is a lot of things. Playful. Loyal. Powerful.

Timid is not one of them.

She is just like Max.

I let him in...

I had to work hard to enjoy the thought of him, the memory. In the beginning, it was impossible to love him from afar. With that affection came so much pain, so much loneliness. I was terrified for him and what he might have been reduced to. A magnificent lion in a cage, his natural instincts crushed, his every moment at the will of far less impressive beings. I was overwhelmed by sadness.

"WHILE I'M IN, *I need you to be the bravest you have ever been. Don't disappear in here. Be you. Bubbly. A silly little girl. Soften my brothers' lives.*"

I'M TRYING, *Max. I'm trying.*

Looking back on that first five months, I suppose I had succumbed to a kind of depression. Every happy event was shadowed by his absence. Seeped into my bones, into my marrow, it festered there. I was low. So low I could barely move.

"I HAD *no idea how good it would feel to make you smile. Fuck me, I'd do just about anything to make you smile.*"

I WORKED HARD at smiling for him, the sad smile that now accompanies his memories, but a smile, nonetheless.

When Clara acts like Max—broody and protective—I like to imagine him kneeling down and giving her a pep talk about what he expects of her while he is gone. Her floppy puppy ears flip to the side as she tilts her head, listening intently to her master. I imagine him telling her to cuddle me every night. To lick all my tears away. To growl whenever a stranger approaches me. To bite any male who touches me.

I imagine this a lot.

With my sad smile.

Max is never to be disobeyed; he'd be very proud of her.

Pulled from my thoughts by her wagging tail, I catch the taillights of a car as it pulls away from the house. I scruff her crown, tighten the drawstring around my waist, and finish making my way to Bronson's room. Without knocking, I push the door open.

"No mommies," I hear her say through a giggle, her voice coming at me from under a canopy of sheets—a blanket forte. The multicoloured fabric hangs like shade sails through the centre of the bedroom, with one pegged at the front to create a wall. I press my lips together to stop my grin because I shouldn't love this so much. I should be firm and consistent with her. I want us to keep to a routine—I *really* do. All the ladies in my mother's group say that it is *all* about a steady routine so that our children feel safe and understand what is expected.

Ugh!

Those ladies don't have a completely love-struck *Nànnu* and four Butcher boys constantly stealing their child away—they aren't that lucky.

We could leave, begin a life of normality. Of structure. Our new house in Brussman is finished, has been for a month now, but I don't want to be there without *him*. So having the boys a few metres away, a constant interruption, a constant distraction, is a great comfort to me. Even if it means no rules, chaos, and a lack of schedules.

I run my fingers down my face, still waking up. "It's six. You should be in bed, Kelly. We spoke about this. We don't leave the room until the sun comes up. Remember the light? Bright out the window?"

Her high-pitched plea meets me again. "Uncle Bonson pay."

I let out a long sigh and try to address the other 'adult' in the room. "Bronson?"

"Tell her that I'm a troll," Bronson whispers.

She giggles. "I. A. Toll."

"No, *I am* a troll," he mutters with feigned secrecy. "Not you, Outlaw."

"*Am*. A. Toll." She tries again.

"Yeah, he's a troll alright. Trolling my schedule," I murmur through a chuckle. "Okay, I'm going to have a shower. Have you at least changed her nappy?"

"Tell her trolls eat nappies." I hear a *nom nom nom* sound and Kelly bursts into a fit of laughter, her broken giggle contagious. He must be pretending to eat her belly or something; I'd recognise that overexcited sound anywhere. Shaking my head with a huge smile etched on my cheeks, I leave them to act like toddlers together.

I nod to myself; at least her nappy is clean.

Or ingested.

After a shower, I get dressed in a pair of black leggings and a dusty-blue shirt and begin my morning ritual. As I sit down on the mattress and pull the bedside drawer out, I can hear Kelly and Bronson wandering down the hallway. She screeches with excitement about something. I dig into the drawer in search of Max's letter, riffling around to no avail. My chest aches as if a fist has broken into the cavity and is squeezing my lungs. I yank the entire drawer out, dislodging it from its track. I slide onto the floor with it in front of me. Where is it? Why can't I find it?

I need to cross it off.

Frick, what if Kelly took it? I jolt up and rush through the bedroom door as flashes of Max's letter in tiny pieces or covered in crayon nearly bring me to my knees. Clara follows me with meaning; she reads me and is on high alert. As I hurry down the staircase, I twist my wedding rings with my thumb, rotating the bands around my finger. A habit that has soothed me since-

"Daddy!"

I jerk to a stop, my feet and lungs motionless.

Warmth spreads through me, and only one person has that effect on me. In my peripherals I can see *him,* but I don't dare twist my head in case it's a lie. A mirage. His face in a shadow. In a crowd. I was so often crippled by hallucinations of him.

Gripping the railing for dear life, I try to stay upright, but my legs lose form and structure and buckle. I don't look down. Don't look at him. I hear Clara growl with uncertainty. Her response to the shift in energy, the quickening of my pulse, the gathering of my pieces, all the pieces that have been missing for so long.

Unable to walk or even stand, I just sink down onto the Jarrah step. Staring straight ahead, I take a few moments to come to terms with what is happening.

Eight hundred and three?

Is that the last one?

Is he here?

Is it a trick of my eye? I can't let the fight go.

Slowly, I lower my uncertain gaze and see Max squatting at the bottom of the staircase. I clasp my hands over my mouth, sobbing relentlessly into them.

It's him; *it's really him.*

I know this because he's... *different,* beautifully so. A lion in the wild—the king of the fricking jungle. He's wearing jeans and a white shirt, the sleeves bunched up around his biceps 'cause that's his style. His physique is strong and defined, perhaps slightly leaner than when he left, and that cool smile, *oh my God*. With those deep-set grey eyes and expressive dark brows set into that masculine face... he's sheer perfection.

Watching him intently, I wonder if he feels my eyes on him like a tangible caress. I wonder if butterflies are dancing in his belly. They are pirouetting in mine.

Kelly has stopped just a few metres away from him. Her wispy golden-blonde hair is in a pile on top of her head. I show her pictures of him every night, saying, "Goodnight, Daddy. We love you." I have told her stories and made him seem almost magical. He's Santa, The Easter Bunny, and The Tooth Fairy combined—he's legendary.

She blinks at him, awestruck by his presence. They stare at each other with matching grey-blue eyes. His mouth moves, saying something to her that isn't audible from where I'm perched. Kelly shuffles slowly over to him, stopping within an arm's length. They are talking now. She swings her hips nervously from side to side, like she isn't sure how to act or respond.

I shake my head into my palms, watching the exchange.

Please don't be asleep.

Fearful I'm in an amazing dream again, I pinch the skin on my forearm, wincing as I do. But my baby girl and my man are still there... *chatting*. She is a talkative little thing when she gets started, reeling off words she learned that day, connecting them in nonsensical ways. He nods as if he understands. When she moves into him and wraps her chubby arms around his neck, he envelops her tightly against him, lovingly, dipping his head into the crook of her neck.

He squeezes his eyes shut, holding them like that for several long beats of my heart. His shoulders move as he tries to control his breaths in and out. The butterflies in my belly are getting dizzy; they really should slow the *frick* down.

When they release each other, Kelly bands Max's finger with her little hand, ready to show him the house or the yard or her new trampoline, ready to take him on an adventure. But Max... he looks emotionally exhausted by the moment. He grips his forehead before briefly dragging his hand down his face and then across his eyes.

No, wait...

Is he crying?

Clara moves to sit beside me and the staircase creaks, the sound steeling my spine, knowing it was loud enough for—

Max drops his hand to his side.

I suck a sharp breath in.

Turning towards the sound, he lifts his gaze up to meet me and I... *I can't.* His eyes mist over further when they connect with mine. I jump up and run away from him, back down the hall and into our room. I rush into the bathroom, move into the shower, and desperately turn the faucet on. Sitting down on the tiles in my yoga pants and shirt, I let the water create a kind of white noise, soothing me, buying me time.

I wasn't always brave, Max.

The door opens and I cuddle my knees in tight. Just like the unapologetic menace he is, he walks straight into the shower, clothes and all, and sits down opposite me. His gaze moves like a magnifying glass over me, scorching a trail that feels tangible—traceable. When I finally look up, finding his gaze too hot and distracting to ignore, he's staring at me with such intensity I am surprised that he hasn't scarred me.

Swallowing hard, I try to consider what to say. What to —"You're here." Well, that was stupid and obvious... Well done, Cassidy Butcher... "You have your clothes on."

Ugh. Just... stop it.

"So do you," he says over the noise of the cascading water. My lip trembles in response to his voice—deep and confident with a hint of gravel and danger. The same voice I hear in my dreams. "Look what you made me while I was gone... She is fucking *incredible*. Thank you, Little One."

The water rushes off my head, soaking every inch of me, mingling with my tears. "I wasn't always brave, Max."

His brows draw a line above his serious gaze. "Neither was I."

I sob desperately, so very thankful to hear he's still soft, still vulnerable, with me. That was my biggest fear, waiting all this time for him and losing him to the dark anyway. But I haven't. I see *my Max* sitting across from me. Our eyes dive into one another, gazes drawn together like magnets. He shakes his head as if the sight of me is so mystifying, so unfathomable, I can't possibly be real.

The feeling is mutual.

"You're so fucking beautiful, Cassidy," he says, the break in his raspy voice choking my heart with vicarious agony. I glance down to watch his throat roll, then up again to catch a single tear as it drops from his eye. "I'm sorry, Little One. I'm so fucking sorry I wasn't here for you."

Max Butcher.

I leap from my position on the tiles and crawl onto his lap, my hands finding his cheeks, my lips finding his lips, my heart pressing against his heart. His big warm palms massage up my back, gripping me with such need, I whimper, overwhelmed, not having had anyone touch me in such a way for over two years. My body responds to him as if we were once one entity now split in two.

My Max.

The one with all the contradictory pieces that match

mine, slotting together like a puzzle of souls. My light into his dark. My nervous into his confidence. My softness into his fierce.

With our chests pressed together, our hearts beating at a collective tempo, we say all the things that are held captive in our emotionally overcome bodies.

We say I missed you, it is over now, are you still soft, are you still fierce, are you still mine, you better still be mine! We say we will never be apart again.

We say never again.

We say all of this with our kiss.

With our needy hands.

With our actions.

THE END

"TU, *sì a chiù bedda carusa ca ancuntrài nda me vita.*"
"You're the most beautiful girl in the world."

epilogue: cassidy

HE HAS BEEN HOME for five emotional hours. After our very expressive kiss, we stripped off our clothes and made love under a warm spray of water. The first time was desperate and rough; the second was savouring and gentle.

Now, I want nothing more than to laze in bed, feet tangled with my husband, and talk his ear off. I want to detail every significant and insignificant event of the past two years, share my thoughts and feelings, and help him connect with this world again. Then I want to collect up all of our things, wrestle Kelly from the clutches of her uncle, and move into our beautiful new home in Brussman. I want to start our life right now. Not tomorrow. Not next week. I don't want to wait another minute... That is what I want to do, but instead, we are walking into Butch's office.

Max squeezes my hand as we enter, refusing to let it go even as three of his brothers jump to their feet to greet him. He uses his free hand to pat each of them on the back, giving Xander a light slap to the cheek.

"Look at this little beefcake. You been working out?" Max laughs.

Xander grins, his beautiful blue eyes sparkling with excitement. "I've been boxing like crazy. Maybe I could kick your arse now."

Max scoffs, sitting down opposite his dad and pulling me onto his lap. "I've been boxing every day for the past ten years. I wouldn't fucking count on it, dickhead."

Konnor straightens from his seat and approaches Max, nodding his head in approval. "Your little girl is the sweetest thing. The coolest kid. So any part of Kelly, I have to like. Even if you are the moodiest son of a bitch I've ever met. So,"—he smiles softly—"welcome home."

"The moodiest? Met Butch?" Max asks, trailing his hand up my belly to cup my right breast.

I swipe his hand away. "Stop it, Menace."

Konnor closes his eyes, cringing. "You're still a dickhead then?"

Max stares blankly at him. "Why would I change?"

Ignoring them, I turn to look at Bronson and say, "Where is Kelly?"

His eyes widen and my heart leaps, but then he grins mischievously and I want to kill him. "Don't worry, she's with my mum." When I jump up with a start, he chuckles. "Or maybe it was the maid... Wait, which of them has *black* hair?"

"Why?" I plop back down on Max's lap, finding him more tense than before I bounced up. "Why torment me?"

"It's our bit." He shrugs, nonchalant. "Looks like I pissed off Maxipad, though. *Oh,* how I've missed that."

Twisting to face my husband... *my husband.*

He's here.

I let out a peaceful sigh and cuddle his neck tightly,

nuzzling in deep. Then I straighten to smooth the knotted brows above his uncertain gaze. "*Max.* She's *fine.* She loves the maid. They hunt fairies together. Lisa makes a trail with flowers and they follow them... She doesn't like *him* though," I admit, smirking playfully as I point at Clay.

"What?" Relaxing in his chair, he crosses his ankle over the top of his knee. "That's not true. We played hide and seek just yesterday."

Giggling, I say, "*Yeah.* And she left you *hidden.*"

"I can't compete with Bronson," he states, folding his arms across his chest. "He has an unfair advantage; they have the same maturity level."

"What about Butch?" Xander says straightaway. "Such a soft cock."

Butch lifts his head, pride plastered across his strong features. "I'm her favourite."

Xander shakes his head through a chuckle, staring at Max. "When Cassidy called us from the hospital to tell us that she had a girl, Butch hung up, opened The Balvenie forty-year-old single barrel, and drank the entire thing."

They all laugh, but I feel Max's heart suddenly rampant against my body. He grips me as though I am his lifeline, like I am the one now grounding *him.* As to not twist around and alert his brothers to how unsettled he is, I just lean back into him, breathing in the scent of perfect masculinity. When my head rolls against him to let him know he's not alone, that I feel his trepidation and it's alright, his arms encircle me tighter in response. He's transitioning and I am right here for him. The light to his dark. My stomach knots up just thinking about what it would feel like to learn all about your own daughter from second-hand information. I wriggle against him, drawing his mind to me and away from the thoughts plaguing him.

"We can move out tomorrow," I whisper sweetly. "Just me, you, and Kelly. You're her hero, Max. Don't worry."

His rough exhale fans my hair. "I'll be earning that title, Little One."

The boys are still chuckling and teasing each other when Max clears his throat. "I spoke with Knight." He's obviously over talking about his daughter and having no anecdote of his own to share.

Everyone quiets down.

"I couldn't tell you any earlier. Couldn't trust the guards not to read the letters. Couldn't trust anyone... except a Butcher, with this information, and they're all in this room."

Butch clasps his fingers together. "Straight to business then?"

Max nods. "You need to know now."

Clay swings in his chair, eyeing Max, unreadable as always. "I hear he died in prison."

"Prison justice. No one saw what happened," Max confirms, flexing his arms around my middle. Turning his head towards Konnor, he says, "He told me that Dustin paid him to kill you."

Konnor blinks, not at all surprised. That's what we expected to hear. "Okay."

Max sighs for a minute. *"Kill* you."

Butch's eyes narrow on Max. "What are you saying?"

"I'm saying that Dustin paid to have Konnor taken from his bed and *killed*. But he was approached by another man. This man offered him twice the amount to keep him alive. Keep him in a basement. For as long as it took. Just in case one day, this man had a use for him."

I strain for breath.

Konnor sinks down into a nearby seat, thrusting a hand through his hair and dragging it back down his face. All of the Butchers are fixed on Max, awaiting further information. The energy crackling around us is like the beginning of a current that has no end. Clay tightens, suspicious and analytical. Xander rubs his hands down his jeans, perhaps a nervous reaction to the impending news. Bronson just stares, shadowed by a palpable darkness that has little restraint.

Max levels them with his eyes. *"Jimmy fucking Storm."*

My mouth drops open and I exhale the words, "*Oh my God.*"

Rolling his fingers into his palms, Butch squeezes until his knuckles turn bone-white. He beats his fist onto the desk. "*Pocca miseria!*"

I flinch, curling into Max.

Butch stares at Konnor, anger like I've never seen before raging in his eyes. "He was going to use you against me," he hisses. "He knew this whole time."

Clay uncrosses his legs, leans forward onto his knees, and cups his forehead. "*Fuck.*" Concern shines through a crack in his usually guarded and emotionless manner.

"You know what this means? Made-men don't lie to made-men," Xander says, standing up. "Jimmy broke a vow. This is war."

War...

I start to scratch a layer of pink polish off my nail. War means casualties, and I only just got Max back. Before I can object, Bronson steps forward, rousing our attention.

He grins and it's anything but nice. "Not for you, Xander."

Xander frowns at his big brother, but Bronson just continues, shifting his gaze to each of us. "This means nothing for any of you. Be good little Butchers." He shares a meaningful exchange with Max and Clay. "Work for the city. Stay clean. Be family men."

Nodding his agreement, Butch states, "Nothing changes. We plant ourselves in the city. We let Jimmy think he's the head and—"

"The fish rots from the head." Bronson winks at Max. "One of his favourite sayings... *I'm* going to be the rot. I'm going to deteriorate that fucker. And he won't even know that it's happening."

"Dustin is mine," Max says through a low growl while my breath shudders at the mention of his name. *Dustin.*

"No," Butch bites out. "I won't see you lose more years and you can't leave the District while you're on parole. They will have eyes on yo—"

"I'll hunt him down for you, my beautiful brother. Bring him to you," Bronson states, vengeance playing with his wicked smirk.

Offering Konnor a quick glance, wanting to reach out to someone on my wavelength, I find only determination in his eyes. A flare of acceptance. He's ready for the people who hurt him to pay for their crimes. I blink at these dangerous men I call my family. And I feel my lips curl, curl up into a smile.

I'm ready for that too.

My mother once told me that 'if you avoid conflict to prevent a battle, you often start a war in your heart.'

My heart belongs to Max. And I *am* willing to support him in this battle. His family—*my family*—is the most powerful family in the District, and they don't need to bully the innocent. Taunt the lambs and the deer. They don't hurt people like me. Butch should be at the head. At that thought, my heart picks up pace. I want to watch him put a torch to the District's web of lies because now I know exactly who will burn along with it...

Jimmy Storm.

I softly stroke my fingernails down Max's forearm, over the red and black tattoos, little hairs rising in response to the gentle stimulation. His sigh rumbles behind my spine.

I'm with you, Menace.

To the end.

her way - bronson butcher's story

"Your love for her is dangerous and unnatural."
I grin. "I'm dangerous and unnatural."

Bronson:
Olive skin. Amber eyes. She has been mine since we were
fourteen.
She was my beautiful distraction from the chaos I was born
into.
From the disturbances in my own mind.
From my legacy.
So when everything we created together is ripped away, I
burn the idea of a peaceful life. Widening my arms to my
inevitable fate, I accept my duties.

Without her, I embrace a single purpose.

To protect my brothers.

To protect my family.

Shoshanna:

Green-blue eyes. A dimpled grin. The world was a mere playground to my nutcase, Bronson Butcher.

But I destroyed him.

So he walked away from me, dragging behind him one half of my severed heart.

Eleven years later, the crazy son of a bitch appears, bleeding out on my hospital table.

A bullet wound. *Of course.*

We have both changed so much.

Bronson now lives by a deranged and bloody moral code.

And he takes whatever he wants...

Whomever he wants.

Get book

harris' notes: a bittersweet goodbye.

Dear Max and Cassidy,

So I was going to write a note to your readers, but instead, I drank a bottle of red wine and this is the result...

You are my favourite book couple. Two individuals with strength and promise and yet, unknowingly living a kind of half existence.

Cassidy with your beauty and talent and hopefulness. Your brother's trauma cloaked a shadow over your life, but you never held any resentment. You are pure and kind.

And Max, with your intelligence and no-bullshit and inner gentleness. You were forced into a life that bred toxic masculinity and crushed weakness, but you managed to hold on to your integrity.

You shine a light on each other, illuminating hidden pieces and becoming whole.

I wanted to break you out of prison, Max. Have you snatch Cassidy away and run, to another place, to a different book world, and protect her and Kelly. I wanted you to be there throughout the pregnancy, irrational in your pursuit to protect her while she's in, as you would put it, a 'delicate condition.'

I daydreamed about you in the delivery room with her, scowling at the doctors and then tearing up when you hear that first high-pitched cry. I imagined you being unwilling to share your baby with anyone besides your wife, being the one to bottle feed her every night so that Cassidy can get some sleep... Kelly falling asleep on your chest.

I'm sorry I didn't give you those moments.

But I did give you the happily ever fricking after. The house. Marriage. Baby. Placemats... peace will come later...

Bronson will make sure of it.

editorial notes: how could you?

Dear Nicci,

An editor shouldn't have favourites. I love every story I work on...
*But this one? **Jeebus.***

I have screamed and cried over Cosa Nostra. I have cursed you and
called you a genius. This book, this couple, is definitely one of my
all time favourites, and you're a monster for making it end. And
*that ending! **Ugh.** That tore me up. How could you?*

Max crying. Cassidy crying. Me crying...

This book had all the feels and I am both nervous and excited to edit the next one. Because I love Bronson, and I know you're going to make him hurt. You're going to tear him apart to build him back up and that is going to absolutely wreck me. Going to kill me as I suggest ways to twist that knife even further...

Perhaps one day, you can write an alternate universe where the boys didn't grow up surrounded by so much darkness. And then another with Max and Cassidy meddling in Kelly's love life as she falls in love. Basically, just keep writing this series, this world, so my favourite couple never ends.

—Mri Grout @writingevolution. www. writingevolution.co.uk

our thing - book one

Have you read book one?

It is the start of something beautiful...

Blurb:

She's a good girl with the whole world at her feet.
He's a bad boy with his foot on the world.

As the youngest leading ballerina in my academy, my days are set. Routine. No time for boys. Unfortunately, my mind didn't get the memo, because there is always one name playing on my lips... Max Butcher.

The notorious bad boy of The District.
Hot to the point of physical discomfort.
Dangerous...

So when he notices me, I struggle to stay *en pointe*. But he finds me infuriating. ***A silly little girl.*** He wants to keep me out of his business and away from him and other men. He wants to protect my body—protect my innocence. But not even Max Butcher can stick to his guns. And the further into his world I'm led, the more danger gathers.

Get book

facing us - the prequel

Have you read the Konnor & Blesk's story?

He is desperate to remember.
She will destroy everything to forget.

Konnor: Up until now, my life has been a mirage of sorts. Of dark, lonely places. Of bourbon and women. I don't care. I think I'm pretty happy really.
But then she happens...

Blesk: He wants me. He'll do anything, drop everything, to have me. But when he uncovers who I am and what I've done, he'll rue ever facing me.
I've already buried everything he loves...

We both have secrets. Mine are harrowing. His, heart-breaking. Just merely being together threatens to expose everything we have tried to escape.

Will finally facing our past bring us peace or... spark chaos?

Get Book!

nicci who?

I'm an Australian chick writing real love stories for dark
souls.
Stalk me.

**Meet other Butcher Boy lovers on Facebook. Join Harris's
Harem of Dark Romance Lovers
Stalk us.**

- facebook.com/authornicciharris
- amazon.com/author/nicciharris
- bookbub.com/books/our-thing-an-australian-mafia-
  romance-kids-of-the-district-by-nicci-harris
- goodreads.com/nicciharris
- instagram.com/author.nicciharris

Printed in Great Britain
by Amazon